"YOU WANT ME TO PLAY ADAM TO A WHOLE NEW RACE?"

"Not at all. I want you to perpetuate your line," Mordan said.

"My answer is still no. I'll tell you why. Conceding that I am a superior survival type—I don't argue that; it's true. I'm smart and I'm able and I know it. Even so, I know of no reason why the human race should survive."

Mordan waited, then said slowly, "Don't you enjoy life, Felix?"

"I certainly do," Hamilton answered emphatically. "I've got a twisted sense of humor, and everything amuses me."

"Then isn't life worth living for itself alone?"

"It is for me. But do most people enjoy life? I doubt it. As near as I can tell from outward appearances it's about fourteen to one against it."

"Your children will be anxious to have children— I can assure you of that."

"What's that to me?" Hamilton demanded. "You can eliminate my misgivings and produce a line that will go on happily breeding for the next ten million years. That still doesn't make sense. Survival? What for? Until you can give me some convincing explanation why the human race should go on at all, my answer is 'no.'"

BEYOND THIS HORIZON

BEYOND THIS HORIZON

ROBERT A. Heinlein

A ROC BOOK

ROC
Published by the Penguin Group
Penguin Books USA Inc., 375 Hudson Street,
New York, New York 10014, U.S.A.
Penguin Books Ltd, 27 Wrights Lane,
London W8 5TZ, England
Penguin Books Australia Ltd, Ringwood,
Victoria, Australia
Penguin Books Canada Ltd, 10 Alcorn Avenue,
Toronto, Ontario, Canada M4V 3B2
Penguin Books (N.Z.) Ltd, 182–190 Wairau Road,
Auckland 10, New Zealand

Penguin Books Ltd, Registered Offices:
Harmondsworth, Middlesex, England

Published by Roc, an imprint of Dutton Signet,
a division of Penguin Books USA Inc.
Previously printed in a Signet edition.

First Roc Printing, July, 1997
10 9 8 7 6 5 4 3 2 1

For Cal, Mickey and both J's

CHAPTER ONE

"All of them should have been very happy—"

Their problems were solved: the poor they no longer had with them; the sick, the lame, the halt, and the blind were historic memories; the ancient causes of war no longer obtained; they had more freedom than Man has ever enjoyed. All of them should have been happy—

Hamilton Felix let himself off at the thirteenth level of the Department of Finance, mounted a slideway to the left, and stepped off the strip at a door marked:

BUREAU OF ECONOMIC STATISTICS
Office of Analysis and Prediction
Director
—— PRIVATE

He punched the door with a code combination, and awaited face check. It came promptly; the door dilated, and a voice inside said, "Come in, Felix."

He stepped inside, glanced at his host and remarked, "You make ninety-eight."

"Ninety-eight what?"

"Ninety-eight sourpusses in the last twenty minutes. It's a game. I just made it up."

Monroe-Alpha Clifford looked baffled, an expression not uncommon in his dealings with his friend Felix. "But what is the point? Surely you counted the opposites, too?"

"Of course. Ninety-eight mugs who'd lost their last friends, seven who looked happy. But," he added, "to make it seven I had to count one dog."

Monroe-Alpha gave Hamilton a quick look in an effort to determine whether or not he was joking. But he could not be sure—he rarely could be sure. Hamilton's remarks often did not appear serious, frequently even seemed technically sense-free. Nor did they appear to follow the six principles of humor—Monroe-Alpha prided himself on his sense of humor, had been known to pontificate to his subordinates on the necessity of maintaining a sense of humor. But Hamilton's mind seemed to follow some weird illogic of its own, self consistent perhaps, but apparently unrelated to the existent world.

"But what is the purpose of your survey?" he asked.

"Does it need a purpose? I tell you, I just made it up."

"But your numbers are too few to be significant. You can't fair a curve with so little data. Besides, your conditions are uncontrolled. Your results don't mean anything."

Hamilton rolled his eyes up. "Elder Brother,

hear me," he said softly. "Living Spirit of Reason, attend Thy servant. In Your greatest and most prosperous city I find vinegar phizzes to grins in a ratio of fourteen to one—and *he* says it's not significant!"

Monroe-Alpha looked annoyed. "Don't be irreverent," he advised. "And the proper ratio is sixteen and a third to one; you should not have counted the dog."

"Oh, forget it!" his friend answered. "How goes the tail chasing?" He wandered around the room, picking things up and putting them down under Monroe-Alpha's watchful eye, and finally stopped in front of the huge integrating accumulator. "It's about time for your quarterly prediction, isn't it?"

"Not 'about time'—it *is* time. I had just completed the first inclusive run when you arrived. Want to see it?" He stepped to the machine, pressed a stud. A photostat popped out. Monroe-Alpha unclipped it and handed it to Hamilton without looking at it. He had no need to—the proper data had been fed into the computer: he knew with quiet certainty that the correct answer would come out. Tomorrow he would work the problem again, using a different procedure. If the two answers did not then agree, within the limits of error of the machine, he would become interested in the figures themselves. But, of course, that would not happen. The figures would interest his superiors; the procedure alone was of interest to him.

Hamilton eyed the answer from a nonprofessional viewpoint. He appreciated, in part at least, the huge mass of detail which had gone into this simple answer. Up and down two continents human beings had gone about their lawful occasions—buying, selling, making, consuming, saving, spending, giving, receiving. A group of men in Altoona, Pennsylvania, had issued unsecured aspirant-stock to subsidize further research into a new method of recovering iron from low grade ores. The issue had been well received down in New Bolivar where there was a superabundance of credit because of the extreme success of the tropical garden cities along the Orinoco ("Buy a Slice of Paradise"). Perhaps that was the canny Dutch influence in the mixed culture of that region. It might have been the Latin influence which caused an unprecedented tourist travel away from the Orinoco during the same period— to Lake Louise, and Patagonia, and Sitka.

No matter. All of the complex of transactions appeared in the answer in Hamilton's hand. A child in Walla Walla broke its piggy bank (secretly, with one eye on the door), gathered up the slowly accumulated slugs and bought a perfectly delightful gadget, which not only *did* things, but made the appropriate noises as well. Some place down in the innards of the auto-clerk which handled the sale for the Gadget Shoppe four holes were punched in a continuous roll of paper; the item appeared in the owner's cost accounting, and was reflected in the accounting of the endless chain of middle distributors, transporters, processors, original producers, service companies, doctors, lawyers, merchants, chiefs—world without end.

The child (a bad-tempered little blond brat, bound to prove a disappointment to his planners and developers) had a few slugs left over which he exchanged for a diet-negative confection ("Father Christmas' Psuedo-Sweets—Not a tummyache in a tankful"); the sale was lumped with many others like it in the accounts of the Seattle Vending Machine Corporation.

The broken piggy bank and its concatenations appeared in the figures in Hamilton's hand, as a sliver of a fragment of a super-microscopic datum, invisible even in the fifth decimal place. Monroe-Alpha had not heard of this particular piggy bank when he set up the problem—nor would he, ever—but there are tens of thousands of piggy banks, a large but countable number of entrepreneurs, lucky, and unlucky, shrewd and stupid, millions of producers, millions of consumers, each with his draft book, each with printed symbols in his pouch, potent symbols—the stuff, the ready, the you-know-what, jack, kale, rocket juice, wampum, the shekels, the sugar, the dough.

All of these symbols, the kind that jingle and the kind that fold and, most certainly, the kind that are only abstractions from the signed promise of an honest man, all of these symbols, or more correctly, their reflected shadows, passed through the bottle neck formed by Monroe-Alpha's computer, and appeared there in terms of angular speeds, settings of three-dimensional cams, electronic flow, voltage biases, *et* complex *cetera.* The manifold constituted a dynamic abstracted structural picture of the economic flow of a hemisphere.

Hamilton examined the photostat. The reinvestment of accumulated capital called for an increase in the subsidy on retail transfers of consumption goods of three point one percent and an increase in monthly citizens' allowance of twelve credits—unless the Council of Policy decided on another means of distributing the social increment.

" 'Day by day, in every way, I'm getting richer and richer,' " Hamilton said. "Say, Cliff, this money machine of yours is a wonderful little gadget. It's the goose that lays the golden egg."

"I understand your classical allusion," Monroe-Alpha conceded, "but the accumulator is in no sense a production machine. It is merely an accounting machine, combined with an integrating predictor."

"I know that," Hamilton answered absently. "Look, Cliff—what would happen if I took an ax and just beat the bejasus out of your little toy?"

"You would be examined for motive."

"Don't be obtuse. What about the economic system?"

"I suppose," Monroe-Alpha told him, "that you want me to assume that no other machine was available for replacement. Any of the regional accumulators could—"

"Sure. Bust the hell out of all of them."

"Then we would have to use tedious methods of actuarial computation. A few weeks delay would result, with accumulated errors which would have to be smoothed out in the next prediction. No important result."

"Not that. What I want to know is this. If nobody computed the amount of new credit necessary to make the production-consumption cycle come out even—what would happen?"

"Your hypothetical question is too far-fetched to be very meaningful," Monroe-Alpha stated, "but it would result in a series of panics and booms of the post-nineteenth century type. Carried to extreme, it could even result in warfare. But of course it would not be—the structural nature of finance is too deeply imbedded in our culture for pseudo-capitalism to return. Any child understands the fundamentals of production accounting before he leaves his primary development center."

"I didn't."

Monroe-Alpha smiled tolerantly. "I find that difficult to believe. You know the Law of Stable Money."

" 'In a stable economy, debt-free new currency must be equated to the net re-investment,' " Hamilton quoted.

"Correct enough. But that is Reiser's formulation. Reiser was sound enough, but he had a positive talent for stating simple things obscurely. There is a much simpler way to look at it. The processes of economic system are so multitudinous in detail and involve so many promises to be performed at later dates that it is a psychological impossibility for human beings to deal with the processes without the use of a symbol system. We call the system 'finance' and the symbols 'money.' The symbolic structure should bear a one-to-one relationship to the physical structure of production and consumption. It's my business to keep track of the actual growth of the physical processes and recommend to the policy board changes in the symbol structure to match those in the physical structure."

"I'm damned if you've made it any simpler," Hamilton complained. "Never mind—I didn't say I didn't understand it; I said I didn't understand it as a kid. But honestly—wouldn't it be simpler to set up a collective system and be done with it?"

Monroe-Alpha shook his head. "Finance structure is a general theory and applies equally to any type of state. A complete socialism would have as much need for structural appropriateness in its cost accounting as do free entrepreneurs. The degree of public ownership as compared with the degree of free enterprise is a cultural matter. For example, food is, of course, free, but—"

"Freeze it, pal. You've just reminded me of one of the two reasons I had for looking in on you. Busy for dinner tonight?"

"Not precisely. I've a tentative date with my orthowife for twenty-one hundred, but I'm free until then."

"Good. I've located a new pay-restaurant in Meridian Tower that will be a surprise to your gastro tract. Guaranteed to give you indigestion, or you have to fight the chef."

Monroe-Alpha looked dubious. He had had previous experience with Hamilton's gastronomic adventures. "Let's go to the refectory here. Why pay out hard cash for bad food when good food is included in your basis dividend?"

"Because one more balanced ration would unbalance me. Come on."

Monroe-Alpha shook his head. "I don't want to contend with the crowds. Honestly, I don't."

"You don't really *like* people, do you?"

"I don't dislike them—not individually."

"But you don't like 'em. Me, I like 'em. People are funnier than anybody. Bless their silly little hearts. They do the craziest things."

Monroe-Alpha looked morose. "I suppose *you* are the only sane one in the lot."

"Me? Shucks, no. I'm one long joke on myself. Remind me to tell you about it sometime. But look—the other thing I came to see you about. Notice my new sidearm?"

Monroe-Alpha glanced at Hamilton's holster. In fact, he had not noticed that his friend was bearing anything new in the way of weapons—had he arrived unarmed Monroe-Alpha would have noticed it, naturally, but he was not particularly observant about such matters, and could easily have spent two hours with a man and never noticed whether he was wearing a Stokes coagulator or a common needlebeam.

But, now that his attention was directed to the

matter, he saw at once that Hamilton was armed with something novel . . . and deucedly odd and uncouth. "What is it?" he asked.

"Ah!" Hamilton drew the sidearm clear and handed it to his host. "Woops! Wait a moment. You don't know how to handle it—you'll blow your head off." He pressed a stud on the side of the grip, and let a long flat container slide out into his palm. "There—I've pulled its teeth. Ever see anything like it?"

Monroe-Alpha examined the machine. "Why, yes, I believe so. It's a museum piece, isn't it? An explosive-type hand weapon?"

"Right and wrong. It's mill new, but it's a facsimile of one in the Smithsonian Institution collection. It's called a point forty-five Colt automatic pistol."

"Point forty-five what?"

"Inches."

"Inches . . . let me see, what is that in centimeters?"

"Huh? Let's see—three inches make a yard and a yard is about one meter. No, that can't be right. Never mind, it means the size of the slug it throws. Here . . . look at one." He slid one free of the clip. "Damn near as big as my thumb, isn't it?"

"Explodes on impact, I suppose."

"No. It just drills its way in."

"That doesn't sound very efficient."

"Brother, you'd be amazed. It'll blast a hole in a man big enough to throw a dog through."

Monroe-Alpha handed it back. "And in the meantime your opponent has ended your troubles with a beam that acts a thousand times as fast. Chemical processes are slow, Felix."

"Not that slow. The real loss of time is in the operator. Half the gunfighters running around loose chop into their target with the beam already hot. They haven't the skill to make a fast sight. You can stop 'em with this, if you've a fast wrist. I'll show you. Got something around here we can shoot at?"

"Mmm . . . this is hardly the place for target practice."

"Relax. I want something I can knock out of the way with the slug, while you try to burn it. How about this?" Hamilton picked up a large ornamental plastic paperweight from Monroe-Alpha's desk.

"Well . . . I guess so."

"Fine." Hamilton took it, removed a vase of flowers from a stand on the far side of the room, and set the target in its place. "We'll face it, standing about the same distance away. I'll watch for you to start to draw, as if we really meant action. Then I'll try to knock it off the stand before you can burn it."

Monroe-Alpha took his place with lively interest. He fancied himself as a gunman, although he realized that his friend was faster. This might be, he thought, the split second advantage he needed. "I'm ready."

"Okay."

Monroe-Alpha started his draw.

There followed a single *CRACK!* so violent that

it could **be fe**lt through the skin and in the nostrils, as well as heard. Piled on top of it came the burbling *Sring-ow-ow!* as the bullet ricocheted around the room, and then a ringing silence.

"Hell and breakfast," remarked Hamilton. "Sorry, Cliff—I never fired it indoors before." He stepped forward to where the target had been. "Let's see how we made out."

The plastic was all over the room. It was difficult to find a shard large enough to show the outer polish. "It's going to be hard to tell whether you burned it, or not."

"I didn't."

"Huh?"

"That noice—it startled me. I never fired."

"Really? Say, that's great. I see I hadn't half realized the advantages of this gadget. It's a psychological weapon, Cliff."

"It's noisy."

"It's more than that. It's a terror weapon. You wouldn't even have to hit with your first shot. Your man would be so startled you'd have time to get him with the second shot. And that isn't all. Think . . . the braves around town are used to putting a man to sleep with a bolt that doesn't even muss his hair. This thing's bloody. You saw what happened to that piece of vitrolith. Think what a man's face will look like after it stops one of those slugs. Why a necrocosmetician would have to use a stereosculp to produce a reasonable facsimile for his friends to admire. Who wants to stand up to that kind of fire?"

"Maybe you're right. I still say it's noisy. Let's go to dinner."

"Good idea. Say—you've got a new nail tint. I like it."

Monroe-Alpha spread his fingers. "It *is* smart, isn't it? *Mauve Iridescent* it's called. Care to try some?"

"No, thank you. I'm too dark for it, I'm afraid. But it goes well with your skin."

They ate in the pay-restaurant Hamilton had discovered. Monroe-Alpha automatically asked for a private room when they entered; Hamilton, at the same moment, demanded a table in the ring. They compromised on a balcony booth, semi-private, from which Hamilton could amuse himself by staring down at the crowd in the ring.

Hamilton had ordered the meal earlier in the day, which was the point which had caused his friend to consent to venture out. It was served promptly. "What is it?" Monroe-Alpha demanded suspiciously.

"Bouillabaisse. It's halfway between a soup and a stew. More than a dozen kinds of fish, white wine, and the Great Egg alone knows how many sorts of herbs and spices. All natural foods."

"It must be terribly expensive."

"It's a creative art and it's a pleasure to pay for it. Don't worry about it. You know I can't help making money."

"Yes, I know. I never could understand why you take so much interest in games. Of course, it pays well."

"You don't understand me. I'm not interested in games. Have you ever seen me waste a slug or a credit on one of my own gadgets—or any other? I haven't played a game since I was a boy. For me, it is already well established that one horse can run faster than another, that the ball falls either on red or on black, and that three of a kind beats two pair. It's that I can't see the silly toys that people play with without thinking of one a little more complicated and mysterious. If I am bored with nothing better to do, I may sketch one and dispatch it to my agent. Presently in comes some more money." He shrugged.

"What are you interested in?"

"People. Eat your soup."

Monroe-Alpha tasted the mess cautiously, looked surprised, and really went to work on it. Hamilton looked pleased, and undertook to catch up.

"Felix—"

"Yes, Cliff."

"Why did you group me in the ninety-eight?"

"The ninety-eight? Oh, you mean the sourpuss survey. Shucks, pal, you rated it. If you are gay and merry-merry be-behind that death mask, you conceal it well."

"I've nothing to be unhappy about."

"No, not to my knowledge. But you don't look happy."

They ate in silence for a few minutes more. Monroe-Alpha spoke again. "It's true, you know. I'm not."

"Not what?"

"Not happy."

"So? Mmmm . . . why not?"

"I don't know. If I did I could do something about it. My family psychiatrist doesn't seem to be able to find the reason."

"You're on the wrong frequency. A psychiatrist is the last man to see about a thing like that. They know everything about a man, except what he is and what makes him tick. Besides, did you ever see a worry-doctor that was sane himself? There aren't two in the country who can count their own fingers and get the same answer twice running."

"It's true that he hasn't been able to help me much."

"Of course not. Why? Because he will start with the assumption that there is something wrong with you. He can't find it, so he's stuck. It doesn't occur to him that there might be nothing wrong with you and that might be what was wrong."

The other man looked weary. "I don't understand you. But he does claim to be following a clue."

"What sort?"

"Well . . . I'm a deviant, you know."

"Yes, I know," Hamilton answered shortly. He was reasonably familiar with his friend's genetic background, but disliked to hear him mention it. Some contrary strain in Hamilton rebelled against the idea that a man was necessarily and irrevocably the gene pattern handed to him by his genetic planners. Furthermore he was not convinced that Monroe-Alpha should be considered a deviant.

"Deviant" is a question-begging term. When the human zygote resulting from the combination of two carefully selected gametes is different from what the geneticists had predicted but not so different as to be classified with certainty as a mutation, that zygote is termed a deviant. It is not, as is generally believed, a specific term for a recognized phenomenon, but a catch-all to cover a lack of complete knowledge.

Monroe-Alpha (this particular Monroe-Alpha—Clifford, 32–847–106–B62) had been an attempt to converge two lines of the original Monroe-Alpha to recapture and reinforce the mathematical genius of his famous ancestor. But mathematical genius is not one gene, nor does it appear to be anything as simple as a particular group of genes. Rather, it is thought to be a complex of genes *arranged in a particular order*.

Unfortunately this gene complex appears to be close-linked in the Monroe-Alpha line to a neurotic contrasurvival characteristic, exact nature undetermined and not assigned to any set of genes. That it is not necessarily so linked appears to be established, and the genetic technicians who had selected the particular gametes which were to produce Monroe-Alpha Clifford believed that they had eliminated the undesired strain.

Monroe-Alpha Clifford did not think so.

Hamilton fixed him with a finger. "The trouble with you, my fine foolish friend, is that you are bothering your head with things you don't understand. Your planners told you that they had done their level best to eliminate from you the thing which caused your great grandfather Whiffenpoof to raise garter snakes in his hat. There is a long chance that they failed, but why assume that they did?"

"My great grandfathers did nothing of the sort. A slight strain of anhedonism, a tendency to—"

"Then why act like they had to be walked on a leash? You make me tired. You've got a cleaner pedigree than ninety-nine out of a hundred, and a chromosome chart that's as neat and orderly as a checker board. Yet you're yiping about it. How would you like to be a control natural? How would you like to have to wear lenses against your eyeballs? How would you like to be subject to a dozen filthy diseases? Or have your teeth fall out, and have to chew your meals with false choppers?"

"Of course, nobody would *want* to be a control natural," Monroe-Alpha said reflectively, "but the ones I've known seemed to be happy enough."

"All the more reason for you to snap out of your funk. What do you know of pain and sickness? You can't appreciate it any more than a fish appreciates water. You have three times the income you can spend, a respected position, and work of your own choosing. What more do you want out of life?"

"I don't know, Felix. I don't know, but I know I'm not getting it. Don't ride me about it."

"Sorry. Eat your dinner."

The fish stew contained several large crab legs; Hamilton ladled one into his guest's trencher. Monroe-Alpha stared at it uneasily. "Don't be so suspicious," Hamilton advised. "Go ahead. Eat it."

"How?"

"Pick it up in your fingers, and crack the shell." Monroe-Alpha attempted to comply, somewhat clumsily, but the greasy, hard surface skidded between his fingers. He attempted to recover and knocked it over the edge of the balcony rail at his elbow.

He started to rise; Hamilton put a hand on his forearm. "My fault," he said. "I will repair it." He stood up and looked down at the table directly beneath their booth.

He did not see the stray bit of seafood at once, but he had no difficulty in telling approximately where it had landed. Seated at the table was a party of eight. Two of them were elderly men who wore the brassards-of-peace. Four women alternated with the males around the table. One of them, quite young and pretty, was dabbing at something which seemed to have stained her gown. The wayward crab leg was floating in a crystal bell of purple liquid directly in front of her; cause and effect were easy to infer.

The two remaining men were both armed, both standing, and staring up at the balcony. The younger, a slender youth in bright scarlet promenade dress, resting his right hand on the grip of his sidearm, seemed about to speak. The older man turned coldly dangerous eyes from Hamilton to his youthful companion. "My privilege, Cyril," he said quietly, "if you please."

The young brave was clearly annoyed and reluctant to comply; nevertheless he bowed stiffly and sat down. His elder returned the bow punctiliously and turned back to Hamilton. The lace of his cuff brushed his holster, but he had not touched his weapon—as yet.

Hamilton leaned over the balcony, both his hands spread and plainly visible on the rail. "Sir, my clumsiness has disturbed the pleasure of your meal and invaded your privacy. I am deeply sorry."

"I have your assurance that it was accidental, sir?" The man's eyes were still frosty, but he made no move to draw. But he did not sit down.

"You have indeed, sir, and with it my humble apology. Will you graciously permit me to make reparation?"

The other glanced down, not at the youth, but at the girl whose gown had been splashed. She shrugged. He answered Hamilton. "The thought is taken for the deed, sir."

"Sir, you leave me indebted."

"Not at all, sir."

They were exchanging bows and were about to resume their seats, when a shouted remark from the balcony booth directly opposite interrupted them. "Where's your brassard?"

They both looked toward the source of the disturbance; one of a party of men—armed citizens all apparently, for no brassards were to be seen—was leaning out of the booth and staring with deliberate rudeness. Hamilton spoke to the man at the table below. "My privilege, is it not, sir?"

"Your privilege. I wish you well." He sat down and turned his attention back to his guests.

"You spoke to me?" asked Hamilton of the man across the ring.

"I did. You were let off lightly. You should eat at home—if you have a home. Not in the presence of gentlefolk."

Monroe-Alpha touched Hamilton's arm. "He's drunk," he whispered. "Take it easy."

"I know," his friend answered in a barely audible aside, "but he gives me no choice."

"Perhaps his friends will take care of him."

"We'll see."

Indeed his friends were attempting to. One of them placed a restraining hand on his weapon arm, but he shook him off. He was playing to a gallery—the entire restaurant was quiet now, the diners ostentatiously paying no attention, a pose contrary to fact. "Answer me!" he demanded.

"I will," Hamilton stated quietly. "You have been drinking and are not responsible. Your friends should disarm you and place a brassard on *you*. Else some short-tempered gentleman may fail to note that your manners were poured from a bottle."

There was a stir and a whispered consultation in the party behind the other man, as if some agreed with Hamilton's estimate of the situation. One of them spoke urgently to the belligerent one, but he ignored it.

"What's that about my manners, you misplanned mistake?"

"Your manners," Hamilton stated, "are as thick as your tongue. You are a disgrace to the gun you wear."

The other man drew too fast, but he drew high, apparently with the intention of chopping down.

The terrific explosion of the Colt forty-five brought every armed man in the place to his feet, sidearm clear, eyes wary, ready for action. But the action was all over. A woman laughed, shortly and shrilly. The sound broke the tension for everyone. Men relaxed, weapons went back to belts, seats were resumed with apologetic shrugs. The diners went back to their own affairs with the careful indifference to other people's business of the urbane sophisticate.

Hamilton's antagonist was half supported by the arms of his friends. He seemed utterly surprised and completely sobered. There was a hole in his chemise near his right shoulder from which a wet dark stain was spreading. One of the men holding him up waved to Hamilton with his free arm, palm out. Hamilton acknowledged the capitulation with the same gesture. Someone drew the curtains of the booth opposite.

Hamilton sank back into the cushions with a relieved sigh. "We lose more crabs that way," he observed. "Have some more, Cliff?"

"Thanks, no," Monroe-Alpha answered. "I'll stick to spoon foods. I hate interruptions at meals. He might have cooled you."

"And left you to pay the check. Such slug pinching ill becomes you, Cliff."

Monroe-Alpha looked annoyed. "You know it's not that. I have few enough friends not to wish to lose them in casual brawls. You should have taken a private room, as I requested." He touched a stud under the railing; the curtains waved across the arch, shutting them off from the public room.

Hamilton laughed. "A little excitement peps up the appetite."

In the booth opposite the man who had waved capitulation spoke savagely to the one who had been wounded. "You fool! You clumsy fool! You muffed it."

"I couldn't help it," the injured man protested. "After he waived privilege, there was nothing to do but play drunk and pretend I meant the other one." He dabbed futilely at his freely bleeding shoulder. "In the Name of the Egg, what did he burn me with?"

"No matter."

"Maybe not to you, but it is to me. I'll look him up."

"You will not. One mistake is too many."

"But I thought he was one of us. I thought it was part of the set-up."

"Hummph! Had it been, you would have been told."

After Monroe-Alpha left to keep his date, Hamilton found himself at loose ends. The night life of the capital offered plenty of opportunity for a man to divest himself of surplus credit, but it was not new to him. He tried, in a desultory fashion, to find professional entertainment, then gave up and let the city itself amuse him. The corridors were thronged as always, the lifts packed; the Great Square under the port surged with people. Where were they all going? What was the hurry? What did they expect to find when they got there?

The presence of some types held obvious explanations. The occasional man with a brassard was almost certainly out at this hour because his business required him to be. The same rule applied without exception to the few armed men who also wore brassards—proclaiming thereby their unique status as police monitors, armed but immune to attack.

But the others, the armed and richly costumed men and their almost as gaudy women—why did they stir about so? Why not remain quietly at home with their wenches? He realized, consciously and sardonically, that he himself was part of the throng, present because it amused him. He knew he had no reason to feel that his own sense of detached amusement was unique. Perhaps they all came to keep from being bored with themselves, to observe their mutual folly and to laugh.

He found himself, later, the last customer in a small bar. The collection of empty cups at his elbow was impressive. "Herbert," he said at last, to the owner back of the bar, "why do you run this joint?"

Herbert paused in his tidying up. "To make money."

"That's a good answer, Herbert. Money and children—what other objectives are there? I've too much of one and none of the other. Set 'em up, Herbert. Let's drink to your kids."

Herbert set out two cups, but shook his head. "Make it something else. I've no kids."

"Sorry—none of my business. We'll drink to the kids I haven't got instead." Herbert poured the drinks, from separate bottles.

"What's that private stock of yours, Herbert? Let me try it."

"You wouldn't like it."

"Why not?"

"Well, to tell the truth, it's flavored water."

"You'd drink a toast in *that*? Why, Herbert!"

"You don't understand. My kidneys . . ."

Hamilton looked at him in sharp surprise. His host looked pleased. "You wouldn't guess, would you? Yes, I'm a natural. But it's my own hair I'm wearing. And my own teeth . . . mostly. Keep myself fit. Good a man as the next." He dumped the liquid from his own cup, and refilled it from the bottle he had used for Hamilton's drink. "Shucks! One won't hurt me." He raised his drink. "Long life!"

"And children," Hamilton added mechanically.

They tossed them down. Herbert filled them up again. "Take children," he began. "Any man wants to see his kids do better than he did. Now I've been married for twenty-five years to the same woman. My wife and I are both First Truthers and we don't hold with these modern arrangements. But children ... we settled that a long time ago. 'Martha,' I said to her, 'it don't matter what the brethren think. What's right is right. Our kids are going to have every advantage that other kids have.' And after a while she came around to my way of thinking. So we went to the Eugenics Board—"

Hamilton tried to think of a way to stop his confidences.

"I must say that they were very kind and polite. First they told us to think it over. 'If you practice gene selection,' they said, 'your children won't receive the control benefit.' As if we don't know that: Money wasn't the object. We wanted our kids to grow up fine and strong and smarter than we were. So we insisted and they made a chromosome chart on each of us.

"It was two, three weeks before they called us back. 'Well, Doc,' I said, soon as we were inside, 'what's the answer? What had we better select for?' 'Are you sure you want to do this?' he says. 'You're both good sound types and the state needs controls like you. I'm willing to recommend an increase in benefit, if you'll drop it.' 'No,' I said, 'I know my rights. Any citizen, even a control natural, can practice gene selection if he wants to.' Then he let me have it, full charge."

"Well?"

"There wasn't anything to select for in either of us."

"Huh?"

" 'S truth. Little things, maybe. We could have

arranged to leave out my wife's hay fever, but that was about all. But as for planning a child that could compete on even terms with the general run of planned children, it just wasn't in the cards. The material wasn't there. They had made up an ideal chart of the best that could be combined from my genes and my wife's and it still wasn't good enough. It showed a maximum of a little over four percent over me and my wife in the general rating scale. 'Furthermore,' he told us, 'you couldn't plan on that score. We might search your germ plasm throughout your entire fertile period and never come across two gametes that could be combined in this combination.' 'How about mutations?' I asked him. He just shrugged it off. 'In the first place,' he said, 'it's damned hard to pick out a mutation in the gene pattern of a gamete itself. You generally have to wait for the new characteristic to show up in the adult zygote, then try to locate the variation in the gene pattern. And you need at least thirty mutations, all at once, to get the child you want. It's not mathematically possible."

"So you gave up the idea of planned children?"

"So we gave up the idea of children period. Martha offered to be host-mother to any child I could get, but I said 'No, if it ain't for us, it ain't for us.' "

"Hmmm. I suppose so. Look—if you and your wife are both naturals, why do you bother to run this place? The citizen's allowances plus two control benefits add up to quite a tidy income. You don't look like a man with extravagant tastes."

"I'm not. To tell you the truth we tried it, after our disappointment. But it didn't work out. We got uneasy and fretful. Martha comes to me and says 'Herbert, please yourself but *I'm* going to start my hairdressing studio again.' And I agreed with her. So here we are."

"Yes, so we are," Hamilton concurred. "It's a queer world. Let's have another drink."

Herbert polished the bar before replying. "Mister, I wouldn't feel right about selling you another unless you checked that gun with me and let me loan you a brassard."

"So? Well, in that case I guess I've had enough. Good night."

"G'night."

CHAPTER TWO

"Rich Man, Poor Man,
Beggar Man, Thief—"

His telephone started to yammer as soon as he was home. "Nuts to you," said Hamilton. "I'm going to get some sleep." The first three words were the code cut-off to which he had set the instrument; it stopped mournfully in the middle of its demand.

Hamilton swallowed eight hundred units of thiamin as a precautionary measure, set his bed for an ample five hours of sleep, threw his clothes in the general direction of the service valet, and settled down on the sheet. The water rose gently under the skin of the mattress until he floated, dry and warm and snug. The lullaby softened as his breathing became regular. When his respiration and heart action gave positive proof of deep sleep, the music faded out unobtrusively, shut off without so much as a click.

"It's like this," Monroe-Alpha was telling him, "we're faced with a surplusage of genes. Next quarter every citizen gets ninety-six chromosomes—'" "But I don't like it," Hamilton protested. Monroe-Alpha grinned gleefully. "You have to like it," he proclaimed. "Figures don't lie. Everything comes out even. I'll show you." He stepped to his master accumulator and started it. The music swelled up, got louder. "See?" he said. "That proves it." The music got louder.

And louder.

Hamilton became aware that the water had drained out of his bed, and that he lay with nothing between him and the spongy bottom but the sheet and the waterproof skin. He reached up and toned down the reveille, whereupon the insistent voice of his telephone cut through to him. "Better look at me, Boss. I got troubles. Better look at me, Boss. I got troubles. Better look at me, Boss. I got troubles—"

"So have I. Thirty minutes!" The instrument shut off obediently. He punched for breakfast and stepped into the shower, eyed the dial, and decided against the luxury of a long workout. Besides, he wanted breakfast. Four minutes would do.

Warm soapy emulsion sprayed over his body, was scrubbed in by air blast, was replaced at the end of the first minute by water of the same temperature in needle jets. The temperature dropped, the needle jets persisted for a few seconds, then changed to a gentle full stream which left him cool and tingling. The combination was his own; he did not care what the physiotherapists thought of it.

The air blast dried him with a full minute to spare for massage. He rolled and stretched against the insistent yielding pressure of a thousand mechanical fingers and decided that it was worthwhile to get up, after all. The pseudodactyls retreated from him. He pushed his face for a moment into the capillotomer. Shave completed, the booth sprayed him with scent and dusted him off. He was beginning to feel himself again.

He tucked away a quarter litre of sweet-lemon juice and went to work seriously on the coffee before turning on the news roundup.

The news contained nothing fit to be recorded permanently. No news, he thought, makes a happy country but a dull breakfast. The machine called out the plugs for a dozen stories while the accompanying flash pictures zipped past without Hamilton's disturbing the setting. When he did so, it was not because the story was important, but because it concerned him. The announcer proclaimed, "Diana's Playground Opened to the Public!"; the flash panned from a crescent moon down to the brutal mountain surface and below to a gaily lighted artificial dream of paradise. Hamilton slapped the tell-me-more.

"Leyburg, Luna. Diana's Playground, long touted by its promoters as the greatest amusement enterprise ever undertaken off earth or on, was invaded by the first shipload of tourists at exactly twelve thirty-two, Earth Prime. These old eyes have seen many a pleasure city, but I was surprised! Biographers relate that Ley himself was fond of the gay spots—I'm going to keep one eye on his tomb while I'm here; he might show up—"

Hamilton gave half an ear to the discourse, half an eye to the accompanying stories, most of his attention to half a kilo of steak, rare.

"—bewilderingly beautiful, weirdly sensuous low-gravity dancing.

"The gaming rooms are thronged; the management may have to open annexes. Particularly popular are the machines offered by Lady Luck, Incorporated—Hamilton's Hazards they are called by the trade. In fact—" The picture that went with the spiel did not show a throng in Hamilton's estimation; he could almost feel the trouble the pick-up man had gone to in order to shoot favorable angles.

"—round trip excursion tickets which entitle the holder to visit every place of amusement in the Playground, with three days hotel accommodations, strictly high-gravity, every room centrifuged."

He switched it off: and turned to the telphone. "Connection—one one one zero."

"Special service," a husky contralto answered him presently.

"Gimme the Moon, please."

"Certainly. To whom do you wish to speak, Mr.—uh, Hamilton?"

"Hamilton is correct. I would like to talk to Blumenthal Peter. Try the manager's office at Diana's Playground."

There was a delay of several seconds before an image appeared on the screen. "Blumenthal speaking. That you, Felix? The image at this end is lousy. All streaked up with incidentals."

"Yeah, it's me. I called to ask about the play, Pete . . . what's the matter? Can't you hear me?"

The face of the image remained quiet for a long three seconds, then said suddenly, "Of course I can hear you. Don't forget the lag."

Hamilton looked sheepish. He *had* forgotten the lag—he always did. He found it difficult to remember, when staring right into a man's live features, that there would be a second and a half delay before that man—if on the Moon—could hear, another second and a half for his voice to travel back, three seconds lag in all. Three seconds lag seems inconsiderable but it is long enough to stride six paces, or fall forty-one metres.

He was glad there was no phone service to the minor planets; it would be maddening to wait ten minutes or so between sentences—easier to stat a letter. "Sorry," he said. "My mistake. How was the play? The crowds didn't look so good."

"Naturally the crowd was light. One shipload isn't Noah's Ark. But the play was okay. They had plenty of scrip and were anxious to spend. We reported to your agent."

"Sure. I'll get the report, but I wanted to know what gadgets were popular."

"*Lost Comet* went strong. And so did *Eclipses*."

"How about *Claiming Race* and *Who's Your Baby*?"

"Okay, but not too heavy. Astronomy is the angle for this dive. I told you that."

"Yes, I should have listened to you. Well, I'll figure out a revamp. You could change *Claiming Race* right now. Call it *High Trajectory* and rename the mobiles after some of the asteroids. Get it?"

"Right. We'll redecorate it in midnight blue and silver."

"That's right. I'll send a stat to confirm. That's all, I guess. I'm clearing."

"Wait a minute. I took a whirl at *Lost Comet* myself, Felix. That's a great game."

"How much did you drop?"

Blumenthal looked suspicious. "Why about eight hundred and fifty, if you must know. Why do you assume I lost? Isn't the game level?"

"Certainly it's level. But I designed that game myself, Pete. Don't forget that. It's strictly for suckers. You stay away from it."

"But look—I've figured out a way to beat it. I thought you ought to know."

"That's what you think. I know. *There is no way to beat the game.*"

"Well—okay."

"Okay. Long life!"

"And kids."

As soon as the circuit was clear the phone resumed its ubiquitous demand. "Thirty minutes. Better look at me, Boss. I got troubles. Better—"

He removed a stat from the receiver; it shut up. "To Citizen Hamilton Felix 65–305–243 B47," it read, "Greetings. The District Moderator for Genetics presents his compliments and requests that Citizen Hamilton visit him at his office at ten hundred tomorrow." It was dated the previous evening and had an added notation requesting him to notify the moderator's office if it were not convenient to keep the appointment, refer to number such-and-so.

It lacked thirty minutes of ten hundred. He decided to comply with the request.

The Moderator's suite struck Hamilton as being rather less mechanized than most places of business, or perhaps more subtly so. It was staffed with humans where one expects auto-gadgets—the receptionist, for example. The staff was mostly female, some grave, some merry, but all were beautiful, very much alive, and obviously intelligent.

"The Moderator will see you now."

Hamilton stood up, chucked his cigaret into the nearest oubliette, and looked at her. "Do I disarm?"

"Not unless you wish. Come with me, please."

She ushered him as far as the door to the Moderator's private office, dilated it, and left him as he stepped through. "Good morning, sir!" a pleasant voice called out.

Hamilton found himself staring at the Moderator. "Good morning to you," he answered mechanically, then, "For the love o'—!" His right hand slid of its own volition toward his sidearm, hesitated, changed its mind, and stopped.

The Moderator was the gentleman whose dinner party had been disturbed by the incident of the wayward crab leg.

Hamilton recovered some of his poise. "Sir," he said stiffly, "this is not proper procedure. If you were not satisfied, you should have sent your next friend to wait on me."

The Moderator stared at him, then laughed in a fashion that would have been rude in another man—but from him it was simply Jovian. "Believe me, sir, this is as much of a surprise to me as it is to you. I had no idea that the gentleman who exchanged courtesies with me yesterday evening was the one I wished to see this morning. As for the little *contretemps* in the restaurant—frankly, I would not have made an issue of the matter, unless you had forced me to the limit. I have not drawn my tickler in public for many years. But I am forgetting my manners—sit down, sir. Make yourself comfortable. Will you smoke? May I pour you a drink?"

Hamilton settled himself. "If the Moderator pleases."

"My name is Mordan"—which Hamilton knew—"my friends call me Claude. And I would speak with you in friendship."

"You are most gentle—Claude."

"Not at all, Felix. Perhaps I have an ulterior motive. But tell me: what was that devil's toy you used on the cocky young brave? It amazed me."

Hamilton looked pleased and displayed his new weapon. Mordan looked it over. "Oh, yes," he said, "a simple heat engine burning a nitrate fuel. I think I have seen its pattern, have I not, on display at the Institution?"

Felix acknowledged the fact, a little crestfallen that Mordan was so little surprised at his toy. But Mordan made up for it by discussing in detail with, apparently, lively interest the characteristics and mechanism of the machine. "If I were a fighting man, I would like to have one like it," he concluded.

"I'll have one fashioned for you."

"No, no. You are kind, but I would have no use for it."

Hamilton chewed his lip. "I say . . . you'll pardon me . . . but isn't it indiscreet for a man who does no fighting to appear in public armed?"

Mordan smiled. "You misconstrue. Watch." He indicated the far wall. It was partly covered with a geometrical pattern, consisting of small circles, all the same size and set close together. Each circle had a small dot exactly in the center.

Mordan drew his weapon with easy swiftness, coming *up*, not down, on his target. His gun seemed simply to check itself at the top of its swing, before he returned it to his holster.

A light puff of smoke drifted up the face of the wall. There were three new circles, arranged in tangent trefoil. In the center of each was a small dot.

Hamilton said nothing. "Well?" inquired Mordan.

"I was thinking," Hamilton answered slowly,

"that it is well for me that I was polite to you yesterday evening."

Mordan chuckled.

"Although we have never met," Mordan said, "you and the gene pattern you carry have naturally been of interest to me."

"I suppose so. I fall within the jurisdiction of your office."

"You misunderstand me. I cannot possibly take a personal interest in every one of the myriad zygotes in this district. But it is my duty to conserve the best strains. I have been hoping for the past ten years that you would show up at the clinic, and ask for help in planning children."

Hamilton's face became completely expressionless. Mordan ignored it and went on. "Since you did not come in voluntarily for advice, I was forced to ask you to visit me. I want to ask you a question: Do you intend to have children any time soon?"

Hamilton stood up. "This subject is distasteful to me. May I have your leave, sir?"

Mordan came to him and placed a hand on his arm. "Please, Felix. No harm can be done by listening to me. Believe me, I do not wish to invade your private sphere—but I am no casual busybody. I am your moderator, representing the interests of all of your own kind. Yours among them."

Hamilton sat down without relaxing. "I will listen."

"Thank you. Felix, the responsibility of improving the race under the doctrines of our republic is not a simple one. We can advise but not coerce. The private life and free action of every individual must be scrupulously respected. We have no weapon but cool reason and the appeal to every man's wish that the next generation be better than the last. Even with co-operation there is little enough we can do—in most cases, the elimination of one or two bad characteristics, the preservation of the good ones present. But your case is different."

"How?"

"You know how. You represent the careful knitting together of favorable lines over four generations. Literally tens of thousands of gametes were examined and rejected before the thirty gametes were picked which constitute the linkage of your ancestral zygotes. It would be a shame to waste all that painstaking work."

"Why pick on me? I am not the only result of that selection. There must be at least a hundred citizens descended from my great gross grandparents. You don't want me—I'm a cull. I'm the plan that didn't pan out. I'm a disappointment."

"No," Mordan said softly, "no, Felix, you are not a cull. You are the star line."

"Huh?"

"I mean it. It is contrary to public policy to discuss these things, but rules were made to be broken. Step by step, back to the beginning of the experiment, your line has the highest general rating. You are the only zygote in the line which combines every one of the favorable mutations with which my predecessors started. Three other favorable mutations showed up after the original combinations; all of them are conserved in you."

Hamilton smiled wryly. "That must make me still more of a disappointment to you. I haven't done very much with the talents you attribute to me, have I?"

Mordan shook his head. "I have no criticism to make of your record."

"But you don't think much of it, do you? I've frittered away my time, done nothing more important than design silly games for idle people. Perhaps you geneticists are mistaken in what you call 'favorable characteristics.' "

"Possibly. I think not."

"What do you call a favorable characteristic?"

"A survival factor, considered in a broad sense. This inventiveness of yours, which you disparage, is a very strong survival factor. In you it lies almost latent, or applied to matters of no importance. You don't need it, because you find yourself in a social matrix in which you do not need to exert yourself to stay alive. But that quality of inventiveness can be of crucial importance to your descendants. It can mean the difference between life and death."

"But—"

"I mean it. Easy times for individuals are bad times for the race. Adversity is a strainer which refuses to pass the ill equipped. But we have no adversity nowadays. To keep the race as strong as it is and to make it stronger requires careful planning. The genetic technician eliminates in the laboratory the strains which formerly were eliminated by simple natural selection."

"But how do you know that the things you select for are survival factors? I've had my doubts about a lot of them."

"Ah! There's the rub. You know the history of the First Genetic War."

"I know the usual things about it, I suppose."

"It won't do any harm to recapitulate. The problem those early planners were up against is typical—"

The problems of the earliest experiments are typical of all planned genetics. Natural selection automatically preserves survival values in a race simply by killing off those strains poor in survival characteristics. But natural selection is slow, a statistical process. A weak strain may persist—for a time—under favorable conditions. A desirable mutation may be lost—for a time—because of exceptionally unfavorable conditions. Or it may be lost through the blind wastefulness of the reproductive method. Each individual animal represents exactly half of the characteristics potential in his parents.

The half which is thrown away may be more desirable than the half which is perpetuated. Sheer chance.

Natural selection is slow—it took eight hundred thousand generations to produce a new genus of horse. But artificial selection is fast, *if* we have the wisdom to know *what* to select for.

But we do not have the wisdom. It would take a superman to plan a superman. The race acquired the techniques of artificial selection without knowing what to select.

Perhaps it was a bad break for mankind that the basic techniques for gene selection were developed immediately after the last of the neo-nationalistic wars. It would be interesting to speculate whether or not the institution of modern finance structure after the downfall of the Madagascar System would have been sufficient to maintain peace if no genetic experiments had been undertaken. But pacifist reaction was at its highest point at this time; the technique of para-ectogenesis was seized on as a God-given opportunity to get rid of war by stamping it out of the human spirit.

After the Atomic War of 1970, the survivors instituted drastic genetic regulations intended for one purpose alone—to conserve the Parmalee-Hitchcock recessive of the ninth chromosome and to eliminate the dominant which usually masks it—to breed sheep rather than wolves.

"It is wryly amusing that most of the "wolves" of the period—the Parmalee-Hitchcock island *is* recessive; there are few natural "sheep"—were caught by the hysteria and co-operated in the attempt to eliminate themselves. But some refused. The Northwest Colony eventually resulted.

That the Northwest Union should eventually fight the rest of the world was a biological necessity. The outcome was equally a necessity and the details are unimportant. The "wolves" ate the "sheep."

Not physically in the sense of complete extermination, but, genetically speaking, we are descended from "wolves," not "sheep."

"They tried to breed the fighting spirit out of men," Mordan went on, "without any conception of its biological usefulness. The rationalization involved the concept of Original Sin. Violence was 'bad'; non-violence was 'good.' "

"But why," protested Hamilton, "do you assume that combativeness is a survival characteristic? Sure—I've got it; you've got it; we've all got it. But bravery is no use against nuclear weapons. What real use is it?"

Mordan smiled. "*The fighters survived.* That is the final test. Natural selection goes on always, regardless of conscious selection."

"Wait a minute," demanded Hamilton. "That doesn't check. According to that, we should have lost the Second Genetic War. Their 'mules' were certainly willing to fight."

"Yes, yes," Mordan agreed, "but I did not say that combativeness was the *only* survival characteristic. If it were, the Pekingese dog would rule the earth. The fighting instinct should be dominated by cool self-interest. Why didn't you shoot it out with me last night?"

"Because there was nothing worth fighting about."

"Exactly. The geneticists of the Great Khan

made essentially the same mistake that was made three hundred years earlier; they thought they could monkey with the balance of human characteristics resulting from a billion years of natural selection and produce a race of supermen. They had a formula for it—efficient specialization. But they neglected the most obvious of human characteristics.

"Man is an unspecialized animal. His body, except for its enormous brain case, is primitive. He can't dig; he can't run very fast; he can't fly. But he can eat anything and he can stay alive where a goat would starve, a lizard would fry, a bird freeze. Instead of special adaptations he has general adaptability—"

The Empire of the Great Khans was a reversion to an obsolete form—totalitarianism. Only under absolutism could the genetic experiments which bred *homo proteus* have been performed, for they required a total indifference to the welfare of individuals.

Gene selection was simply an adjunct to the practices of the imperial geneticists. They made use also of artificial mutation, by radiation and through gene-selective dyes, and they practiced endocrine therapy and surgery on the immature zygote. They tailored human beings—if you could call them that—as casually as we construct buildings. At their height, just before the Second Genetic War, they bred over three thousand types including the hyperbrains (thirteen sorts), the almost brainless matrons, the clever and repulsively beautiful pseudo-feminine freemartins, and the neuter "mules."

We tend to identify the term mule with fighters, since we knew them best, but in fact, there was a type of mule for every sort of routine job in the Empire. The fighters were simply those specialized for fighting.

And what fighters! They needed no sleep. They had three times the strength of ordinary men. There is no way to compare their endurance since they simply kept on going, like well designed machines, until disabled. Each one carried fuel— "fuel" seems more appropriate than "food"—to last it for a couple of weeks, and could function beyond that time for at least another week.

Nor were they stupid. In their specialization their minds were keen. Even their officers were mules, and their grasp of strategy and tactics and the use of scientific weapons was masterly. Their only weakness lay in military psychology; they did not understand their opponents—but men did not understand them; it worked both ways.

The basic nature of their motivation has been termed a "substitute for sex sublimation," but the tag does not explain it, nor did we ever understand it. It is best described negatively by saying that captured mules became insane and suicided in not over ten days time, even though fed on captured rations. Before insanity set in they would ask for something called *vepratoga* in their tongue, but our semanticists could discover no process referent for the term.

They needed some spark that their masters could give them, and which we could not. Without it they died.

The mules fought us—yet the true men won. Won because they fought and continued to fight, as individuals and guerilla groups. The Empire had one vulnerable point, its co-ordinators, the Khan, his satraps and administrators. Biologically the Empire was a single organism and could be killed at the top, like a hive with a single queen bee. At the end, a few score assassinations accomplished a collapse which could not be achieved in battle.

No need to dwell on the terror that followed the collapse. Let is suffice that no representative of *homo proteus* is believed to be alive today. He joined the great dinosaurs and the sabre-toothed cats.

He lacked adaptability.

"The Genetic Wars were brutal lessons," Mordan added, "but they taught us not to tamper casually with human characteristics. If a characteristic is not already present in the germ plasm of the race we don't attempt to put it in. When natural mutations show up, we leave them on trial for a long time before we attempt to spread them around through the race. Most mutations are either worthless, or definitely harmful, in the long run. We eliminate obvious disadvantages, conserve obvious advantages; that is about all. I note that the backs of your hands are rather hairy, whereas mine are smooth. Does that suggest anything to you?"

"No."

"Nor to me. There appears to be no advantage, one way or the other, to the wide variations in hair patterns of the human race. Therefore we leave them alone. On the other hand—have you ever had a toothache?"

"Of course not."

"Of course not. But do you know why?" He waited, indicating that the question was not rhetorical.

"Well . . . it's a matter of selection. My ancestors had sound teeth."

"Not all of your ancestors. Theoretically it would have been enough for one of your ancestors to have naturally sound teeth, provided his dominant characteristics were conserved in each generation. But each gamete of that ancestor contains only half of his chromosomes; if he inherited his sound teeth from just one of his ancestors, the dominant will be present in only half of his gametes.

"We selected—our predecessors, I mean—for sound teeth. Today, it would be hard to find a citizen who does not have that dominant from both his parents. We no longer have to select for sound teeth. It's the same with color blindness, with cancer, with hemophilia, with a great many other heritable defects—we selected and eliminated them, without disturbing in any way the ordinary, normal, biologically commendable tendency for human beings to fall in love with other human beings and produce children. We simply enabled each couple to have the best children of which they were potentially capable by combining their gametes through selection instead of blind chance."

"You didn't do that in my case," Hamilton said bitterly. "I'm a breeding experiment."

"That's true. But yours is a special case, Felix. *Yours is a star line*. Every one of your last thirty ancestors entered voluntarily into the creation of your line, not because Cupid had been out with his bow and arrow, but because they had a vision of a race better than they were. Every cell in your body contains in its chromosomes the blueprint of a stronger, sounder, more adaptable, more resistant race. I'm asking you not to waste it."

Hamilton squirmed uncomfortably. "What do you expect me to do? Play Adam to a whole new race?"

"Not at all. I want you to perpetuate your line."

Hamilton leaned forward. "Gotcha!" he said. "You're trying to do what the Great Khans did. You're trying to separate out one line and make it different from the rest . . . as different as we are from the control naturals. It's no good. I won't have it."

Mordan shook his head slowly. "Wrong on both counts. We intend to follow a process similar to that used to get sound teeth. Have you ever heard of Deaf Smith County?"

"No."

"Deaf Smith County, Texas, was a political sub-
division of the old United States. Its natives had
sound teeth, not by inheritance, but because of
the soil. It gave them a diet rich in phosphates
and fluorides. You can hardly appreciate the curse
of dental caries in those days. Teeth actually rot-
ted in the head, and were the cause of a large
part of the continual sicknesses of the time. There
were nearly a hundred thousand technicians in
North America alone who did nothing but remove
and repair diseased teeth—even at that, four fifths
of the population had no such help. They simply
suffered and died, with their rotten teeth poisoning their whole bodies."

"What has this to do with me?"

"It will have. The data from Deaf Smith County
was seized on by the contemporary technicians—
medicine men, they called them—as a solution
for the problem. Duplicate the diet of the Deaf
Smithians—no more caries. They were perfectly
right and biologically quite wrong, for an advantage is no good to a *race* unless it can be inherited. The clue was there, but they used it the
wrong way. What we looked for finally were men
and women who had perfect teeth despite poor
diet and lack of attention. In time it was proved
that all such cases had a group of three genes,
previously uncharted. Call it a favorable mutation.
Or call the susceptibility to tooth decay an unfavorable mutation which didn't quite kill off the
race.

"My predecessors conserved this particular gene

group. You know how inheritance fans out; go back enough generations and all of us are descended from the whole population. But, genetically, our teeth are descended from one small group—because we selected to preserve that dominant. What we want to do with you, Felix, is to conserve the favorable variations present in you until the whole race has your advantages. You won't be the only ancestor of coming generations—oh, no!—but you will be, genetically, the ancestor of them all in the respects in which you are superior to the majority."

"You've picked the wrong man. I'm a failure."

"Don't tell me that, Felix. I know your chart. I know you better than you know yourself. You are a survivor type. I could set you down on an island peopled by howling savages and dangerous animals—in two weeks you would own the place."

Hamilton grudged a smile. "Maybe so. I'd like to try it."

"We don't need to try it. *I know*! You've got the physique and the mentality and the temperament. What's your sleep ration?"

"Around four hours."

"Fatigue index?"

"It runs around a hundred and twenty-five hours, maybe more."

"Reflex?"

Hamilton shrugged. Mordan suddenly whipped his sidearm clear, aimed it at Hamilton. Hamilton had his own out and had Mordan covered at appreciably the same instant. He returned it at once.

Mordan laughed and replaced his own. "I was in no danger," he declared. "I knew that you could draw, evaluate the situation, and decide not to fire, before a slower man would see that anything was going on."

"You took a long chance," Hamilton complained.

"Not at all. *I know your chart.* I counted not only on your motor reactions, but your intelligence. Felix, your intelligence rating entitles you to the term genius even in these days."

There followed a long silence. Mordan broke it. "Well?"

"You've said all you have to say?"

"For the moment."

"Very well, then, I'll speak my piece. You haven't said anything that convinces me. I wasn't aware that you planners took such an interest in my germ plasm, but you didn't tell me anything else that I did not already know. My answer is 'No'—"

"But—"

"My turn—Claude. I'll tell you why. Conceding that I am a superior survival type—I don't argue that; it's true. I'm smart and I'm able and I know it. Even so, I know of no reason why the human race *should* survive . . . other than the fact that their make-up insures that they will. But there's no sense to the whole bloody show. There's no point to being alive at all. I'm damned if I'll contribute to continuing the comedy."

He paused. Mordan waited, then said slowly, "Don't you enjoy life, Felix?"

"I certainly do," Hamilton answered emphatically. "I've got a twisted sense of humor, and everything amuses me."

"Then isn't life worth living for itself alone?"

"It is for me. I intend to live as long as I can and I expect to enjoy most of it. But do most people enjoy life? I doubt it. As near as I can tell from outward appearances it's about fourteen to one against it."

"Outward appearances may be deceiving. I am inclined to think that most people are happy."

"Prove it!"

Mordan smiled. "You've got me. We can measure most things about the make-up of a man, but we've never been able to measure that. However—don't you expect your own descendants to inherit your zest for living?"

"Is it inheritable?" Hamilton asked suspiciously.

"Well, truthfully, we don't know. I can't point to a particular spot on a particular chromosome and say, 'There lies happiness.' It's more subtle than blue eyes versus brown eyes. But I want to delve into this more deeply. Felix, when did you begin to suspect that life was not worth living?"

Hamilton stood up and paced nervously, feeling in himself such agitation as he had not felt since adolescence. He knew the answer to that question. He knew it well. But did he wish to bare it to this stranger?

No one speaks to a little child of chromosome charts. There was nothing to mark Hamilton Felix out from other infants in the first development center he could remember. He was a nobody, kindly and intelligently treated, but of importance to no one but himself. It had dawned on him slowly that his abilities were superior. A bright child is dominated in its early years by other, duller children, simply because they are older, larger, better informed. And there are always those remote omniscient creatures, the grown ups.

He was ten—or was it eleven?—when he began to realize that in competition he usually excelled. After that he tried to excel, to be conspicuously superior, cock-o'-the-walk. He began to feel the strongest of social motivations, the desire to be appreciated. He knew now what he wanted to be when he "grew up."

The other fellows talked about what they wanted to do. ("I'm going to be a rocket pilot when *I* grow up." "So am I." "*I'm* not. My father says a business man can hire all the rocket pilots he wants." "He couldn't hire *me*." "He could *so*.")

Let them talk. Young Felix knew what he wanted to do. He would be an encyclopedic synthesist. All the really great men were synthesists. The whole world was their oyster. Who stood a chance of being elected to the Board of Policy but a synthesis? What specialist was there who did not, in the long run, take his orders from a synthesist? They were the leaders, the men who knew everything, the philosopher-kings of whom the ancients had dreamed.

He kept his dream to himself. He appeared to

be pulling out of his pre-adolescent narcissist period and to be undergoing the social integration of adolescence with no marked trouble. His developers were unaware that he was headed for an insuperable obstacle. Youths seldom plan to generalize their talents; it takes more subtle imagination than they usually possess to see romance in being a policy former.

Hamilton looked at Mordan. The man's face invited confidence. "You're a synthesist, aren't you? You aren't a geneticist."

"Naturally. I couldn't specialize in the actual techniques. That takes a lifetime."

"The best geneticist on your staff can't hope to sit where you are sitting."

"Of course not. They wouldn't wish to."

"Could I become your successor? Go ahead—answer me. You know my chart."

"No, you couldn't."

"Why not?"

"You know why. You have an excellent memory, more than adequate for any other purpose, but it's not an eidetic memory. A synthesist must have complete memory in order to be able to cover the ground he must cover."

"And without it," Hamilton added, "a man can never be recognized as a synthesist. He just isn't one, any more than a man can claim to be an engineer who can't solve fourth degree equations in his head. I wanted to be a synthesist and I wasn't equipped for it. When it was finally pounded into my head that I couldn't take first prize, I wasn't interested in second prize."

"Your son could be a synthesist."

Hamilton shook his head. "It doesn't matter any more. I still have the encyclopedic viewpoint, but I wouldn't want to trade places with you. You asked me when and how it was that I first came to the conclusion that life doesn't mean anything. I've told you how I first began to have my doubts, but the point is: I still have 'em."

"Wait," Mordan put in. "You still have not heard the whole story. It was planned that eidetic memory would be incorporated in your line either in your generation, or in your father's. Your children will have it, if your co-operate. There is still something lacking which needs to be added and will be added. I said you were a survival type. You are—except for one thing. You don't want children. From a biological standpoint that is as contra-survival as a compulsion to suicide. You got that tendency from your dexter great-grandfather. The tendency had to be accepted at the time as he was dead before his germ plasm was used and we hadn't much supply in the bank to choose from. But it will be corrected at this linkage. Your children will be anxious to have children—I can assure you of that."

"What's that to me?" Hamilton demanded. "Oh, I don't doubt that you can do it. You can wind 'em up and make 'em run. You can probably eliminate my misgivings and produce a line that will go on happily breeding for the next ten million years. That still doesn't make it make sense. Survival! What for? Until you can give me some convincing explanation why the human race should go on at all, my answer is 'no.' " He stood up.

"Leaving?" asked Mordan.

"If you will excuse me."

"Aren't you interested in knowing something about the woman whom we believe is suitable for your line?"

"Not particularly."

"I choose to interpret that as permission," Mordan answered affably. "Look over there." He touched a control on his desk; Hamilton looked where he had been directed to. A section of the wall faded away and gave place to a stereo scene. It was as if they were looking out through an open window. Before them lay a garden swimming pool, its surface freshly agitated . . . by diving, apparently, for a head broke the surface of the water. The swimmer took three easy strokes toward the pick-up, and climbed out on the bank with effortless graceful strength. She rolled to her knees, stood up bare and lovely. She stretched and laughed, apparently from sheer animal spirits, and glided out of the picture. "Well?" asked Mordan.

"She's comely, but I've seen others."

"It's not necessary that you ever lay eyes on her," the Moderator added hastily. "She's your fifth cousin, by the way. The combination of your charts will be simple." He snapped off the scene, replaced it with a static picture. "Your chart is on the right; hers is on the left." Two additional diagrams then appeared, one under his, one under hers. "Those are the optimum haploid charts for your respective gametes. They combine so—" He touched another control; a fifth chart formed itself in the center of the square formed by the four others.

The charts were not pictures of chromosomes, but were made up of the shorthand used by genetic technicians to represent the extremely microscopic bits of living matter which are the arbiters of human make-up. Each chromosome was represented by a pattern which more nearly resembled a spectogram than any other familiar structure. But the language was a language of experts; to a layman the charts were meaningless.

Even Mordan could not read the charts unassisted. He depended on his technicians to explain them to him when necessary. Thereafter his unfailing memory enabled him to recall the significance of the details.

One thing alone was evident to the uninstructed eye: the two upper charts, Hamilton's and the girl's, contained twice as many chromosome patterns—forty-eight to be exact—as the charts of the gametes underneath them. But the chart of the proposed offspring contained forty-eight representations of chromosomes—twenty-four from each of its parents.

Hamilton ran his eye over the charts with interest, an interest he carefully repressed. "Intriguing, I'm sure," he said indifferently. "Of course I don't understand it."

"I'd be glad to explain it to you."

"Don't bother. It's hardly worth while, is it?"

"I suppose not." Mordan cleared the controls; the pictures snapped off. "I must ask you to excuse me, Felix. Perhaps we can talk another day."

"Certainly, if you wish." He glanced at his host in surprise, but Mordan was as friendly and as smilingly urbane as ever. Hamilton found himself in the outer office a few moments later. They had exchanged goodbyes with all the appropriate intimate formality of name-friends; nevertheless Hamilton felt a vague dissatisfaction, a feeling of incompleteness, as if the interview had terminated before it was over. To be sure, he had said no, but he had not said it in all the detail he had wished to.

Mordan went back to his desk and switched the charts on again. He studied them, recalling all that he had been taught about them and dwelling with interest on the middle one.

A chime played the phrase announcing his chief technical assistant. "Come in, Martha," he invited without looking around.

"I'm in, Chief," she replied almost at once.

"Ah—so you are," he answered, turning to her. "Got a cigaret?"

"Help yourself." She did so from the jeweled container on his desk, inhaled it into life, and settled down comfortably . . . She was older than he, iron grey, and looked as competent as she was. Her somber laboratory coveralls were in marked contrast to the dignified dandyism of his costume, but they fitted her character.

"Hamilton 243 just left, didn't he?"

"Yes."

"When do we start?"

"Mmmm . . . How would the second Tuesday of next week do?"

She raised her brows. "As bad as that?"

"I'm afraid so. He said so. I kicked him out—gently—before he had time to rationalize himself into a position from which he would not care to back down later."

"Why did he refuse? Is he in love?"

"No."

"Then what's the catch?" She got up, went to the screen and stared at Hamilton's chart, as if she might detect the answer there.

"Mmmm . . . He posed me a question which I must answer correctly—else he will not co-operate."

"Huh? What was the question?"

"I'll ask you. Martha, what is the meaning of life?"

"What! Why, what a stupid question!"

"He did not ask it stupidly."

"It's a psychopathic question, unlimited, unanswerable, and, in all probability, sense free."

"I'm not so sure, Martha."

"But—Well, I won't attempt to argue with you outside my own field. But it seems to me that 'meaning' is a purely anthropomorphic conception. Life simply *is*. It exists."

"He used the idea anthropomorphically. What does life mean to men, and why should he, Hamilton, assist in its continuance? Of course I couldn't answer him. He had me. And he proposed to play Sphinx and not let us proceed until I solve his riddle."

"Fiddlesticks!" She snapped the cigaret away savagely. "What does he think this clinic is—a place to play word games? a man should not be allowed to stand in the way of racial progress. He doesn't own the life in his body. It belongs to all of us—to the race. He's a fool."

"You know he's not, Martha." He pointed to the chart.

"No," she admitted, "he's not a fool. Nevertheless, he should be required to co-operate. It's not as if it would hurt him or inconvenience him in any way."

"Tut, tut, Martha. There's a little manner of constitutional law."

"I know. I know. I abide by it, but I don't have to worship it. Granted, it's a wise law, but this is a special case."

"They are all special cases."

She did not answer him but turned back to the charts. "My oh my," she said half to herself, "what a chart! What a *beautiful* chart, chief."

CHAPTER THREE

"This we covenant in the Name of Life Immortal"

To this we pledge our lives and sacred honor:

"To destroy no fertile life,

"To hold as solemn secret that which may be divulged to us, directly, or indirectly through the techniques of our art, concerning the private matters of our clients,

"To practice our art only with the full and uninfluenced consent of our client zygotes,

"To hold ourselves, moreover, guardian in full trust for the future welfare of infant zygotes and to do only that which we soberly and earnestly believe to be in their best interests,

"To respect meticulously the laws and customs of the group social in which we practice,

"This we covenant in the Name of Life Immortal."

Extract from the Mendelian Oath
Circa 2075 A.D. (Old Style)

Sweet peas, the evening primrose, the ugly little fruit fly *Drosophila*—back in the XIXth and XXth centuries the Monk Gregor Mendel and Doctor Morgan of the ancient University of Columbia used these humble tools to establish the basic laws of genetics. Simple laws, but subtle.

In the nucleus of every cell of every zygote, whether man or fruit fly, sweet pea or race horse, is a group of threadlike bodies—chromosomes. Along the threads are incredibly tiny somethings, on the order of ten times the size of the largest protein molecules. They are the genes, each one of which controls some aspect of the entire structure, man, animal, or plant, in which the cell is lodged. Every living cell contains within it the plan for the entire organism.

Each man's cells contain forty-eight chromosomes—twenty-four pairs. Half of them he derived from his mother, half from his father. In each one of a pair of chromosomes, there are genes, thousands of them, in one-to-one correspondence with the genes from the chromosomes of the other parent. Thus each parent "casts a vote" on each characteristic. But some "votes" carry more weight than others. Such "votes" are called dominant, the weaker, recessive. If one parent supplies the gene for brown eyes, while the other parent supplies the gene for blue eyes, the child will have brown eyes—brown is "dominant." If both parents supply the gene for brown eyes, the vote is unanimous, but the result is the same—for that generation. But it always requires "unanimous vote" to produce blue eyes.

Nevertheless, the gene for blue eyes may be passed on from generation to generation, unnoticed but *unchanged*. The potentialities of a race are passed on unchanged—except for mutation—from parent to child. They may be shuffled and dealt and shuffled again, producing an inconceivable number of unique individuals, but the genes are unchanged.

Chess men may be arranged on the board in many combinations, but the unit men do not vary. Fifty-two playing cards may be dealt to produce an enormous number of different hands, but the cards are the original fifty-two. One hand may be full of high cards; another may be worthless—pure chance.

But suppose you were permitted to make up the best hand of five cards possible out of the first ten cards dealt? The chance of getting the best possible hand has been increased two hundred and fifty-two times! (Check it.)

Such is the method of racial improvement by gene selection.

A life-producing cell in the gonads of a male is ready to divide to form gametes. The forty-eight chromosomes intertwine frantically, each with its opposite number. So close is this conjugation that genes or groups of genes may even trade places with their opposites from the other chromosomes. Presently this dance ceases. Each member of a pair of chromosomes withdraws from its partner as far as possible, until there is a cluster of twenty-four chromosomes at each end of the cell. The cell splits, forming two new cells, each with only twenty-four chromosomes, each containing exactly half of the potentialities of the parent cell and parent zygote.

One of these cells contains a chromosome—the X-chromosome—which declares that any zygote formed with its help will be female.

The two cells divide again. But in this fission the chromosomes themselves divide, endwise, thereby conserving every gene and every one of the twenty-four chromosomes. The end product is four wigglers—male gametes, spermatozoa—half of whom can produce females; half, males. The male producers are exactly alike in their gene assortments *and are exact complements of the female producers*. This is the key point in the technique of gene selection.

The heads of the male producers average four microns in length; the heads of the female producers average five microns in length—another key point.

In the female gonad the evolution of the gamate, or ovum, is like that described for the male gametes, with two exceptions. After the reduction-division in which the number of chromosomes per cell is reduced from forty-eight to twenty-four the result is not two ova, but one ovum and one "polar body." The polar body is a pseudo egg, containing a chromosome pattern complementary to that of the true gamete, but it is sterile. It's a nobody that never will be anybody.

The ovum divides again, throwing off another polar body which has the same pattern as the ovum. The original polar body divides again, producing two more polar bodies of complementary pattern. Thus the polar bodies of pattern complementary to the ovum always exceed in number those of identical pattern. This is a key fact. All ova may become either male or female. Sex of the infant zygote is determined by the cell provided by the father; the mother has no part in it.

The above is a very rough picture. It is necessary to compress, to exaggerate, to omit detail, to use over-simplified analogy. For example, the terms "dominant" and "recessive" are relative terms; and characteristics are rarely determined by one gene alone. Furthermore, mutations—spontaneous changes in the genes themselves—occur with greater frequency than this account has emphasized. But, the picture is reasonably correct in its broad outlines.

How can these facts be used to produce the sort of man or woman one wishes to produce? Offhand, the question appears simple. An adult male produces hundreds of billions of gametes. Ova are produced on no such wholesale scale, but in quite adequate numbers. It would appear to be a simple matter to determine what combination you want and then wait for it to show up . . . or at least to wait for a combination near enough to be satisfactory.

But it is necessary to recognize the combination wanted when it shows up. And that can be done only by examining the gene patterns in the chromosomes.

Well? We can keep gametes alive outside the

body . . . and genes, while infinitesimally small, are large enough to be recognized under our ultra-microscopes. Go ahead. Take a look. Is it the gamete we want, or is it one of its lesser brothers? If the latter, then reject it, and look again.

Wait a moment! Genes are such tiny things that to examine one is to disturb it. The radiations used to see a gamete closely enough to tell anything about its chromosomes will produce a storm of mutations. Sorry, what you were looking for isn't there any more. You've changed it—more probably killed it.

So we fall back on the most subtle and powerful tool of research . . . inference. You will remember that a single male gonad cell produces two groups of gametes, complementary in their chromosome patterns. The female producers have the larger heads; the males are more agile. We can separate them.

If, in a given small constellation of male gametes, enough members are examined to determine that they all stem from the same parent cell, then we may examine in minute detail the group producing the sex we do *not* want. From the chromosome-gene pattern of the group examined we can infer the complementary pattern of the group kept free of the perils of examination.

With female gametes the problem is similar. The ovum need not leave its natural environment in the body of the female. The polar bodies, worthless and non-viable in themselves, are examined. Their patterns are either identical with that of their sister cell, or complementary. Those that are complementary are more numerous than those identical. The pattern of the ovum may be inferred with exactness.

Half the cards are face up. Therefore we *know* the value of the cards face down. We can bet—or wait for a better hand.

Romantic writers of the first days of genetics dreamed of many fantastic possibilities—test-tube babies, monsters formed by artificial mutation, fatherless babies, babies assembled piece by bit from a hundred different parents. All these horrors are possible, as the geneticists of the Great Khans proved, but we citizens of this Republic have rejected such tampering with our life stream. Infants born with the assistance of the neo-Ortega-Martin gene selection technique are normal babies, stemming from normal germ plasm, born of normal women, in the usual fashion.

They differ in one respect only from their racial predecessors: they are the *best* babies their parents can produce!

CHAPTER FOUR

Boy Meets Girl

Monroe-Alpha called for his ortho-wife again the next evening. She looked up and smiled as he came into her apartment. "Two nights running," she said. "Clifford, you'll have me thinking you are courting me."

"I thought you wanted to go to this party," he said woodenly.

"I do, my dear. And I appreciate your taking me. Half a minute, while I gown." She got up and slipped out of the room with a slow-seeming, easy glide. Larsen Hazel had been a popular dancing star in her day, both record and beamcast. She had wisely decided to retire rather than fight it out with younger women. She was now just thirty, two years younger than her spouse.

"All ready," she announced after an interval hardly longer than her promise mentioned.

He should have commented on her costume; it deserved comment. Not only did it do things with respect to her laudable figure, but its color, a live Mermaid green, harmonized with her hair and with her sandals, her hair ornaments, and her costume clips. They all were of the same dull gold as the skin-tight metallic habit he had chosen.

He should at least have noticed that she had considered what he was wearing in selecting her own apparel. Instead he answered, "Fine. We'll be right on time."

"It's a new gown, Clifford."

"It's very pretty," he answered agreeably. "Shall we go?"

"Yes, surely."

He said very little during the ride, but watched the traffic as if the little car were not capable of finding its way through the swarming traffic without his supervision. When the car finally growled to a stop at the top floor of an outlying residence warren he started to raise the shell, but she put a hand on his arm. "Let it be, for a moment, Clifford. Can we talk for a little before we get lost in a swarm of people?"

"Why surely. Is something the matter?"

"Nothing—and everything. Clifford, my dear—there's no need for us to go on as we have been going."

"Huh? What do you mean?"

"You know what I mean if you stop to think about it. I'm not necessary to you any more—am I?"

"Why, uh—Hazel, I don't know why you should say a thing like that. You've been swell. You're a swell girl, Hazel. Nobody could ask for anything more."

"Mmmm . . . that's as may be. I don't have any

secret vices and I've never done you any harm that I know of. But that's not what I mean. You don't get any pleasure out of my company any more—any *lift*."

"Uh . . . that's not so. I couldn't ask for any better pal than you've been. We've never had an argu—"

She checked him with her hand. "You still don't understand me. It might be better if we did quarrel a little. I'd have a better idea of what goes on behind those big solemn eyes of yours. You don't dislike me. In fact, I think you like me as well as you like anybody. You even like to be with me, sometimes, if you're tired and I happen to fit your mood. But that isn't enough. And I'm fond enough of you to be concerned about you, darling. You need something more than I've been able to give you."

"I don't know how any woman could do any more than you've done for me."

"I do. I do, because I was once able to do it. Do you remember when we first registered? I gave you a lift then. You were happy. It made me happy, too. You were so pathetically pleased with me and with everything about me that sometimes I could cry, just to look at you."

"I haven't stopped being pleased with you."

"Not consciously. But I think I know what happened."

"What?"

"I was still dancing then. I was the great Hazel, premiere danseuse. I was everything you had never been. Glamour and bright lights and music. I remember how you used to call for me after a performance, looking so proud and so glad to see me. And I was so impressed by your intellect (I still am, dear) and I was so flattered that you paid attention to me."

"Why you could have had your pick of all the braves in the country."

"They didn't look at me the way you did. But that isn't the point. I'm not really glamorous and never was. I was just a working girl, doing the job she could do best. Now the lights are out and the music has stopped and I'm no longer any help to you."

"Don't say that, kid."

She placed a hand on his arm. "Be honest with yourself, Cliff. My feelings aren't hurt. I'm not a romantic person. My feelings have always been maternal, rather than anything else. You're my baby. You aren't happy and I want you to be happy."

He shrugged helplessly. "What is there to do about it? Even if everything you say is true, what is there to do?"

"I could make a guess. Somewhere there is a girl who is everything you thought I was. Someone who can do for you what I once did by just being herself."

"Hunnh! I don't know where I'd find her. There isn't any such person. No, kid, the trouble is with me, not with you. I'm a skeleton at the feast. I'm morose by nature. That's what."

"Hummph right back at you. You haven't found her because you haven't been looking for her. You've fallen into a rut, Cliff. Tuesdays and Fridays, dinner with Hazel. Mondays and Thursdays, work out at the gymnasium. Weekends, go to the country and soak up some natural vitamin D. You need to be shaken out of that. I'm going down tomorrow and register a consent."

"You wouldn't really!"

"I certainly shall. Then, if you find someone who pleases your fancy, you can confirm it without any delay."

"But Hazel, I don't *want* you to turn me loose."

"I'm not turning you loose. I'm just trying to encourage you to have a roving eye. You can come to see me whenever you like, even if you remarry. But no more of this Tuesday-and-Friday stuff. That's out. Try phoning me in the middle of the night, or duck out of your sacred office during working hours."

"Hazel, you don't really *want* me to go chasing after other women, do you?"

She took his chin in her hand. "Clifford, you are a big sweet dope. You know all there is to know about figures, but what you don't know about women would fill reels." She kissed him. "Relax. Mamma knows best."

"But—"

"The party waits."

He raised the shell of the car. They got out and went on in.

The town house of the Johnson-Smith Estaire

occupied the entire top platform of the warren. It was a conspicuous example of conspicuous waste. The living quarters (that great pile of curiously assembled building materials could hardly be called a home) occupied perhaps a third of the space, the rest was given over to gardens, both open and covered. Her husband's ridiculously large income was derived from automatic furniture; it was her fancy to have her house display no apparent evidence of machine domination.

So it was that real live servants offered to take their wraps—they had none—and escorted them to the foot of the broad flight of stairs at the top of which the hostess was greeting her guests. She extended both arms as Clifford and Hazel approached. "My dear!" she bubbled to Hazel. "So gentle of you to come! And your brilliant husband." She turned to her guest of honor, standing at her side. "Doctor Thorgsen, these are two of my *dearest* friends. Larsen Hazel—such a clever little person, really. And Master Monroe-Alpha Clifford. He does things about money at the Department of Finance. Dreadfully intricate. I'm sure you would understand it—I don't."

Thorgsen managed to frown and smile simultaneously. "*The* Larsen Hazel? But you are—I recognize you. Will you be dancing for us tonight?"

"I no longer dance."

"What a pity! That is the first unfavorable change I've found on earth. I've been away ten years."

"You've been on Pluto. How fares it there, Doctor?"

"Chilly." He repeated his somewhat frightening mixed expression. Clifford caught his eye and bowed deeply. "I am honored, learned sir."

"Don't let it—I mean, not at all. Or something like that. Damn it, sir, I'm not used to all this fancy politeness. Forgotten how to do it. We have a communal colony, you know. No weapons."

Monroe-Alpha had noticed with surprise that Thorgsen was unarmed and brassarded, yet he carried himself with the easy arrogance of an armed citizen, sure of his position. "The life must be quite different," he offered.

"It is. It is. Nothing like this. Work, a little gossip, bed, and back to work again. You're in finance, eh? What sort of thing?"

"I compute the re-investment problem."

"That? Now I know who you are. We heard of your refinement of the general solution—even out on Pluto. High computation, that. Makes our little stereo-parallax puzzles look fiddlin'."

"I would hardly say so."

"I would. Perhaps we can find a chance to talk later. You could give me some advice."

"I would be honored."

Several latecomers were waiting in line. Hazel could see that their hostess was becoming impatient. They moved on. "Enjoy yourselves, my dears," she invited them. "There are, well, things—" She waved vaguely.

There were indeed "things." Two theaters were

available, one of which was giving a continuous performance of all the latest and smartest stereo-reels, the other provided the current spot news for anyone who could not relax without knowing what was going on out of his sight. There were gaming rooms, of course, and dozens of little snuggeries where small groups or couples could enjoy each other's company *tête-à-tête*. A currently popular deceiver circulated through the crowd, displaying his jests and deceptions and sophisticated legerdemain to any who cared to watch. Food and drink in lavish variety, quality, and quantity were available everywhere.

The sweeping tesselated ballroom floor was lightly filled. Pattern dancing would come later. The huge room faced, with no wall intervening, into one of the covered gardens, unlighted save for lights below the surface of numerous rocky little pools. The other side of the ballroom was limited by the transparent wall of the swimming bath, the surface of which was on the floor above. In addition to ornate decoration and moving colored lights on the water side of the crystal wall, the swimmers themselves, with the inescapable gracefulness of underwater movement, gave life and harmony to that side of the room.

Clifford and Hazel seated themselves at that wall and leaned against the glass. "Shall we dance?" he asked.

"No, not just yet." A girl, swimming on the other side of the wall, glided down toward them and blew bubbles against the glass. Hazel followed the girl's nose with her forefinger, tracing against the glass. The swimmer grinned, she smiled back. "I think I'd like a dip, if you don't mind."

"Not at all."

"Join me?"

"No, thanks."

After she had gone he wandered around aimlessly for a few minutes. The recreations at hand left him cold; he was searching half-heartedly for a niche in which he could be alone to nurse his own melancholy and, perhaps, a drink as well. But couples—not melancholy!—had had the same idea; the smaller hide-aways were populated. He gave up and entered a medium-sized lounge, already occupied by a stag group of half a dozen or so. They were engaged in the ancient sport of liquidating world problems in liquid.

He hesitated at the door, elevated his brows in query, received casual gracious consent from one who caught his eye, came on in and found a seat. The hot-air session went on.

"Suppose they do release the field?" one of the men present was saying. "What will it amount to? What will it contain? Some artifacts possibly, perhaps some records of the period in which it was set up. But nothing more than that. The notion that life could be preserved in it, unchanged, in absolute stasis, for several centuries is preposterous."

"How do you know? It's certain that they thought they had found a way of suspending, uh, shall we say *freezing* entropy. The instructions with the field are perfectly plain."

Monroe-Alpha began to understand what they were talking about. It was the so-called Adirondack stasis field. It had been a three-day wonder when it was discovered, a generation earlier, in a remote part of the mountain from which it got its name. Not that the field itself was spectacular— it was simply an impenetrable area of total reflection, a cubical mirror. Perhaps not impenetrable, for no real effort had been made to penetrate it— because of the plaque of instructions found with it. The plaque stated quite simply that the field contained living specimens of the year 1926 (old style, of course) which could be released by the means given below—but there was nothing below.

Since the field had not been passed down in the custody of recognized institutions there was a strong tendency to regard the whole matter as a hoax. Nevertheless, attempts had been made to guess the secret of the blank plaque.

Monroe-Alpha had heard that it had at last been read, but he had not paid much attention. The newscasts were always full of wonders which amounted to little in the long run. He did not even recall how the inscription had been read—a reflected image, using polarized light, or something equally trivial.

"That isn't the matter of real interest," spoke up a third man. "Let us consider the purely intellectual problem of the hypothetical man who might thus be passed down to us, out of the Dark

Ages." He was a slender, youngish man—in his late twenties, Clifford judged—and was dressed in a turquoise blue satin which brought out the pallor of his face. He spoke with slow intensity. "What would he think of this world in which he suddenly finds himself? What have we to offer him in exchange for that which he has left behind?"

"What have we to offer him! Everything! Look around you."

The young man answered with a superior smile. "Yes—look around you. Gadgets—but what need has he for gadgets? He comes from an earlier, braver world. A world of independence and dignity. Each man tilled his own plot of ground with his woman by his side. He raised his own children, straight and strong, and taught them to wrest their food from Mother Earth. He had no artificial lights, but he had no need for them. He was up with the dawn and busy with his serious, fundamental affairs. At sundown he was tired and welcomed the rest of night. If his body was sweaty and dusty with honest labor, he took a dip in his own brook. He needed no fancy swimming baths. He was based, rock solid, on primitive essentials."

"And you think he actually *liked* that better than modern comforts?"

"I certainly do. Those men were happy. They lived naturally, as the Great Egg intended they should."

Monroe-Alpha turned the idea over in his mind. There was something devilishly appealing about it. He felt, quite sincerely, that he cared nothing for gadgets. Not even for his master accumulator. It was not the machine he cared about but the mathematical principles involved. And since when did a mathematician need any tools but his own head? Pythagoras had done well enough with a stick and a stretch of sand. As for other matters, if he and Hazel were partners in the old, old, fight to win a living from the eternal soil, would they have drifted apart?

He closed his eyes and visualized himself back in the simple, golden days of 1926. He was dressed in homespun, woven by his wife's capable hands—or even in the skins of animals, cured on their cabin door. There would be children some-where about—three, he thought. When the day's work was over, he would walk to the top of the hill with his oldest son, and show him the beauty of the sunset. When the stars came out he would explain to him the intricate wonders of astronomy. Wisdom would be passed down from father to son, as it had been.

There would be neighbors—strong, silent men, whose curt nod and hard handclasp meant more than the casual associations of modern "civili-zation."

There were others present who did not accept the thesis as readily as Monroe-Alpha. The argu-ment was batted back and forth until it grew somewhat acrimonious. The young man who had started it—Gerald seemed to be his name—got up and asked the company to excuse him. He seemed slightly miffed at the reception his ideas had gotten.

Monroe-Alpha arose quickly and followed him out of the room. "Excuse me, gentle sir."

Gerald paused. "Yes?"

"Your ideas interest me. Will you grant me the boon of further conversation?"

"Gladly. You do me honor, sir."

"The benefit is mine. Shall we find a spot and sit?"

"With pleasure."

Hamilton Felix showed up at the party somewhat late. His credit account was such that he rated an invitation to any of Johnson-Smith Estaire's grand levees, although she did not like him—his remarks confused her; she half suspected the amused contempt he had for her.

Hamilton was troubled by no gentlemanly scruples which might have kept him from accepting hospitality under the circumstances. Estaire's parties swarmed with people in amusing combinations. Possessing no special talents of her own, she nevertheless had the knack of inducing brilliant and interesting persons to come to her functions. Hamilton liked that.

In any case there were always swarms of people present. People were always funny—the more, the merrier!

He ran across his friend Monroe-Alpha almost at once, walking in company with a young fellow dressed in a blue which did not suit his skin. He touched his shoulder. "Hi, Cliff."

"Oh—hello, Felix."

"Busy?"

"At the moment, yes. A little later?"

"Spare me a second. Do you see that bucko leaning against a pillar over there. Now—he's looking this way."

"What about him?"

"I think I should recognize him, but I don't."

"I do. Unless I am misled by a close resemblance, he was in the party of the man you burned, night before last."

"Sooo! Now that's interesting."

"Try to stay out of trouble, Felix."

"Don't worry. Thanks, Cliff."

"Not at all."

They moved on, left Hamilton watching the chap he had inquired about. The man evidently became aware that he was being watched, for he left his place and came directly to Hamilton. He paused a ceremonious three paces away and said, "I come in friendship, gentle sir."

" 'The House of Hospitality encloses none but friends,' " Hamilton quoted formally.

"You are kind, sir. My name is McFee Norbert."

"Thank you. I hight Hamilton Felix."

"Yes, I know."

Hamilton suddenly changed his manner. "Ah! Did your friend know that when he chopped at me?"

McFee glanced quickly to the right and left, as if to see whether or not the remark had been overheard. It was obvious that he did not like the tack. "Softly, sir. Softly," he protested. "I tell you I come in friendship. That was a mistake, a regrettable mistake. His quarrel was with another."

"So? Then why did he challenge me?"

"It was a mistake, I tell you. I am deeply sorry."

"See here," said Hamilton. "Is this procedure? If he made an honest error, why does he not come to me like a man? I'll receive him in peace."

"He is not able to."

"Why? I did no more than wing him."

"Nevertheless, he is not able to. I assure you he has been—disciplined."

Hamilton looked at him sharply. "You say 'disciplined'—and he is not able to meet with me. Is he—perhaps—so 'disciplined' that he must tryst with a mortician instead?"

The other hesitated a moment. "May we speak privately—under the rose?"

"There is more here than shows above water. I don't like the rose, my friend Norbert."

McFee shrugged. "I am sorry."

Hamilton considered the matter. After all, why not? The set-up looked amusing. He hooked an arm in McFee's. "Let it be under the rose, then. Where shall we talk?"

McFee filled the glass again. "You have admitted, Friend Felix, that you are not wholly in sympathy with the ridiculous genetic policy of our so-called culture. We knew that."

"How?"

"Does it matter? We have our ways. I know you are a man of courage and ability, ready for anything. Would you like to put your resources to work on a really worthwhile project?"

"I would need to know what the project is."

"Naturally. Let me say—no, perhaps it is just as well not to say anything. Why should I burden you with secrets?"

Hamilton refused the gambit. He just sat. McFee waited, then added, "Can I trust you, my friend?"

"If you can't, then what is my assurance worth?"

The intensity of McFee's deep-set eyes relaxed a little for the first time. He almost smiled. "You have me. Well . . . I fancy myself a good judge of men. I choose to trust you. Remember, this is still under the rose. Can you conceive of a program, scientifically planned to give us the utmost from the knowledge we have, which would not be inhibited by the silly rules under which our official geneticists work?"

"I can conceive of such a program, yes."

"Backed by tough-minded men, men capable of thinking for themselves?"

Hamilton nodded. He still wondered what this brave was driving at, but he had decided to see the game through.

"There isn't much more I can say . . . here," McFee concluded. "You know where the Hall of the Wolf is?"

"Certainly."

"You are a member?"

Hamilton nodded. Everybody, or almost everybody, belonged to the Ancient Benevolent and Fraternal Order of the Wolf. He did not enter its portals once in six months, but it was convenient to have a place to rendezvous in a strange city. The order was about as exclusive as a rain storm.

"Good. Can you meet me there, later tonight?"

"I could."

"There is a room there where some of my friends sometimes gather. Don't bother to inquire at the desk—it's in the Hall of Romulus and Remus, directly opposite the escalator. Shall we say at two hundred?"

"Make it half past two."

"As you wish."

Monroe-Alpha Clifford saw her first during the grand promenade. He could not have told truthfully why she caught his eye. She was beautiful, no doubt, but beauty alone is, of course, no special mark of distinction among girls. They cannot help being beautiful, any more than can a Persian cat, or a luna moth, or a fine race horse.

What she did possess is less easy to tag. Perhaps it will do to say that, when Monroe-Alpha caught sight of her, he forgot about the delightful and intriguing conversation he had been having with Gerald, he forgot that he did not care much for dancing and had been roped into taking part in the promenade only through his inadvertent presence in the ballroom when the figure was announced, he forgot his own consuming melancholy.

He was not fully aware of all this. He was only

aware that he had taken a second look and that he thereafter spent the entire dance trying to keep track of her. As a result of which he danced even worse than usual. He was forced to apologize to his temporary partners more than once for his awkwardness.

But he continued to be clumsy, for he was trying to work out in his head the problem of whether or not the figures of the dance would bring them together, make them partners for an interval. If he had been confronted with the question as an abstract problem—Given: the choreographic score of the dance. Required: will unit A and unit B ever come in contact?—had it been stated thus, he could have found the answer almost intuitively, had he considered it worthy of his talents.

To attempt to solve it after the dynamics had commenced, when he himself was one of the variables, was another matter. Had he been in the second couple? Or the ninth?

He had decided that the dance would *not* bring them together, and was trying to figure out some way to fudge—to change positions with another male dancer—when the dance did bring them together.

He felt her finger tips in his. Then her weight was cradled against his hand as he swung her by the waist. He was dancing lightly, beautifully, ecstatically. He was outdoing himself—he could feel it.

Fortunately, she landed on top.

Because of that he could not even help her to her feet. She scrambled up and attempted to help *him*. He started laboriously to frame his apology in the most abjectly formal terms he could manage when he realized that she was laughing.

"Forget it," she interrupted him. "It was fun. We'll practice that step on the quiet. It will be a sensation."

"Most gracious madame—" he began again.

"The dance—" she said. "We'll be lost!" She slipped away through the crowd, found her place.

Monroe-Alpha was too demoralized by the incident to attempt to find his proper place. He slunk away, too concerned with his own thalamic whirlwind to worry over the gaucherie he was committing in leaving a figure dance before the finale.

He located her again, after the dance, but she was in the midst of a group of people, all strangers to him. A dextrous young gallant could have improvised a dozen dodges on the spot whereby the lady could have been approached. He had no such talent. He wished fervently that his friend Hamilton would show up—Hamilton would know what to do. Hamilton was resourceful in such matters. People never scared him.

She was laughing about something. Two or three of the braves around her laughed too. One of them glanced his way. Damn it—were they laughing at *him*?

Then *she* looked his way. Her eyes were warm and friendly. No, she was not laughing at him. He felt for an instant that he knew her, that he had known her for a long time, and that she was inviting him, as plain as speech, to come join her. There was nothing coquettish about her gaze. Nor was it tomboyish. It was easy, honest, and entirely feminine.

He might have screwed up his courage to approach her then, had not a hand been placed on his arm. "I've been looking everywhere for you, young fellow."

It was Doctor Thorgsen. Monroe-Alpha managed to stammer, "Uh . . . How do you fare, learned sir?"

"As usual. You aren't busy, are you? Can we have a gab?"

Monroe-Alpha glanced back at the girl. She was no longer looking at him, was instead giving rapt attention to something one of her companions was saying. Oh well, he thought, you can't expect a girl to regard being tumbled on a dance floor as the equivalent of a formal introduction. He would look up his hostess later and get her to introduce them. "I'm not busy," he acknowledged. "Where shall we go?"

"Let's find some place where we can distribute the strain equally on all parts," Thorgsen boomed. "I'll snag a pitcher of drinks. I see by this morning's news that your department announces another increase in the dividend," he began.

"Yes," Monroe-Alpha said, a little mystified. There was nothing startling in an increase in the productivity of the culture. The reverse would have been news; an increase was routine.

"I suppose there is an undistributed surplus?"

"Of course. There always is." It was a truism that the principal routine activity of the Board of Policy was to find suitable means to distribute new currency made necessary by the ever-increasing productive capital investment. The simplest way was by the direct issue of debt-free credit—fiat money—to the citizens directly, or indirectly in the form of a subsidized discount on retail sales. The indirect method permitted a non-coercive control against inflation of price symbols. The direct method raised wages by decreasing the incentive to work for wages. Both methods helped to insure that goods produced would be bought and consumed and thereby help to balance the books of every businessman in the hemisphere.

But man is a working animal. He likes to work. And his work is infernally productive. Even if he is bribed to stay out of the labor market and out of production by a fat monthly dividend, he is quite likely to spend his spare time working out some gadget which will displace labor and increase productivity.

Very few people have the imagination and the temperament to spend a lifetime in leisure. The itch to work overtakes them. It behooved the planners to find as many means as possible to distribute purchasing power through wages in spheres in which the work done would not add to the flood of consumption goods. But there is a reasonably, if not an actual, limit to the construction, for example, of non-productive public works. Subsidizing scientific research is an obvious way to use up credit, but one, however, which only postpones the problem, for scientific research, no matter how "pure" and useless it may seem, has an annoying habit of paying for itself many times, in the long run, in the form of greatly increased productivity.

"The surplus," Thorgsen went on, "have they figured out what they intend to do with it?"

"Not entirely, I am reasonably sure," Monroe-Alpha told him. "I haven't given it much heed. I'm a computer, you know, not a planner."

"Yes, I know. But you're in closer touch with these planning chappies than I am. Now I've got a little project in my mind which I'd like the Policy Board to pay for. If you'll listen, I'll tell you about and, I hope, get your help in putting it over."

"Why don't you take it up with the Board directly?" Monroe-Alpha suggested. "I have no vote in the matter."

"No, but you know the ins-and-outs of the Board and I don't. Besides I think you can appreciate the beauty of the project. Offhand, it's pretty expensive and quite useless."

"That's no handicap."

"Huh? I thought a project had to be useful?"

"Not at all. It has to be worthwhile and that generally means that it has to be of benefit to the whole population. But it should not be useful in an economic sense."

"Hmmm . . . I'm afraid this one won't benefit anybody."

"That is not necessarily a drawback. 'Worthwhile' is an elastic term. But what is it?"

Thorgsen hesitated a moment before replying. "You've seen the ballistic planetarium at Buenos Aires?"

"No, I haven't. I know about it, of course."

"It's a beautiful thing! Think of it, man—a machine to calculate the position of any body in the solar system, at any time, past or future, and give results accurate to seven places."

"It's nice," Monroe-Alpha agreed. "The basic problem is elementary, of course." It was—to him. To a man who dealt in the maddeningly erratic variables of socio-economic problems, in which an unpredictable whim of fashion could upset a carefully estimated prediction, a little problem involving a primary, nine planets, a couple of dozen satellites, and a few hundred major planetoids, all operating under a single invariable rule, was just that—elementary. It might be a little complex to set up, but it involved no real mental labor.

"Elementary!" Thorgsen seemed almost offended. "Oh, well, have it your own way. But what would you think of a machine to do the same thing for the entire physical universe?"

"Eh? I'd think it was fantastic."

"So it would be—now. But suppose we attempted to do it for this galactic island only."

"Still fantastic. The variables would be of the

order of three times ten to the tenth, would they not?"

"Yes. But why not? If we had time enough— and money enough. Here is all I propose," he said earnestly. "Suppose we start with a few thousand masses on which we now have accurate vector values. We would assume straight-line motion for the original set up. With the stations we now have on Pluto, Neptune, and Titan, we could start checking at once. Later on, as the machine was revised we could include some sort of empirical treatment of the edge effect—the limit of our field, I mean. The field would be approximately an oblate ellipsoid."

"Double oblation, wouldn't it be, including parallax shown by our own stellar drift?"

"Yes, yes. That would become important."

"I suppose you will include the Solar Phoenix devolution?"

"Huh?"

"Why, I should think that was obvious. You'll type the stars, won't you? The progression of the hydrogen-helium transformation in each body is certainly a key datum."

"Brother, you're way ahead of me. I was thinking only of a master ballistic solution."

"Why stop with that? When setting up a structural analogue why not make the symbolic mechanism as similar to the process as possible?"

"Sure, sure. You're right. I just wasn't that ambitious. I was willing to sell out for less. Tell me— d'you think the Board would go for it?"

"Why not? It's worthwhile, it's very expensive, it will run on for years, and it doesn't show any prospect of being economically productive. I would say it was tailor-made for subsidy."

"It does me good to hear you say so."

They made a date for the following day.

As soon as he could gracefully do so, Monroe-Alpha excused himself from Thorgsen and went back to where he had last seen the girl. She was no longer there. He spent more than an hour looking for her, and was finally forced to the conclusion that she had left the party, or had hidden herself very cleverly. She was not in the swimming bath, or, if she were, she was capable of remaining under water longer than ten minutes. She was not in any of the accessible rooms—he had risked his life quite unconsciously, so thoroughly had he searched the dark corners.

He intended to tell Hazel of the incident on the way to her home, but he could not find the words. What was there to tell, really? He had seen an attractive girl, and had managed to trip her by his clumsiness. What was there in that? He did not even know her name. And it did not, somehow, seem like just the evening to speak to Hazel of other women. Good old Hazel!

She noticed his preoccupation, noticed that it differed in character from his earlier glumness. "Enjoy yourself, Clifford?"

"I think so. Yes."

"Meet any attractive girls?"

"Why, uh, yes. Several."

"That's nice."

"See here, Hazel—you don't intend to go through with this silly divorce business, do you?"

"I do."

One might think that he lay awake that night, filled with romantic thoughts of the nameless beauty. One would be wrong. He did think of her, but only for long enough to work out a suitable face-rehabilitating day dream, one in which he made killingly witty remarks anent his own awkwardness to which she responded with proper appreciation. It had not even been necessary to bulldoze any of the braves who surrounded her. They, too, had applauded his wit.

Nor did he think long of Hazel. If she saw fit to break the contract, it was her business. Not that there was any sense to it; it did not occur to him that anything could greatly change their relations. But he would stop his twice-a-week dine-and-visit. A woman appreciated a few surprises, he supposed.

All this was simply to clear the circuits for the serious getting-to-sleep thoughts. Thorgsen's proposal. A really pretty problem, that. A nice problem—

Hamilton Felix had a much busier night. So busy, that he had much on his mind at breakfast the next morning. Decisions to make, matters to evaluate. He did not even turn on the news, and, when the annunciator informed him that a visitor waited outside his door, he punched the "welcome" key absent-mindedly, without stopping to consider whether he really wished to see anyone. Some woman, he had noticed, from the mug plate. His thoughts went no further.

She came in and perched herself on the arm of a chair, one leg swinging. "Well," she said, "good morning, Hamilton Felix!"

He looked at her in puzzlement. "Do we know each other?"

"Noooo," she said calmly, "but we will. I thought it was about time I looked you over."

"I know!" He stabbed the air with a forefinger. "You are the woman Mordan picked for me!"

"That's right. Of course."

"Why, damn your impudence! What the devil do you mean by invading my privacy like this?"

"Tut! Tut! Tut! Mamma spank. Is that any way to talk to the future mother of your children?"

"Mother of my fiddlesticks! If I needed anything to convince me that I want to have nothing to do with the scheme, you have given it to me. If I ever do have children, it won't be by you!"

She had on shorts and a boyish corselet. In defiance of usual custom for her sex she wore, belted to her side, a hand weapon, small but deadly. She stood up at his words, resting her hands on her hips. "What's wrong with me?" she said slowly.

"Hunh! What's wrong with you! What isn't wrong with you? I know your type. You're one of these 'independent' women, anxious to claim all the privileges of men but none of the responsibilities. I can just see you, swaggering around town with that damned little spit gun at your side, demanding all the rights of an armed citizen, picking fights in the serene knowledge that no brave will call your bluff. Arrgh! You make me sick."

She remained still, but her face was cold. "You are a shrewd judge of character, aren't you? Now you listen to me for a while. I haven't drawn this gun, except in practice, for years. I don't go around insisting on privileges and I am just as punctiliously polite as the next brave."

"Then why do you wear it?"

"Is there anything wrong with a woman preferring the dignity of an armed citizen? I don't like to be coddled and I don't like to be treated like a minor child. So I waive immunity and claim my right—I go armed. What's wrong with that?"

"Nothing—if that were really the case. Which it isn't. You give the lie to your own words by the fashion in which you broke in on me. A man couldn't get away with it."

"So! So? Let me remind you, you ill-mannered oaf, that you signalled 'welcome' and let me in. You did not have to. Once inside, before I could say yes, no, or maybe, you started to snarl at me."

"But—"

"Never mind! You think you have a grievance. I said I hadn't drawn this gun in years—that doesn't mean I'm not ready to! I'm going to give you a chance, my fine bucko boy, to work out that grievance. Belt on your gun."

"Don't be silly."

"Strap on your gun! Or, so help me, I'll take it away from you and hang it in the Square."

Instead of answering he moved toward her. She gripped her weapon, half drew it. "Stand back! Stand back, or I'll burn you."

He checked himself and looked at her face. "Great Egg!" he said delightedly. "I believe you would. I honestly believe you would."

"Of course I would."

"That," he admitted, "puts a different face on things, doesn't it?" He eased back a step, as if to parley. She relaxed a trifle, and removed her fist from the grip of the weapon.

He lunged forward, low, tackling her around the knees. They rolled on the floor, tussled briefly. When events slowed down a little, it could be seen that he had her right wrist grasped firmly, as firmly, indeed, as her right hand gripped her gun.

He banged her knuckles hard against the polished floor, grabbed the shank of the weapon with his other hand and broke it out of her grasp. Still grasping her wrist, he struggled to his knees and moved away from the spot, half dragging her behind him. He ignored the minor violences that were happening to his person in the process. When he was within reach he chucked her gun in the oubliette and turned his attention back to her.

Heedless of her struggles he picked her up and carried her to a large chair where he seated himself with her on his lap. He pinned her legs between his knees, forced her arms behind her back until he managed to get both her wrists in one of his fists. She bit him in the process.

With her thus effectively immobilized, he settled back, holding her away from him, and looked at her face. "Now we can talk," he said cheerily. He measured her face with his eye, and slapped her once, not too hard but with plenty of sting in it. "That's for biting. Don't do it again."

"Let me go."

"Be reasonable. If you look closely you will see that I am nearly forty kilos heavier than you are, and a lot taller. You are tough and strong—I've got to hand it to you—but I'm a hell of a sight stronger and tougher. What you want doesn't matter."

"What do you intend to do with me?"

"Talk to you. Yes, and I think I'll kiss you."

She answered this by giving a brief but entirely futile imitation of a small cyclone, with wildcat overtones. When it was over he said, "Put your face up."

She did not. He took a handful of hair and snapped her head back. "No biting," he warned, "or I'll beat holy hell out of you."

She did not bite him, but she did not help with the kiss either. "That," he observed conversationally, "was practically a waste of time. You 'independent' girls don't know anything about the art."

"What's wrong with the way I kiss?" she said darkly.

"Everything. I'd as lief kiss a twelve-year-old."

"I can kiss all right if I want to."

"I doubt it. I doubt if you've ever been kissed before. Men seldom make passes at girls that wear guns."

"That's not true."

"Caught you on the raw, didn't I? But it is true and you know it. See here—I'll give you a chance to prove that I'm wrong, and then we'll talk about letting you go."

"You're hurting my arm."

"Well—"

This kiss was longer than the first one, about eight times as long. Hamilton released her, drew his breath, and said nothing.

"Well?"

"Young lady," he said slowly, "I've misjudged you. Twice, I've misjudged you."

"Will you let me go now?"

"Let you go? That last deserves an encore."

"That's not fair."

"My lady," he said quite seriously, " 'fair' is a purely abstract concept. By the way, what is your name?"

"Longcourt Phyllis. You're changing the subject."

"How about the encore?"

"Oh well!" He relaxed his hold on her completely. Nonetheless, it was as long and as breath-consuming as the last. At its conclusion she ran a hand through his hair, mussing it. "You heel," she said. "You dirty heel!"

"From you, Phyllis, that's a compliment. Have a drink?"

"I could use one."

He made a ceremony of selecting the liquor, fetching glasses, and pouring. He paused with his glass in the air. "Shall we pledge peace?"

She checked her own glass before it reached her mouth. "At this point? I think not. I want to catch you armed."

"Oh, come now. You fought valiantly and were licked with honor. To be sure I slapped you, but you bit me. It's even."

"How about the kisses?"

He grinned. "That was an even exchange. Don't be stuffy. I don't want you hunting me down. Come on. Peace, and let bygones be bygones." He raised his glass a trifle.

He caught her eye and she smiled in spite of herself. "All right—peace."

"Have another drink?"

"No, thanks. I've got to go."

"What's the hurry?"

"I really must go. May I have my blazer now?"

He opened the oubliette, reached in, recovered it, and dusted it off. "It's mine, you know. I won it."

"You wouldn't keep it, would you?"

"That's what I mean," he said, "about the armed women just pretending to take a man's part. A man would never ask for his gun back. He would wear a brassard first."

"Are you going to keep it?"

"No, but I wish you wouldn't wear it."

"Why not?"

"Because I want to take you to dinner tonight. I'd feel a fool, escorting an armed woman."

She looked at him. "You're an odd one, Hamilton Felix. Slap a girl around, then ask her to dinner."

"You'll come?"

"Yes, I'll come." She unsnapped her gun belt and tossed it to him. "Tube them back to me. The address is on the nameplate."

"Twenty hundred?"

"Or a few minutes after."

"Do you know, Phyllis," he said as he dilated the door for her, "I have a feeling that you and I are going to have lots and lots of fun."

She gave him a slow, sidelong look. "You'll find out!"

CHAPTER FIVE

"I myself am but indifferent honest"

Hamilton turned away from the door purposefully. There were things to be done, urgent things. He stepped to his phone and called Monroe-Alpha. "Cliff? In your office. I see. Stay there." He clicked off without offering explanation.

"Good morning, Felix," Monroe-Alpha said with his usual formality as he ushered him in. "You seemed perturbed. Anything wrong?"

"Not exactly. I want you to do me a favor. Say—what's gotten into you?"

"Me? What do you mean?"

"Yesterday you looked like a six-day corpse. Today you sparkle, you glow. There's a song on your lips and a hey, nonny, nonny. How come?"

"I didn't know that it showed in my face, but it is true that I am feeling somewhat elated."

"Why? Did the money machine declare another dividend?"

"Didn't you see the news this morning?"

"As a matter of fact, no. Why?"

"They opened the Adirondack Stasis!"

"Well?"

"It had a man in it, a live man."

Hamilton's eyebrows crawled up. "That's interesting, if true. But do you mean to tell me that the discovery of this human fossil is the cause of your childlike glee?"

"But don't you see it, Felix? Don't you *feel* the significance of it? He's an actual representative out of the golden days when the race was young—back when life was simple and good, before we messed up with a lot of meaningless complications. Think what he can tell us!"

"Maybe. What year is he from?"

"Uh . . . 1926, on the old scale."

"1926 . . . let's see . . . I'm no historian but I didn't know that that period was such glowing Utopia. I had a notion it was pretty primitive."

"That's just what I mean—simple and beautiful. I'm not a historian either, but I met a chap last night who told me a lot about it. He's made quite a study of it." He launched into an enthusiastic description of Frisby Gerald's concept of life in the early XXth century.

Hamilton waited for him to run out of breath, then said, "I don't know. I wouldn't know, but it seems to me your gears don't mesh."

"Why?"

"Well, I don't think this present day is everything it might be, but I will say I think it is probably the best set-up the human race has ever managed. No, Cliff, this 'Back-to-the-Good-Old-Days' stuff is the bunk. We get more for less, with less trouble, nowadays, than ever before in history."

"Well, of course," Monroe-Alpha answered tartly, "if you have to have an automaton to rock you to sleep at night—"

"Save it. I can sleep on a pile of rock, if necessary, but I think it foolish to go out of your way to seek discomforts."

Monroe-Alpha did not answer. Hamilton saw that his words had rankled and added, "That was strictly a personal opinion. Maybe you're right. Let's forget it."

"What was the favor you wanted?"

"Oh, yes! Cliff, you know Mordan?"

"The district moderator?"

"The same. I want you to call him up and make a date for him to meet me—I mean, to meet you."

"Why should I want to see him?"

"You don't. I'll keep the date."

"Why all the fancy business?"

"Cliff, don't ask me questions. Do it for me."

Monroe-Alpha still hesitated. "You ask me to do this blind. Is it . . . everything it should be?"

"Cliff!"

Monroe-Alpha flushed. "Sorry, Felix. I know it's all right if you want it. How shall I get him to agree?"

"Make it insistent enough and he'll be there."

"Where, by the way?"

"At my—no, that won't do. Let me use your flat."

"Certainly. What time?"

"Noon."

Mordan came into the flat looking slightly puzzled. He looked still more puzzled and surprised when he saw Hamilton. "Felix! What brings you here?"

"To see you, uh, Claude."

"So? Where is our host?"

"He won't be here. Claude, I arranged this. I had to see you and I couldn't do it openly."

"Really? Why not?"

"Because," Hamilton said, "there is a spy in your office."

Mordan simply waited.

"Before we go into that," Hamilton went on, "I want to ask you one question: Did you sic Longcourt Phyllis on me?"

Mordan looked apprehensive. "Decidedly not. Have you seen her?"

"Decidedly yes. A sweet little hell cat you picked for me."

"Don't be too hasty in your judgment, Felix. I admit she is a bit startling, but she is absolutely sound. Her chart is admirable."

"Okay, okay. To tell the truth, I rather enjoyed the encounter. But I wanted to make sure you had not been trying to maneuver me."

"Not at all, Felix."

"Fine. I didn't get you up here just to ask you that. I said there was a spy in your office. I know that because our private conversation the other day leaked and leaked badly." He plunged into an account of his encounter with McFee Norbert, and his subsequent visit to the Hall of the Wolf. "They call themselves the 'Survivors Club,' " he went on. "Superficially it's a drinking club within the lodge. As a matter of fact, it's the front for a revolutionary clique."

"Go on."

"They picked me as likely material, and I played along with them, more out of curiosity, at first. Presently I found myself in too deep to back out." He paused.

"Yes?"

"I joined up. It seemed healthy to do so. I don't know for sure, but I suspect that I wouldn't have lived very long if I hadn't taken their oath. They are playing for keeps, Claude." He paused for a moment, then continued, "You know that little shooting scrape I got into the other night?"

"Yes, surely."

"I can't prove this, but it's the only explanation that makes sense. They weren't gunning for me; they were gunning for you. You are one of the persons they have to rub out in order to put over their plans."

"What are their plans?"

"I don't know in detail . . . yet. But the sense of it is this: they've got no use at all for the present genetic policy. Nor for democratic freedom. They want to set up what they call a 'scientific' state, with the 'natural' leaders running things. They are the 'natural' leaders, self appointed. They have a great contempt for guys like you—synthesists—who help to maintain this present 'backward' state. When they are in control they intend to go all out for biological experimentation. They say that a culture should be an organic whole, with the parts specialized according to function. True men—supermen—sitting on top (that's themselves) and the rest of the population bred to fit requirements."

Mordan smiled slowly. "I seem to have seen all this before."

"Yeah, I know what you mean. The Empire of the Great Khans. They've got an answer for that one. The Khans were fools and did not know what they were up to. These boys know how. This is strictly 100% homegrown and any resemblance between it and the policies of the Khans is purely due to your lack of appreciation."

"So . . ." Mordan said nothing more for a long time. Hamilton became impatient.

"Well?"

"Felix, why do you tell me this?"

"Why? So you can do something about it!"

"But why should you want anything done about it? Wait a moment . . . please. You told me the other day that life is not worth living, as it is. If you go along with these people, you could make of life anything you want it to be. You could redesign the world to a pattern of your own choosing."

"Hm! I'd have some opposition. They have their own plans."

"You could change them. I know you, Felix. In any group, it's a foregone conclusion that you will dominate if you choose to. Not in the first ten minutes, but in the course of time. You must have known that. Why didn't you seize the opportunity?"

"What makes you think I could do anything of the sort?"

"Now, Felix!"

"All right! All right! Suppose I could. But I didn't. Call it patriotism. Call it anything you like."

"As a matter of fact it's because you approve of our culture as it is. Isn't that true?"

"Maybe. In a way. I never did say that I disliked the way things were being run. I just said that I couldn't see any sense to any manner of life, in any final absolute terms." Hamilton was feeling slightly bewildered. He had approached this interview feeling romantically heroic and expecting to be patted on the back for having unmasked the villains. But Mordan failed to get excited at the proper places, and insisted on discussing purely philosophical matters. It threw him off stride. "In any case, I don't want to see those conceited young punks running things. I can't see them building a Utopia."

"I see. Have you any more to tell me? Very well, then—" Mordan began to stir in the fashion of one about to leave.

"Hey, wait a minute!"

"Yes?"

"Look, I— The fact is, since I am already on the inisde, I thought I might do a little amateur sleuthing. We could arrange some way for me to report to you, or to someone."

"Oh, so that's it. No, Felix, I could not approve that."

"Why not?"

"Too dangerous for you."

"I don't mind."

"I do. Your life is very valuable, from my professional point of view."

"*That?* Hell's delight—I thought I made it clear that there is no chance, simply none at all, of me co-operating in the genetic program."

"You did. But so long as you are alive and fertile, I am bound to take into account the possibility that you might change your mind. I can't let you risk your life, therefore."

"Well! How are you going to stop me? You can't coerce me—I know the law."

"No . . . no, it's true that I can't prevent you from risking your valuable life, but I can remove the danger, and shall. The members of the Survivors Club will be picked up at once."

"But, but—look, Claude. If you do that today, you haven't a full case against them. The proper thing to do is to wait until we know all about them. Arresting this one group might mean that a hundred or a thousand others would simply take cover more thoroughly."

"I know that. It's the chance the government will have to take. But we won't risk your germ plasm."

Hamilton threw out his hands. "Damn it, Claude. This is blackmail. That's what it is—blackmail! It's sheer coercion."

"Not at all. I do not plan to do a thing . . . to you."

"But it is, just the same."

"Suppose we compromise."

"How?"

"Your life is your own. If you want to lose it, playing Fearless Frank, you may. My interest is in your potentialities as an ancestor. My professional interest, that is. Personally, I like you and prefer that you live a long and happy life. But that's beside the point. If you would deposit in the plasm bank a few million of your gametes, I would be willing not to interfere."

"But that's just what I was saying! You are trying to blackmail me into co-operating."

"Not so hasty. The life cells you leave with me would not be stirred into being without your consent. They would remain in escrow and you could break the escrow at will—unless you are killed in this adventure. In that case, I will use them to continue the genetic policy."

Hamilton sat down again. "Let's get this straight. You wouldn't touch them, if I don't get knocked over. No tricks?"

"No tricks."

"When it's over, I can withdraw them. Still no tricks?"

"Still no tricks."

"You wouldn't frame me into a position where I would be darned near certain to be killed, I suppose? No, you wouldn't do that. All right, I agree!

I'll bet my ability to stay alive when the shooting starts against your chance to use my deposit."

When Mordan returned to his office, he sent for his chief technician. He caused her to leave the building with him, found a suitable bit of neutral ground where there was no chance of being overheard—a bench in a deserted corner of North roofpark—and told her of his talk with Hamilton.

"I suppose you told him that all this about the Survivors Club was no news to us."

"No," Mordan said judiciously, "no, I can't say that I did. He didn't ask me."

"Mmmm ... You know, chief, you are as crooked as a random incidence curve. A sophist."

"Why, Martha!" Nevertheless his eyes twinkled.

"Oh, I'm not criticizing. You've talked him into a position whereby we stand a much better chance of getting on with the work. Just the same, you did it by letting him think that we didn't already know all about this pipsqueak conspiracy."

"We don't know 'all about it,' Martha. He'll be useful. He has already dug up one significant fact. There is a leak in our own office."

"Um, yes. That's why you dragged me away from the clinic. Well, there'll be some changes made."

"Not too hastily. We'll assume that you can trust any of the women. This scheme, by its nature, is masculine. Women are not a part of it and their interests aren't considered. But be wary of the men on the staff. I think you had better handle the deposit of Hamilton's plasm yourself—today. Better keep an eye on the women, though."

"I shall. Honest, chief, don't you think you should have told him what he was getting into?"

"You forget that it's not my secret."

"No, I suppose not. Just the same, he's much too good stock to risk in such games. Why do you think they recruited him?"

"*He* thinks it's because he's a handy man with a gun and rich as well. But I think you have answered your own question—he's starline stock. He's good breeding material. The 'Survivors' aren't entirely fools."

"Oh ho! I hadn't thought of that. Well, I still say it's a damn shame to risk him in such business."

"Public custodians must not permit themselves the luxury of personal sentimentality, Martha. They have to take the long view."

"Hmmm . . . There is something a little terrifying about a man with too long a view."

CHAPTER SIX

"We don't speak the same lingo"

Hamilton Felix discovered that a conspirator can be a busy person, especially if he is also engaged in counter-conspiracy. He tried to present a convincing picture to McFee Norbert and his other associates in the Survivors Club of an enthusiastic neophyte, anxious in every way to promote the cause. Indoctrination classes, dull in themselves but required before advancement in the organization could be expected, took a good deal of time. He endured these patiently, trying his best to maintain actually the frame of mind of romantic acceptance during instruction, in order that his questions and reactions in general would arouse no suspicion.

In addition to lessons in the principles of the New Order new members were assigned tasks to perform. Since the organization was ruled with an absolute from-the-top-down discipline, the reasons for the tasks were never explained nor were questions permitted. The assigned job might actually have significance to the conspiracy, or it might simply be a test, with every person concerned in the matter actually a brother club-member. The recruit had no way of knowing.

Hamilton saw what happened to one candidate who neglected to take the instruction seriously.

He was tried in the presence of the chapter. Attendance on the part of junior members was compulsory. McFee Norbert acted as prosecutor and judge. The accused was not represented by spokesman, but was permitted to explain his actions.

He had been directed to deliver in person a specific message to a specific person. This he had done, but recognizing the man to whom he had been sent as one he had seen at the club, he had revealed himself. "You had not been told that this man was one in whom you could confide?" McFee persisted.

"No, but he—"

"Answer me."

"No, I had not been told that."

McFee turned to the company present and smiled thinly. "You will note," he stated, "that the accused had no means whatsoever of knowing the exact status of the man he was to contact. He might have been a brother we suspected and wished to test; he might have been a government operative we had unmasked; the accused might have been misled by a chance resemblance. The accused had no way of knowing. Fortunately the other man was none of these things, but was a loyal brother of superior rank."

He turned back to the accused. "Brother

Hornby Willem, stand up." The accused did so. He was unarmed.

"What is the first principle of our doctrines?"

"The Whole is greater than the parts."

"Correct. You will understand, then, why I find it necessary to dispense with you."

"But I didn't—" He got no further. McFee burned him down where he stood.

Hamilton was part of the task group which took the body and spirited it to a deserted corridor, then disposed it so that it would appear to have become deceased in an ordinary private duel, a matter of only statistical interest to police monitors. McFee commanded the group himself and earned Hamilton's reluctant admiration for the skill with which he handled the ticklish matter. Hamilton won McFee's approval by the intelligent alacrity which he showed in carrying out his orders.

"You are getting ahead fast, Hamilton," he said to him when they had returned to the clubroom. "You'll be up with me soon. By the way, what did you think of the object lesson?"

"I don't see what else you could have done," Hamilton declared. "You can't make an omelet without breaking eggs."

" 'You can't make an—' Say, that's a good one!" McFee laughed and dug him in the ribs. "Did you make it up, or hear it somewhere?"

Hamilton shrugged. He promised himself that he would cut off McFee's ears for that dig in the ribs—after all this was over.

He reported the matter in detail, through devious channels, to Mordan, including his own part as an accessory before and after the fact. Getting his reports to Mordan occupied a good portion of his time and thoughts. Neither of his secret lives could be permitted to show above water. His daily conduct had to conform, superficially, with his public *persona*; it was necessary to continue his social life as usual, see his agent when his affairs required it, be seen in public in his habitual manner. It is not necessary to enumerate the varied means by which he found safe channels of communication to Mordan in the midst of this pattern; the methods of intrigue have varied little through the millennia. One example will suffice; Mordan had provided him with a tube address to which (he maintained) messages might be safely sent. He dare not assume that it was safe to stat a letter over his own telephone, but he could and did assume that a public phone picked at random could be used for dictation recording. The spool containing his report would then be consigned at once to the anonymity of the postal system.

Longcourt Phyllis took up much of his free time. He freely admitted that the woman intrigued him; he did not admit even to himself that she represented anything more than diversion to him. Nevertheless he was quite likely to be found waiting for her at the end of her working day. For she was a working woman—four hours a day, seven days a week, forty weeks a year, as a practical psycho-pediatrician in the Wallingford Infant Development Center.

Her occupation disturbed him a little. Why anyone should voluntarily associate day after day with a mob of yelling sticky little brats was beyond him. She seemed normal otherwise—normal but stimulating.

He was too preoccupied to take much interest in the news of the world these days, which was why he did not follow the career of J. Darlington Smith, the "Man from the Past," very closely. He was aware that Smith had been a news sensation for a few days, until crowded out by lunar field trials, and a report (erroneous) of intelligent life on Ganymede. The public soon filed him away with the duckbill platypus and the mummy of Rameses II—interesting relics of the past no doubt, but nothing to get excited about. It might have been different if his advent had been by means of the often discussed and theoretically impossible time-travel, but it was nothing of the sort—simply an odd case of suspended animation. A sight-sound record from the same period was just as interesting—if one were interested.

Hamilton had seen him once, for a few minutes, in a newscast. He spoke with a barbarous accent and was dressed in his ancient costume, baggy pantaloons described by the interlocutor as "plus fours" and a shapeless knitted garment which covered his chest and arms. None of which prepared Hamilton for the reception of a stat relating to J. Darlington Smith.

"Greetings," it began, etc. etc. The gist of it was that the interlocutor appointed by the Institution as temporary guardian for Smith desired that Hamilton grant the favor of an hour of his no-doubt valuable time to Smith. No explanation.

In his bemused frame of mind his first impulse was to ignore it. Then he recalled that such an act would not have fitted his former, pre-intrigue, conduct. He would have seen the barbarian, from sheer curiosity.

Now was as good a time as any. He called the Institution, got hold of the interlocutor, and arranged for Smith to come to his apartment at once. As an afterthought he called Monroe-Alpha, he having remembered his friend's romantic interest in Smith. He explained what was about to take place. "I thought you might like to meet your primitive hero."

"My hero? What do you mean?"

"I thought you were telling me what a bucolic paradise he came from?"

"Oh, that! Slight mistake in dates. Smith is from 1926. It seems that gadgeting was beginning to spoil the culture, even then."

"Then you wouldn't be interested in seeing him?"

"Oh, I think I would. It was a transition period. He may have seen something of the old culture with his own eyes. I'll be over, but I may be a little late."

"Fine. Long life." He cleared without waiting for a reply.

Smith showed up promptly, alone. He was dressed, rather badly, in modern clothes, but was unarmed. "I'm John Darlington Smith," he began.

Hamilton hesitated for a moment at the sight of the brassard, then decided to treat him as an equal. Discrimination, he felt, under the circumstances would be sheer unkindness. "I am honored that you visit me, sir."

"Not at all. Awfully good of you, and so forth."

"I had expected that there would be someone with you."

"Oh, you mean my nursemaid." He grinned boyishly. He was, Hamilton decided, perhaps ten years younger than Hamilton himself—discounting the years he had spent in stasis. "I'm beginning to manage the lingo all right, well enough to get around."

"I suppose so," Hamilton agreed. "Both lingos are basically Anglic."

"It's not so difficult. I wish lingo were the only trouble I had."

Hamilton was a little at a loss as to how to handle him. It was utterly inurbane to display interest in a stranger's personal affairs, dangerous, if the stranger were an armed citizen. But this lad seemed to invite friendly interest. "What is troubling you, sir?"

"Well, lots of things, hard to define. Everything is different."

"Didn't you expect things to be different?"

"I didn't expect anything. I didn't expect to come to . . . to *now*."

"Eh? I understand that—never mind. Do you mean that you did not know that you were entering the 'stasis'?"

"I did and I didn't."

"What do you mean?"

"Well . . . Listen, do you think you could stand a long story? I've told this story about forty-eleven times, and I know it doesn't do any good to try to shorten it. They just don't understand."

"Go ahead."

"Well, I'd better go back a little. I graduated from Eastern U in the spring of '26 and—"

"You what?"

"Oh, dear! You see in those days the schools—"

"Sorry. Just tell it your own way. Anything I can't pick up I'll ask you about later."

"Maybe that would be better. I had a pretty good job offered to me, selling bonds—one of the best houses on the Street. I was pretty well known—All-American back two seasons." Hamilton restrained himself, and made about four mental notes.

"That's an athletic honor," Smith explained hastily. "You'll understand. I don't want you to think I was a football bum, though. To be sure the fraternity helped me a little, but I worked for every cent I got. Worked summers, too. And I studied. My major was Efficiency Engineering. I had a pretty thorough education in business, finance, economics, salesmanship. It's true that I got my job because Grantland Rice picked me—I mean football helped a lot to make me well known—but I was prepared to be an asset to any firm that hired me. You see that, don't you?"

"Oh, most certainly!"

"It's important, because it has a bearing on what happened afterwards. I wasn't working on my second million but I was getting along. Things were slick enough. The night it happened I was celebrating a little—with reason. I had unloaded an allotment of South American Republics—"

"Eh?"

"Bonds. It seemed like a good time to throw a party. It was a Saturday night, so everybody started out with the dinner-dance at the country club. It was the usual thing. I looked over the flappers for a while, didn't see one I wanted to dance with, and wandered into the locker room, looking for a drink. The attendant used to sell it to people he could trust."

"Which reminds me," said Hamilton, and returned a moment later with glasses and refreshment.

"Thanks. His gin was pure bathtub, but usually reliable. Maybe it wasn't, that night. Or maybe I should have eaten dinner. Anyway, I found myself listening to an argument that was going on in one end of the room. One of these parlor bolsheviks was holding forth—maybe you still have the type? Attack anything, just so long as it was respectable and decent."

Hamilton smiled.

"You do, eh? He was one of 'em. Read nothing but the American Mercury and Jurgen and then knew it all. I'm not narrow-minded. I read those things, too, but I didn't have to believe 'em. I read the Literary Digest, too, and the Times, something they would never do. To get on, he was panning the Administration and predicting that the whole country was about to go to the bowwows . . . go to pieces. He didn't like the Gold Standard, he didn't like Wall Street, he thought we ought to write off the War Debts.

"I could see that some of our better members were getting pretty sick of it, so I jumped in. 'They hired the money, didn't they,' I told him.

"He grinned at me—sneered I should say, 'I suppose you voted for *him.*'

" 'I certainly did,' I answered, which was not strictly true; I hadn't gotten around to registering, such things coming in the middle of the football season. But I wasn't going to let him get away with sneering at Mr. Coolidge. 'I suppose *you* voted for Davis.'

" 'Not likely,' he says. 'I voted for Norman Thomas.'

"Well, that burned me up. 'See here,' I said, 'the proper place for people like you is in Red Russia. You're probably an atheist, to boot. You have the advantage of living in the greater period in the history of the greatest country in history. We've got an Administration in Washington that understands business. We're back to normalcy and we're going to stay that way. We don't need you rocking the boat. We are levelled off on a plateau of permanent prosperity. Take it from me—Don't Sell America Short!'

"I got quite a burst of applause.

" 'You seem pretty sure of that,' he says, weakly.

" 'I ought to be,' I told him. 'I'm in the Street.'

" 'Then there is no point in me arguing,' he said, and just walked out.

"Somebody poured me another drink, and we got to talking. He was a pleasant, portly chap, looking like a banker or a broker. I didn't recognize him, but I believe in establishing contacts. 'Let me introduce myself,' he said. 'My name is Thadeus Johnson.'

"I told him mine.

" 'Well, Mr. Smith,' he said, 'you seem to have confidence in the future of our country.'

"I told him I certainly did.

" 'Confident enough to bet on it?'

" 'At any odds you want to name, money, marbles, or chalk.'

" 'Then I have a proposition that might interest you.'

"I pricked up my ears. 'What is it?' I said.

" 'Could you take a little joyride with me?' he said. 'Between the saxophones and those Charleston-crazy kids, a man can't hear himself think.' I didn't mind—those things don't break up until 3 A.M.; I knew I could stand a spell of fresh air. He had a long, low wicked-looking Hispano-Suiza. Class.

"I must have dozed off. I woke up when we stopped at his place. He took me in and fixed me a drink and told me about the stasis—only he called it a 'level-entropy field.' And he showed it to me. He did a lot of stunts with it, put a cat in it, left it in while we killed a drink. It was all right.

" 'But that isn't the half of it,' he said. 'Watch.' He took the cat and *threw* it, right through where the field would be if it was turned on. When the cat was right spang in the center of the area, he threw the switch. We waited again, a little longer this time. Then he released the switch. *The cat came sailing out, just the way it was heading when we saw it last.* It landed, spitting and swearing.

" 'That was just to convince you,' he said, 'that inside that field, time doesn't exist—no increase of entropy. The cat never knew the field was turned on.'

"Then he changed his tack. 'Jack,' he says, 'what will the country be like in twenty-five years?'

"I thought about it. 'The same—only more so,' I decided.

" 'Think A.T. & T. will still be a good investment?'

" 'Certainly!'

" 'Jack,' he says softly, 'would you enter that field for ten shares of A.T. & T.?'

" 'For how long?'

" 'Twenty-five years, Jack.'

"Naturally, it takes a little time to decide a thing like that. Ten of A.T. & T. didn't tempt me; he added ten of U. S. Steel. And he laid 'em out on the table. I was as sure as I'm standing here that the stock would be worth a lot more in a quarter of a century, and a kid fresh out of college doesn't get blue chips to play with very easily. But a quarter of a century! It was like dying. When he added ten of National City, I said, 'Look Mr. Johnson, let me try it for five minutes. If it didn't kill the cat, I ought to be able to hold my breath that long.'

"He had been filling out the assignments in my name, just to tempt me. He said, 'Surely, Jack.' I stepped to the proper spot on the floor while I still had my courage up. I saw him reach for the switch.

"That's all I know."

Hamilton Felix sat up suddenly. "Huh? How's that?"

"That's all I know," repeated Smith. "I started to tell him to go ahead, when I realized he wasn't there any more. The room was filled with strangers, it was a different room. I was here. I was *now*."

"That," said Hamilton, "deserves another drink."

They drank it in silence.

"My real trouble is this," said Smith. "I don't understand this world at all. I'm a business man, I'd like to go into business here. (Mind you, I've got nothing against this world, this period. It seems okay, but I don't understand it.) I can't go into business. Damn it, nothing *works* the same. All they taught me in school, all I learned on the Street, seems utterly foreign to the way they do business now."

"I should think that business would be much the same in any age—fabrication, buying, selling."

"Yes and no. I'm a finance man—and, damn it, finance is cockeyed nowadays!"

"I admit that the details are a little involved," Hamilton answered, "but the basic principles are evident enough. Say—I've a friend coming over who is the chief mathematician for the department of finance. He'll straighten you out."

Smith shook his head decisively. "I've been experted to death. They don't speak my lingo."

"Well," said Hamilton, "I might tackle the problem myself."

"Would you? Please?"

Hamilton thought about it. It was one thing to kid sober-sided Clifford about his "money-machine"; another matter entirely to explain the workings of finance economics to . . . to the hypothetical Man from Arcturus. "Suppose we start this way," he said. "It's basically a matter of costs and prices. A business man manufactures something. That costs him money—materials, wages, housing, and so forth. In order to stay in business he has to get his costs back in prices. Understand me?"

"That's obvious."

"Fine. He has put into circulation an amount of money exactly equal to his costs."

"Say that again."

"Eh? It's a simple identity. The money he has had to spend, put into circulation, *is* his costs."

"Oh . . . but how about his profit?"

"His profit is part of his cost. You don't expect him to work for nothing."

"But profits aren't costs. They're ... they're *profits.*"

Hamilton felt a little baffled. "Have it your own way. Costs—what you call 'costs'—plus profit must equal price. Costs and profits are available as purchasing power to buy the product at a price exactly equal to them. That's how purchasing power comes into existence."

"But ... but he doesn't buy from himself."

"He's a consumer, too. He uses his profits to pay for his own and other producers' products."

"But he *owns* his own products."

"Now you've got *me* mixed up. Forget about him buying his own products. Suppose he buys what he needs for himself from other business men. It comes out the same in the long run. Let's get on. Production puts into circulation the amount of money—*exactly*—needed to buy the product. But some of that money put into circulation is saved and invested in new production. There it is a cost charge against the new production, leaving a net shortage in necessary purchasing power. The government makes up that shortage by issuing new money."

"That's the point that bothers me," said Smith. "It's all right for the government to issue money, but it ought to be *backed* by something—gold, or government bonds."

"Why, in the Name of the Egg, should a symbol

represent anything but the thing it is supposed to accomplish?"

"But you talk as if money was simply an abstract symbol."

"What else is it?"

Smith did not answer at once. They had reached an impasse of different concepts, totally different orientations. When he did speak it was to another point. "But the government simply *gives away* all this new money. That's rank charity. It's demoralizing. A man should work for what he gets. But forgetting that aspect for a moment, you can't run a government that way. A government is just like a business. It can't be all outgo and no income."

"Why can't it? There's no parallel between a government and a business. They are for entirely different purposes."

"But it's not *sound*. It leads to bankruptcy. Read Adam Smith."

"I don't know this Adam Smith. Relative of yours?"

"No, he's a— Oh, Lord!"

"Crave pardon?"

"It's no use," Smith said. "We don't speak the same lingo."

"I am afraid that *is* the trouble, really. I think perhaps you should go to see a corrective semantician."

"Anyhow," Smith said, one drink later, "I didn't come here to ask you to explain finance to me. I came for another purpose."

"Yes?"

"Well, you see I had already decided that I couldn't go into finance. But I want to get to work, make some money. Everybody here is rich—except me."

"Rich?"

"They look rich to me. Everybody is expensively dressed. Everybody eats well—Hell! They give food away—it's preposterous."

"Why don't you live on the dividend? Why worry about money?"

"I could, of course, but shucks, I'm a workingman. There are business chances all around. It drives me nuts not to do something about them. But I can't—I don't know the ropes. Look—there is just one thing else besides finance that I know well. I thought you might be able to show me how to capitalize on it."

"What is it?"

"Football."

"Football?"

"Football. I'm told that you are the big man in games. Games 'tycoon' they called you." Hamilton conceded it wordlessly. "Now football is a game. There ought to be money in it, handled right."

"What sort of a game? Tell me about it."

Smith went into a long description of the sport. He drew diagrams of plays, describing tackling, blocking, forward passing. He described the crowds and spoke of gate receipts. "It sounds very colorful," Hamilton admitted. "How many men get killed in an engagement?"

"Killed? You don't hurt anybody—barring a broken collar bone, or so."

"We can change that. Wouldn't it be better if the men defending the ball handlers were armored? Otherwise we would have to replace them with every maneuver."

"No, you don't understand. It's—well . . ."

"I suppose I don't," Hamilton agreed. "I've never seen the game played. It's a little out of my line. My games are usually mechanicals—wagering machines."

"Then you aren't interested?"

Hamilton was not, very. But he looked at the youth's disappointed face and decided to stretch a point. "I'm interested, but it isn't my line. I'll put you in touch with my agent. I think he could work something out of it. I'll talk with him first."

"Say, that's white of you!"

"I take it that means approval. It's no trouble to me, really."

The annunciator warned of a visitor—Monroe-Alpha. Hamilton let him in, and warned him, *sotto voce*, to treat Smith as an armed equal. Some time was consumed in polite formalities, before Monroe-Alpha got around to his enthusiasm. "I understand that your background is urban industrial, sir."

"I was mostly a city boy, if that's what you mean."

"Yes, that was the implication. I was hoping that you would be able to tell me something of the brave simple life that was just dying out in your period."

"What do you mean? Country life?"

Monroe-Alpha sketched a short glowing account of his notion of rustic paradise. Smith looked exeedingly puzzled. "Mr. Monroe," he said, "somebody has been feeding you a lot of cock-and-bull, or else I'm very much mistaken. I don't recognize anything familiar in the picture."

Monroe-Alpha's smile was just a little patronizing. "But you were an urban dweller. Naturally the life is unfamiliar to you."

"What you describe may be unfamiliar, but the circumstances aren't. I followed the harvest two summers, I've done a certain amount of camping, and I used to spend my summers and Christmases on a farm when I was a kid. If you think there is anything romantic, or desirable *per se,* in getting along without civilized comforts, well, you just ought to try tackling a two-holer on a frosty morning. Or try cooking a meal on a wood-burning range."

"Surely those things would simply stimulate a man. It's the primitive, basic struggle with nature."

"Did you ever have a mule step on your foot?"

"No, but—"

"Try it some time. Honest—I don't wish to seem impertinent, but you have your wires crossed. The simple life is all right for a few days vacation, but day in and day out it's just so much dirty back-breaking drudgery. Romantic? Hell, man, there's no time to be romantic about it, and damned little incentive."

Monroe-Alpha's smile was a little bit forced. "Perhaps we aren't talking about the same thing. After all, you came from a period when the natural life had already been sullied by over-emphasis on machines. Your evaluations were already distorted."

Smith himself was beginning to get a little heated. "I hate to tell you, but you don't know what you're talking about. Country life in my day, miserable as it was, was tolerable in direct proportion to the extent to which it was backed by industrialization. They may not have had electric light and running water, but they had Sears Roebuck, and everything that implies."

"Had what?" asked Hamilton.

Smith took time out to explain mail-order shopping. "But what you're talking about means giving up all that—just the noble primitive, simple and self-sufficient. He's going to chop down a tree— *who sold him the ax?* He wants to shoot a deer— *who made his gun?* No, mister, I know what I'm talking about—I've studied economics." (*That* to Monroe-Alpha, thought Hamilton, with a repressed grin.) "There never was and there never could be a noble simple creature such as you described. He'd be an ignorant savage, with dirt on his skin and lice in his hair. He would work sixteen hours a day to stay alive at all. He'd sleep in a filthy hut on a dirt floor. And his point of view and his mental processes would be just two jumps above an animal."

Hamilton was relieved when the discussion was broken into by another chime from the annunciator. It was just as well—Cliff was getting a little white around the lips. He couldn't take it. But, damn it, he had it coming to him. He wondered how a man could be as brilliant as Monroe-Alpha undoubtedly was—about figures—and be such a fool about human affairs.

The plate showed McFee Norbert. Hamilton would have liked not to have admitted him, but it was not politic. The worm had the annoying habit of dropping in on his underlings, which Hamilton resented, but was helpless to do anything about—as yet.

McFee behaved well enough, for McFee. He was visibly impressed by Monroe-Alpha, whose name and position he knew, but tried not to show it. Toward Smith he was patronizingly supercilious. "So you're the man from out of the past? Well, well—how amusing! You did not time it very well."

"What do you mean?"

"Ah, that would be telling! But ten years from now might have been a better time—eh, Hamilton?" He laughed.

"Perhaps," Hamilton answered shortly, and tried to turn attention away from Smith. "You might talk to Monroe-Alpha about it. He thinks we could improve things." He regretted the remark at once, for McFee turned to Monroe-Alpha with immediate interest.

"Interested in social matters, sir?"

"Yes—in a way."

"So am I. Perhaps we can get together and talk."

"It would be a pleasure, I'm sure, Felix, I must leave you now."

"So must I," McFee said promptly. "May I drop you off?"

"Don't trouble."

Hamilton broke in. "Did you wish to see me, McFee?"

"Nothing important. I hope to see you at the Club tonight."

Hamilton understood the circumlocution. It was a direct order to report—at McFee's convenience. McFee turned back to Monroe-Alpha, adding, "No trouble at all. Right on my way."

Hamilton watched them leave together with vague discomfort.

CHAPTER SEVEN

"Burn him down at once—"

Longcourt Phyllis showed up for a moment in the waiting room of the development center and spoke to Hamilton. "Hello, Filthy."

"H'lo, Phil."

"Be with you in a moment. I've got to change." She was dressed in complete coveralls, with helmet. An inhaler dangled loose about her neck.

"Okay."

She returned promptly, dressed in more conventional and entirely feminine clothes. She was unarmed. He looked her over approvingly. "That's better," he said. "What was the masquerade?"

"Hmm? Oh, you mean the aseptic uniform. I'm on a new assignment—control naturals. You have to be terrifically careful in handling them. Poor little beggars!"

"Why?"

"You know why. They're subject to infections. We don't dare let them roll around in the dirt with the others. One little scratch, and anything can happen. We even have to sterilize their food."

"Why bother? Why not let the weak ones die out?"

She looked annoyed. "I could answer that conventionally by saying that the control naturals are an invaluable reference plane for genetics—but I won't. The real point is that they are human beings. They are just as precious to their parents as you were to yours, Filthy."

"Sorry. I didn't know my parents."

She looked suddenly regretful. "Oh—Felix, I forgot!"

"No matter. I never could see," he continued, "why you want to bury yourself in that cage of monkeys. It must be deadly."

"Huh uh. Babies are fun. And they're not much trouble. Feed 'em occasionally, help them when they need it, and love them a lot. That's all there is to it."

"I've always favored the bunghole theory myself."

"The what?"

"You take the child at an early age and place it in a barrel. You feed it through the bunghole. At the age of seventeen, you drive in the bung."

She grinned at him. "Filthy, for a nice man you have a nasty sense of humor. Seriously, your method leaves out the most essential part of a child's rearing—the petting he gets from his nurses."

"I don't seem to recall much of it. I thought the basic idea was to take care of its physical needs and otherwise leave it strictly alone."

"You're way out of date. They used to have a notion of that sort, but it was silly—contra-biological." It occurred to her that Hamilton's faulty orientation might have its origin in the inju-dicious application of that outmoded, unfounded theory. The natural urges of mothers had pre-vented it ever being applied thoroughly in most cases, but his case was different. He had been what was, to her, the most tragic thing on earth—a baby that never left the development center. When she found one of these exceptions among her own charges she lavished on it extra affection and a little over. But she said nothing of this to him.

"Why," she continued, "do you think animals lick their young?"

"To cleanse them, I suppose."

"Nonsense! You can't expect an animal to ap-preciate cleanliness. It's a caress, an expression of instinctive affection. So-called instincts are in-structive, Felix. They point to survival values."

He shrugged. "We're here."

They entered the restaurant—a pay-restaurant—he had chosen, and went to a private room re-served for them. They started the meal in silence. His usual sardonic humor was dampened by the thing in the back of his mind. This business of the Survivors Club—he had entered into it light-heartedly, but now it was developing ominous overtones which worried him. He wished that Mordan—the government, rather—would *act*.

He had not gotten ahead as fast in the organization as he had hoped. They were anxious to use him, willing to accept, to demand, his money, but he still had not obtained a clear picture of the whole network. He still did not know who was senior to McFee Norbert, nor did he know the numbers of the whole organization.

Meantime, daily the tightrope became more difficult to walk.

He had been permitted to see one thing which tended to show that the organization was older and larger than he had guessed. McFee Norbert had escorted him personally, as one of the final lessons in his education in the New Order, to a place in the country, location carefully concealed from Hamilton, where he was permitted to see the results of clandestine experiments in genetics.

Beastly little horrors!

He had viewed, through one-way glass, "human" children whose embryonic gills had been retained and stimulated. They were at home in air or water, but required a humid atmosphere at all times. "Useful on Venus, don't you think?" McFee had commented.

"We assumed too readily," he continued, "that the other planets in this system were not useful. Naturally the leaders will live here, most of the time, but with special adaptation, quite useful supporting types could remain permanently on any of the planets. Remind me to show you the anti-radiation and low-gravity types."

"I'd be interested," Hamilton stated truthfully

but incompletely. "By the way, where do we get our breeding stock?"

"That's an impertinent and irrelevant question, Hamilton, but I'll answer you. You are a leader type—you'll need to know eventually. The male plasm we supply ourselves. The females were captured among the barbarians—usually."

"Doesn't that mean rather inferior stock?"

"Yes, surely. These are simple experiments. None of them will be retained. After the Change, it will be another story. We'll have superior stock to start with—you, for example."

"Yes, of course." He did not care to pursue that line. "No one has ever told me just what our plans are for the barbarians."

"No need for juniors to discuss it. We'll save some of them for experimentation. In time, the rest will be liquidated."

A neat but sweeping plan, Hamilton had thought. The scattered tribes of Eurasia and Africa, fighting their way back up to civilization after the disasters of the Second War, consigned without their consent or knowledge to the oblivion of the laboratory or death. He decided to cut off McFee's ears a bit at a time.

"This is possibly the most stimulating exhibit," McFee had continued, moving on. Hamilton had looked where he was directed. The exhibit appeared to be a hydrocephalic idiot, but Hamilton had never seen one. His eyes saw an obviously sick child with a head much too big for it. "A tetroid type," McFee stated. "Ninety-six chromosomes. We once thought that was the secret of the hyperbrain, but we were mistaken. The staff geneticists are now on the right track."

"Why don't you kill it?"

"We will, presently. There is still something to be learned from it."

There were other things—things that Hamilton preferred not to think about. He felt now that, if he managed to get through that test without displaying his true feelings, he had been damned lucky!

The proposed extermination of the barbarians reminded him of another matter. Most curiously, the strange advent of John Darlington Smith had had an indirect effect on the plans of the Survivors Club. The compelling logic of the plans for the New Order called automatically for the deaths of the inefficient and sickly control naturals, as well as the deaths of synthesists, recalcitrant geneticists, counter-revolutionaries in general.

The plans for the latter aroused no opposition to speak of, but many of the club members had a sentimental fondness for control naturals. They regarded them with the kindly paternal contempt that members of a ruling class frequently feel for subject "inferior" races. Just what to do about this psychological problem had delayed the zero hour of the Change.

The Adirondack stasis gave a means.

McFee had announced the tactical change the evening of the very day that Smith had called on Hamilton. Control naturals were to be placed in stasis for an indefinite period. It was an entirely humane procedure; the prisoners would be unhurt by their stay and would emerge in the distant future. McFee had asked Hamilton what he thought of the scheme, after the meeting.

"It should be popular," Hamilton had admitted. "But what happens after they are let out?"

McFee had looked surprised, then laughed. "We are practical men, you and I," he had said in a low voice.

"You mean . . ."

"Surely. But keep your mouth shut."

Phyllis decided that it was time to interrupt his morose preoccupation. "What's eating you, Filthy?" she inquired. "You haven't said two words since we sat down."

He returned to his surroundings with a start. "Nothing important," he lied—wishing that he could unburden himself to her. "You haven't been chatty yourself. Anything on your mind?"

"Yes," she admitted, "I've just selected the name for our son."

"Great jumping balls of fire! Aren't you being just a little premature? You know damned well we aren't ever going to have children."

"That remains to be seen."

"Hummph! What name have you picked for this hypothetical offspring?"

"Theobold—'Bold for the People,'" she answered dreamily.

" 'Bold for the—' better make it Jabez."

"Jabez? What does it mean?"

" 'He will bring sorrow.' "

" 'He will bring sorrow!' Filthy, you're filthy!"

"I know it. Why don't you forget all this business, give that noisy nursery a miss, and team up with me?"

"Say that slowly."

"I'm suggesting matrimony."

She appeared to consider it. "Just what do you have in mind?"

"You write the ticket. Ortho-spouse, registered companion, legal mate—any contract you want."

"To what," she said slowly, "am I to attribute this sudden change of mind?"

"It isn't sudden. I've been thinking about it ever since . . . ever since you tried to shoot me."

"Something's wrong here. Two minutes ago you were declaring that Theobald was impossibly hypothetical."

"Wait a minute," he said hastily. "I didn't say a word about children. That's another subject. I was talking about us."

"So? Well, understand this, Master Hamilton. When I get married, it will not be to a man who regards it as sort of a super-recreation." She turned her attention back to her dinner.

A thick silence followed for several minutes. He broke it.

"Sore at me?"

"No. Filthy, you're such a rat."

"Yeah, I know that, too. Finished?"

"Yes. Coming home with me?"

"I'd like to, but I can't tonight."

After he left her he went straight to the Hall of the Wolf. A full round-up had been ordered for that evening, no reason given but no excuses accepted. It happened also to be his first meeting since he had been promoted to the minor dignity of section leader.

The door of the clubroom stood open. A few members assembled inside were being moderately noisy and convivial, in accordance with doctrine. It was even possible that a stranger, or two, was present. Such presence was desired when nothing was going on. Later, they would be gently dismissed.

Hamilton wandered in, said hello to a couple of people, drew himself a stein of beer, and settled down to watch a dart game taking place in one end of the lounge.

Some time later, McFee bustled in, checked over the company by sight, picked up two section leaders by eye, and signalled them with a jerk of his head to get rid of the one remaining outsider. The stranger had been well lubricated; he was reluctant to leave, but presented no real problem. When he was gone and the doorway had relaxed, he said, "To business, brothers." To Hamilton he added, "You attend conference tonight, you know."

Hamilton started to acknowledge the order, when he felt a touch on his shoulder and a voice behind him. "Felix. Oh, Felix!"

He turned around, half recognizing the voice. Nevertheless, it was only his animal quickness which enabled him to cover up in time. It was Monroe-Alpha.

"I knew you were one of us," his friend said happily. "I have been wondering when—"

"Get to your section room," McFee said sternly.

"Yes, sir! See you later, Felix."

"Sure thing, Cliff," Hamilton responded heartily.

He followed McFee into the council room, glad of the brief chance to get his raging thoughts in order. Cliff! Great Egg—*Cliff!* What in the Name of Life was he doing in this nest of vermin? Why hadn't he seen him? He knew why, of course—a member of one section was extremely unlikely to meet a member of another. Different instruction nights and so on. He cursed the whole system. But why Cliff? Cliff was the gentlest, kindest man who ever packed a gun. Why would he fall for this rot?

He considered the idea that Monroe-Alpha might be an *agent provocateur,* like himself—and amazed to find *him* there. Or perhaps not amazed—he might know Hamilton's status even though Hamilton did not know his. No, that did not make sense. Cliff didn't have the talent for the deception required. His emotions showed on his sleeve. He was as pellucid as air. He couldn't act worth a damn.

McFee was speaking. "Leaders, I have been ordered to transmit to you great news!" He paused. "The Change is upon us."

They stirred, alert, attentive. Hamilton sat up.

Hell's delight! he thought, the ship about to raise and I have to be saddled with that holy fool Cliff.

"Bournby!"

"Yes, sir."

"You and your section—prime communications. Here's your spool. Memorize it at once. You'll co-operate with the chief of propaganda."

"Right."

"Steinwitz, your section is assigned to Power Center. Take your spool. Harrickson!"

"Yes, sir."

It went on and on, Hamilton listened with half his mind, face impassive, while he tried to think himself out of his predicament. Mordan had to be warned—that was primary!—at the earliest possi-ble moment at which he could break clear. After that, if there was some way to save the fool from his folly, he would try it.

"Hamilton!"

"Yes, sir."

"Special assignment. You will—"

"Just a moment, Chief. Something has come to my attention that constitutes a danger to the movement."

"Yes?" McFee's manner was impatient and frosty.

"Junior member Monroe-Alpha. I want him as-signed to me."

"Impossible. Attend your orders."

"I am not being undisciplined," Hamilton stated evenly. "I happen to know this man better than any of you. He is erratic and inclined to be hysterical. He's a deviant type, but personally devoted to me. I want him where I can keep an eye on him."

McFee tapped the table impatiently. "Utterly impossible. Your zeal exceeds your sense of subordination. Don't repeat the error. Furthermore, if what you say is true, he is better off where he is—you couldn't use him. Mosely—you're his section leader. Watch him. If necessary, burn him down."

"Yes, sir."

"Now, Hamilton—" Hamilton realized with sinking heart that his attempt to find a way out for Monroe-Alpha had simply placed his friend in greater jeopardy. He was snapped to attention by McFee's succeeding words. "At the time of action, you will get yourself admitted to the Moderator for Genetics—Mordan. Burn him down at once, being particularly careful not to give him a chance to draw."

"I know his speed," Hamilton said dryly.

McFee relaxed a trifle. "You need no help on the assignment, as you are one man who can get in to see him easily—as you and I know."

"That's correct."

"So it's just as well that you haven't been assigned a section. I imagine you'll enjoy this assignment; you have a personl interest, I think." He favored Hamilton with a sly smile.

Very, very small pieces, thought Hamilton. But he managed an appropriately grim smile and answered, "There's something in what you say."

"Ah, yes! That's all, gentlemen. No one is to

leave until I give the word—then by ones and twos. To your sections!"

"When do we start?" someone ventured.

"Read your spools."

Hamilton stopped McFee on the way to the lounge. "I have no spool. When is the zero time?"

"Oh, yes. As a matter of fact, it hasn't been assigned yet. Be ready from now on. Stay where you can be reached."

"Here?"

"No. At your apartment."

"I'll leave, then."

"No, don't. Leave when the rest do. Come have a drink with me and help me relax. What was that song about the *Rocket Pilot's Children*? It tickled me."

Hamilton spent the next hour helping The Great Man relax.

Monroe-Alpha's section was dismissed shortly before McFee released them. Hamilton used his new seniority to see to it that he and his friend were among the first groups to filter out. Once outside Monroe-Alpha, tense and excited by the prospect of action, started to babble. "Shut up," Hamilton snapped.

"Why, Felix!"

"Do as you're told," he said savagely. "To your apartment."

Monroe-Alpha continued in sulky silence, which was just as well. Hamilton wanted no talk with him until he had him alone. In the meantime he had his eye open for a telephone. The distance was short—a few flights and a short slide-a-way. They passed two booths. The first was occupied, the second showed a glowing transparency: OUT OF SERVICE. He swore to himself and continued.

They passed a monitor, but he despaired of getting his message across to a routine-indoctrinated mind. They hurried on to Monroe-Alpha's home. Once inside and the door sealed behind them, Hamilton stepped quickly to his friend's side and relieved him of his weapon before Monroe-Alpha had time to realize what he was up to.

Monroe-Alpha stepped back in surprise. "What did you do that for, Felix?" he cried. "What's up? Don't you trust me?"

Hamilton looked him up and down. "You fool," he said bitterly. "You utter, stupid, hysterical fool!"

CHAPTER EIGHT

"Thou, beside me, in the wilderness"

Felix! What do you mean? What's come over you?" His expression was so completely surprised, so utterly innocent of wrongdoing, that Hamilton was momentarily disconcerted. Was it possible that Monroe-Alpha, like himself, was in it as an agent of the government and knew that Hamilton was one also?

"Wait a minute," he said grimly. "What's your status here? Are you loyal to the Survivors Club, or are you in it as a spy?"

"A spy? Did you think I was a spy? Was that why you grabbed my gun?"

"No," Hamilton answered savagely, "I was afraid you *weren't* a spy."

"But—"

"Get this. I *am* a spy. I'm in this thing to bust it up. And, damn it, if I were a good one, I'd blow your head off and get on with my work. You bloody fool, you've gummed the whole thing up!"

"But . . . but Felix, I *knew* you were in it. That was one of the things that persuaded me. I knew you wouldn't—"

"Well, I'm not! Where does that put you? Where do you stand? Are you with me, or against me?"

Monroe-Alpha looked from Hamilton's face to the gun in his fist, then back to his face. "Go ahead and shoot," he said.

"Don't be a fool!"

"Go ahead. I may be a fool—I'm not a traitor."

"Not a traitor—you! You've already sold out the rest of us."

Monroe-Alpha shook his head. "I was born into this culture. I had no choice and I owe it no loyalty. Now I've had a vision of a worthwhile society. I won't sacrifice it to save my own skin."

Hamilton swore. " 'God deliver us from an idealist.' Would you let that gang of rats run the country?"

The telephone said softly but insistently, "Someone's calling. Someone's calling. Someone's—" They ignored it.

"They aren't rats. They propose a truly scientific society and I'm for it. Maybe the change will be a little harsh but that can't be helped. It's for the best—"

"Shut up. I haven't time to argue ideologies with you." He stepped toward Monroe-Alpha, who drew back a little, watching him.

Hamilton suddenly, without taking his eyes off Monroe-Alpha's face, kicked him in the groin. "Someone's calling. Someone's calling." Hamilton holstered his gun—fast—bent over the disabled man and punched him in the pit of the stomach, not with his fist but with stiffened fingers. It was nicely calculated to paralyse the diaphragm—and did. He dragged Monroe-Alpha to a point under the telephone, placed a knee in the small of his back, and seized his throat with the left hand.

"One move is all you'll get," he warned. With his right hand he cut in the phone. His face was close to the pick-up; nothing else would be transmitted.

McFee Norbert's face appeared in the frame. "Hamilton!" he said. "What in the hell are you doing there?"

"I went home with Monroe-Alpha."

"That's direct disobedience. You'll answer for it—later. Where's Monroe-Alpha?"

Hamilton gave a brief, false, but plausible, explanation.

"A fine time to have to do that," McFee commented. "Give him these orders: he is relieved from duty. Tell him to get far away and stay away for forty-eight hours. I've decided to take no chances with him."

"Right," said Hamilton.

"And you—do you realize how near you came to missing your orders? You should be in action ten minutes before the section group moves in. Get going."

"Now?"

"Now."

Hamilton cleared the circuit. Monroe-Alpha had started to struggle the second the phone came to life. Hamilton had ground his knee into his spine and clamped down hard on his throat, but it was a situation which could not be maintained indefinitely.

He eased up on Monroe-Alpha a little. "You heard those orders?"

"Yes," Monroe-Alpha acknowledged hoarsely.

"You are going to carry them out. Where's your run-about?"

No answer. Hamilton dug in viciously. "Answer me. On the roof?"

"Yes."

Hamilton did not bother to answer. He took his heavy automatic from its holster and struck Monroe-Alpha behind his right ear. The man's head jerked once, then sagged limply. Hamilton turned to the phone and signalled Mordan's personal number. He waited apprehensively while distant machinery hunted, fearful that the report would come back, "NOWHERE AVAILABLE." He was relieved when the instrument reported instead, "Signalling."

After an interminable time—all of three or four seconds—Mordan's face lighted up the frame. "Oh—hello, Felix."

"Claude—the time's come! This is it."

"Yes, I know. That's why I'm here." The background behind him showed his office.

"You—*knew*?"

"Yes, Felix."

"But . . . Never mind. I'm coming over."

"Yes, certainly." He cut off.

Hamilton reflected grimly that one more surprise would be just enough to cause him to start picking shadows off the wall. But he had no time to worry about it. He rushed into his friend's bedchamber, found whiat he wanted immediately— small pink capsules, Monroe-Alpha's habitual relief from the peril of sleepless worry. He returned then and examined Monroe-Alpha briefly. He was still out cold.

He picked him up in his arms, went out into the corridor, and sought the lift. He passed one startled citizen on the way. Hamilton looked at him, said, "Sssh—you'll waken him. Open the lift for me, will you please?"

The citizen looked dubious, shrugged, and did as he was requested.

He found Monroe-Alpha's little skycar without trouble, removed the key from his friend's pocket, and opened it. He dumped his burden inside, set the pilot for the roof of the Clinic, and depressed the impeller bar. He had done all he could for the moment; in over-city traffic automatic operation was faster than manual. It would be five minutes, or more, before he reached Mordan, but, even at that, he had saved at least ten minutes over what it would have taken by tube and slideway.

It consoled him somewhat for the time he had wasted on Monroe-Alpha.

The man was beginning to stir. Hamilton took a cup from the cooler, filled it with water, dissolved three of the capsules in it, and went to his side. He slapped him.

Monroe-Alpha sat up. "Whassa matter?" he said. "Stop it. What's happened?"

"Drink this." Hamilton put the cup to his lips.

"What happened? My head hurts."

"It ought to—you had quite a fall. Drink it. You'll feel better."

Monroe-Alpha complied docilely. When he had finished, Hamilton watched him narrowly, wondering if he would have to slug him again before the hypnotic took hold. But Monroe-Alpha said nothing more, seemed still dazed, and shortly was sleeping soundly.

The car grounded gently.

Hamilton raised the panel of the communicator, shoved his foot inside, and pushed. There was a satisfying sound of breaking crystal and snapping wires. He set the pilot on due South, without destination, opened the door, and stepped out. He turned, reached inside, sought the impeller bar— but hesitated without depressing it. He stepped back inside and removed the selector key from the pilot. He stepped out again, depressed the impeller—and ducked. As the door slammed shut, the little runabout angled straight up, seeking cruising altitude.

He did not wait for it to go out of sight, but turned and started below.

Monroe-Alpha awoke with a dry mouth, an excruciatingly throbbing head, a nauseous feeling at his midriff, and a sense of impending disaster. He became aware of things in that order.

He knew that he was in the air, in a skycar,

and alone, but how had he gotten there, why he was there, escaped him. He had had some dreadful nightmares—they seemed to have some bearing on it. There was something he should be doing.

This was the Day, the Day of the Change! That was it!

But why was he here? He should be with his section. No. No, McFee had said—

What was it he had said? And where was Hamilton? *Hamilton was a spy!* Hamilton was about to betray them all!

He must inform McFee at once. Where was he? No matter—call him!

It was then that he found the wrecked communicator. And the bright sunlight outside told him it was too late, too late. Whatever had come of Hamilton's treachery had already happened. Too late.

The pieces were beginning to fall into place. He recalled the ugly interview with Hamilton, the message from McFee, the fight. Apparently he had been knocked out. There was nothing left to do but to go back, turn himself in to his leader, and confess his failure.

No. McFee had given him orders to stay out, to stay away for two days. He must obey. The Whole is greater than the parts.

But those orders did not apply—McFee had not known about Hamilton.

He knew now. That was certain. Therefore, the

orders *did* apply. What was it McFee had said?
"I've decided to take no chances on him."

They didn't trust him. Even McFee knew him
for what he was—a thumb-fingered idiot who
could be depended on to do the wrong thing at
the wrong time.

He never had been any good. All he was fit for
was to do fiddling things with numbers. He knew
it. Everybody knew it. Hazel knew it. If he met a
girl he liked, the best he could do was to knock
her off her feet. Hamilton knew it. Hamilton
hadn't even bothered to kill him—he wasn't
worth killing.

They hadn't really wanted him in the Survivors
Club—not in a pinch. They just wanted him available to set up the accounting for the New Order.
McFee had spoken to him about that, asked him
if he could do it. Naturally, he could. That's all
he was—a clerk.

Well, if they wanted him for that, he'd do it.
He wasn't proud. All he asked was to serve. It
would be a fairly simple matter to set up foolproof
accounting for a collective-type state. It would not
take him long; after that, his usefulness ended,
he would be justified in taking the long sleep.

He got up, having found some comfort in complete self-abnegation. He rinsed out his mouth,
drank more than a litre of water, and felt a little
better. He rummaged in the larder, opened a seal
of tomato juice, drank it, and felt almost human,
in a deeply melancholy way.

He then investigated his location. The car was

hovering; it had reached the extreme limit of its automatic radius. The ground was concealed by clouds, though it was bright sunlight where he was. The pilot showed him the latitude and longitude; a reference to the charts placed him somewhere over the Sierra Nevada Mountains—almost precisely over the Park of the Giant Redwoods, he noticed.

He derived a flicker of interest from that. The Survivors Club, in their public, social guise, claimed the Generalsherman Tree as president emeritus. It was a nice jest, he thought—the unkillable, perfectly adapted Oldest Living Thing on Earth.

The sabotaged pilot put wrinkles between his eyes. He could fly it manually, but he could not enter the traffic of the Capital until it was repaired. He would have to seek some small town—

No, McFee had said to go away and stay away—and McFee meant what he said. If he went to any town, he would be mixed up in the fighting.

He did not admit to himself that he no longer had any stomach for it—that Hamilton's words had left him with unadmitted doubts.

Still, it must be repaired. There might be a repair station at the Park—must be, in fact, in view of the tourist traffic. And surely the Change would not cause any fighting there.

He cut in the fog eyes and felt his way down.

When he grounded a single figure approached.

"You can't stay," the man said, when he was in earshot. "The Park's closed."

"I've got to have a repair," said Monroe-Alpha. "Why is the Park closed?"

"Can't say. Some trouble down below. The rangers were called on special duty hours ago, and we sent the tourists out. There's nobody here but me."

"Can you repair?"

"Could . . . maybe. What's the trouble?"

Monroe-Alpha showed him. "Can you fix it?"

"Not the talkie box. Might scare up some parts for the pilot. What happened? Looks like you smashed it yourself."

"I didn't." He opened a locker, located his car gun, and stuck it in his holster. The caretaker was brassarded; he shut up at once. "I think I'll take a walk while you fix it."

"Yes sir. It won't take long."

Monroe-Alpha took out his credit folder, tore out a twenty credit note, and handed it to the man. "Here. Leave it in the hangar." He wanted to be alone, to talk to no one at all, least of all this inquisitive stranger. He turned and walked away.

He had seen very little of the Big Trees in landing; he had kept his eyes glued to the fog eyes and had been quite busy with the problem of landing. Nor had he ever been in the Park before. True, he had seen pictures—who has not?—but pictures are not the trees. He started out, more intent on his inner turmoil than on the giants around him.

But the place got him.

There was no sun, no sky. The trees lost themselves in a ceiling of mist, a remote distance overhead. There was no sound. His own footsteps lost themselves in a carpet of evergreen needles. There was no limiting horizon; endless succession only of stately columns, slim green columns of sugar pine, a mere meter in thickness, massive redbrown columns of the great ones themselves. They receded from him on all sides, the eye could see nothing but trees—trees, the mist overhead, and the carpet of their debris, touched in spots by stubborn patches of old snow.

An occasional drop of purely local rain fell, dripping from the branches far above.

There was no time there. This had been, was and would be. Time was not. There was no need for time here; the trees negated it, ignored it. Seasons they might recognize, lightly, as one notes and dismisses a passing minute. He had a feeling that he moved too frantically for them to notice, that he was too small for them to see.

He stopped, and approached one of the elders, cautiously, as befits a junior in dealing with age. He touched its coat, timidly at first, then with palm-flat pressure, as he gained confidence. It was not cool, as bark is, but warm and live in spite of the moisture that clung to it. He drew from the tree, through its warm shaggy pelt, a mood of tranquil strength. He felt sure, on a level of being just below that of word-shaped thoughts, that the tree was serene and sure of itself, and, in some earth-slow somber fashion, happy.

He was no longer capable of worrying over the remote problems of his own ant hill. His scale had changed, and the frenetic struggles of that world had faded both in time and distance until he no longer discerned their details.

He came upon the Old One unexpectedly. He had been moving through the forest, feeling it rather than thinking about it. If there were signs warning him of what lay ahead he had not seen them. But he needed no signs to tell him what he saw. The other giants had been huge and old; this one dwarfed them as they dwarfed the sugar pines.

Four thousand years it had stood there, maintaining, surviving, building its giant thews of living wood. Egypt and Babylon were young with it—it was still young. David had sung and died. Great Caesar stained the Senate floor with his ambitious blood. Mohamet fled. Colon Christopher importuned a queen, and the white men found the tree, still standing, still green. They named him for a man known only through that fact—Generalsherman. The Generalsherman Tree.

It had no need of names. It was itself, the eldest citizen, quiet, untroubled, alive and unworried.

He did not stay near it long. It helped him, but its presence was overpowering to him, as it has been to every man who has ever seen it. He went back through the woods, finding the company of those lesser immortals almost jovial by contrast.

When he got back near the underground hangar in front of which he had left his runabout, he skirted around it, not wishing to see anyone as yet. He continued on.

Presently he found his way blocked by a solid grey mass of granite which labored on up out of sight in the mist. A series of flights of steps, cleverly shaped to blend into the natural rock, wound up through its folds. There was a small sign at the foot of these stairs: MORO ROCK. He recognized it, both from pictures and a brief glimpse he had had of it through the fog in landing. It was a great grey solid mass of stone, peak-high and mountain-wide, a fit place for a Sabbat.

He started to climb. Presently the trees were gone. There was nothing but himself, the grey mist, and the grey rock. His feeling for up-and-down grew shaky, he had to watch his feet and the steps to hang on to it.

Once he shouted. The sound was lost and nothing came back.

The way led along a knife edge, on the left a sheer flat slide of rock, on the right bottomless empty grey nothingness. The wind cut cold across it. Then the path climbed the face of the rock again.

He began to hurry; he had reached a decision. He could not hope to emulate the serene, eternal certainty of the old tree—he was not built for it. Nor was he built, he felt sure, for the life he knew. No need to go back to it, no need to face it out with Hamilton nor McFee, whichever won their deadly game. Here was a good place, a place to die with clean dignity.

There was a clear drop of a thousand meters down the face of the rock.

He reached the top at last and paused, a little breathless from his final exertion. He was ready and the place was ready—when he saw that he was not alone. There was another figure, prone, resting on elbows, looking out at the emptiness.

He turned, and was about to leave. His resolution was shaken by another's presence. He felt nakedly embarrassed.

Then she turned and looked at him. Her gaze was friendly and unsurprised. He recognized her—without surprise, and was surprised that he had not been. He saw that she recognized him.

"Oh, hello," he said stupidly.

"Come sit down," she answered.

He accepted silently, and squatted beside her. She said nothing more at the time, but remained resting on one elbow, watching him—not narrowly, but with easy quietness. He liked it. She gave out warmth, as the redwoods did.

Presently she spoke. "I intended to speak to you after the dance. You were unhappy."

"Yes. Yes, that is true."

"You are not unhappy now."

"No," he found himself saying and realized with a small shock that it was true. "No, I am happy now."

They were silent again. She seemed to have no need for small speech, nor for restless movement.

He felt calmed by her manner himself, but his own calm was not as deep. "What were you doing here?" he asked.

"Nothing. Waiting for you, perhaps." The answer was not logical, but it pleased him.

Presently the wind became more chill and the fog a deeper grey. They started down. The way seemed shorter this time. He made a show of helping her, and she accepted it, although she was more surefooted than he and they both knew it. Then they were on the floor of the forest and there was no further excuse to touch her hand or arm.

They encountered a group of mule deer—a five-point buck who glanced at them and returned to the serious business of eating, his dignity undisturbed; two does who accepted them with the calm assurance of innocence long protected; and three fawns. The does were passively friendly, but enjoyed being scratched, especially behind their ears.

The fawns were skittishly curious. They crowded around, stepping on their feet and nuzzling their clothes, then would skitter away in sudden alarm at an unexpected movement, their great soft ears flopping foolishly.

The girl offered them leaves plucked from a shrub, and laughed when her fingers were nibbled. Monroe-Alpha tried it and smiled broadly—the nibbling tickled. He would have liked to have wiped his fingers, but noticed that she did not, and refrained.

He felt a compulsion to unburden himself to her, as they walked along, and tried to, stumbling. He stopped long before he had made himself clear, and looked at her, half expecting to see disgusted disapproval in her eyes. There was none. "I don't know what it is you have done," she said, "but you haven't been bad. Foolish, perhaps, but not bad." She stopped, looked a little puzzled, and added reflectively, "I've never met any bad people."

He tried to describe some of the ideals of the Survivors Club. He spoke of the plans for dealing with the control naturals as being the easiest and clearest to explain. No inhumanity, a bare minimum of necessary coercion, a free choice between a simple sterilizing operation and a trip to the future—all this in the greater interest of the race. He spoke of these things as something that might be done if the people were wise enough to accept it.

She shook her head. "I don't think I would care for it," she said gently, but with clear finality. He dropped the subject.

He was surprised when it became dark. "I suppose we should hurry on to the lodge," he said.

"The lodge is closed." That was true, he remembererd. The Park was closed; they were not supposed to be there. He started to ask her if she had a skycar there, or had she come up through the tunnel, but checked himself. Either way, she would be leaving him. He did not want that; he himself was not pressed for time—his forty-eight hours would not be up until the morrow. "I saw some cabins as I came this way," he suggested.

They found them, nestling half hidden in a hollow. They were unfurnished and quite evidently out of service, but strong and weather-tight. He rummaged around in the cupboards and found a little glow-heater with more than enough charge showing on its dial for their needs. Water there was, but no food. It did not matter.

There were not even cushion beds available, but the floor was warm and clean. She lay down, seemed to nestle out a bed in the floor as an animal might, said, "Good night," and closed her eyes. He believed that she went to sleep at once.

He expected to find it hard to get to sleep, but he fell asleep before he had time to worry about it.

When he awoke it was with a sense of well-being such as he had not enjoyed in many days— months. He did not attempt to analyze it at once, but simply savored it, wallowed in it, stretching luxuriously while his soul fitted itself, catlike, back into its leasehold.

Then he caught sight of her face, across the cabin floor, and knew why he felt cheerful. She was still asleep, her head cradled on the curve of her arm. Bright sun flooded in through the window and illuminated her face. It was, he decided, not necessarily a beautiful face, although he could find no fault with it. Its charm lay more in a child-like quality, a look of fresh wonder, as if she greeted each new experience as truly new and wholly delightful—so different, he thought, from the jaundiced melancholy he had suffered from.

Had suffered from. For he realized that her enthusiasm was infectious, that he had caught it, and that he owed his present warm elation to her presence.

He decided not to wake her. He had much to think of, anyhow, before he was ready to talk with another. He saw now that his troubles of yesterday had been sheer funk. McFee was a careful commander; if McFee saw fit to leave him off the firing line, he should not complain or question. The Whole was greater than the parts. McFee's decision was probably inspired by Felix, anyhow—from the best of intentions.

Good old Felix! Misguided, but a good sort anyhow. He would have to see if he couldn't intercede for Hamilton, in the reconstruction. They could not afford to hold grudges—the New Order had no place for small personal emotions. Logic and science.

There would be much to be done and he could still be useful. The next phase started today—rounding up control naturals, giving them their choice of two humane alternatives. Questioning public officials of every sort and determining whether or not they were temperamentally suited to continue to serve under the New Order. Oh, there was much to be done—he wondered why he had felt yesterday that there was no place for him.

Had he been as skilled in psychologics as he was in mathematics he might possibly have recognized his own pattern for what it was—religious enthusiasm, the desire to be a part of a greater whole and to surrender one's own little worries to the keeping of an over-being. He had been told, no doubt, in his early instruction, that revolutionary political movements and crusading religions were the same type-form process, differing only in verbal tags and creeds, but he had never *experienced* either one before. In consequence, he failed to recognize what had happened to him. Religious frenzy? What nonsense—he believed himself to be an extremely hard-headed agnostic.

She opened her eyes, saw him and smiled, without moving. "Good morning," she said.

"Good morning, good morning," he agreed. "I neglected to ask your name yesterday."

"My name is Marion," she answered. "What is yours?"

"I am Monroe-Alpha Clifford."

" 'Monroe-Alpha,' " she mused. "That's a good line, Clifford. I suppose you—" She got no further with her remark; her expression was suddenly surprised; she made two gasping quick intakes of breath, buried her face in her hands, and sneezed convulsively.

Monroe-Alpha sat up abruptly, at once alert and no longer happy. She? Impossible!

But he faced the first test of his new-found resolution firmly. It was going to be damned unpleasant, he realized, but he had to do it. The Whole is greater than the parts.

He even derived unadmitted melancholy satisfaction from the realization that he could do his duty, no matter how painful. "You sneezed," he said accusingly.

"It was nothing," she said hastily. "Dust—dust and the sunshine."

"Your voice is thick. Your nose is stopped up. Tell me the truth. You're a 'natural'—*aren't you?*"

"You don't understand," she protested. "I'm a— oh, dear!" She sneezed twice in rapid succession, then left her head bowed.

Monroe-Alpha bit his lip. "I hate this as much as you do," he said, "but I'm bound to assume that you are a control natural until you prove the contrary."

"Why?"

"I tried to explain to you yesterday. I've got to take you in to the Provisional Committee—what I was talking about is already an established fact."

She did not answer him. She just looked. It made him still more uncomfortable. "Come now," he said. "No need to be tragic about it. You won't have to enter the stasis. A simple, painless operation that leaves you unchanged—no disturbance of your endocrine balance at all. Besides, there may be no need for it. Let me see your tattoo."

Still she did not answer. He drew his gun and levelled it at her. "Don't trifle with me. I mean it." He lowered his sights and pinged the floor just in front of her. She flinched back from the burnt wood and the little puff of smoke. "If you force me, I'll burn you. I'm not joking. Let me see your tattoo."

When still she made no move, he got up, went to her, grabbed her roughly by the arm, dragging her to her feet. "Let's see your tattoo."

She hesitated, then shrugged her shoulders. "All right . . . but you'll be sorry." She lifted her left arm. As he lowered his head to read the figures tattooed near the arm pit she brought her hand down sharply near the wrist joint of his right hand. At the same instant her right fist made a painful surprise in the pit of his stomach.

He dropped his gun.

He dived after the gun before it had clattered to a stop and was up after her. But she was already gone. The cabin door stood open, framing a picture of sugar pines and redwoods, but no human figure. A bluejay cursed and made a flicker of blue; nothing else moved.

Monroe-Alpha leaped to the door and looked both ways, covering the same arc with his weapon, but the Giant Forest had swallowed her. She was somewhere close at hand, of course; her flight had disturbed the jay. But where? Behind which of fifty trees? Had there been snow on the ground he would have known, but the snow had vanished, except for bedraggled hollows, and the pine needles carpet of an evergreen forest left no tracks perceptible to his untrained eye—nor was it cluttered with undergrowth to impede and disclose her flight.

He cast around uncertainly like a puzzled hound. He caught a movement from the corner of his eye, turned, saw a flash of white, and fired instantly.

He had hit—that was sure. His target had fallen behind a baby pine which blocked his veiw, thrashed once, and was quiet. He went toward the little tree with reluctant steps, intending to finish her off mercifully, if, by chance, his first bolt had merely mutilated her.

It was not she, but a mule deer fawn. His charge had burnt away half the rump and penetrated far up into the vitals. The movement he had seen and heard could have been no more than dying reflex. Its eyes were wide open, deer soft, and seemed to him to be filled with gentle reproach. He turned away at once, feeling a little sick. It was the first non-human animal he had ever killed.

He spent only a few minutes more searching for her. His sense of duty he quieted by telling himself that she stood no chance of getting away here in the mountain forest anyhow, infected, as he knew her to be, with a respiratory ailment. She would have to give up and turn herself in.

Monroe-Alpha did not return to the cabin. He had left nothing there, and he assumed that the little glow-heater which had kept them warm through the night was equipped with automatic cut-off. If not, no matter—it did not occur to him to weigh his personal convenience against the waste involved. He went at once to the parking lot underground where he found his runabout, climbed in, and started its impeller. There was an immediate automatic response from the Park's traffic signal system, evidenced by glowing letters on the runabout's annunciator: NO CRUISING OVER GIANT FOREST—ANGLE THREE THOUSAND AND SCRAMBLE. He obeyed without realizing it; his mind was not on the conning of the little car.

His mind was not on anything in particular. The lethargy, the bitter melancholy, which had enervated him before the beginning of the Readjustment, descended on him with renewed force. For what good? To what purpose was this blind senseless struggle to stay alive, to breed, to fight? He drove the little capsule as fast as its impeller would shove it straight for the face of Mount Whitney, with an unreasoned half-conscious intention of making an ending there and then.

But the runabout was not built to crash. With the increase in speed the co-pilot extended the range of its feelers; the klystrons informed the tracker; solenoids chattered briefly and the car angled over the peak.

CHAPTER NINE

"When we die, do we die all over?"

As he turned his back on the lifting runabout into which he had shanghaied Monroe-Alpha, Hamilton dismissed his friend from his mind— much to do and damned little time. Hurry!

He was surprised and not pleased to find that the door giving down into the building from the roof responded at once to the code used by the Clinic staff—a combination Mordan had given him. Nor were there guards beyond that door. Why, the place might as well be wide open!

He burst into Mordan's office with the fact on his mind. "This place is as unprotected as a church," he snapped. "What's the idea?" He looked around. In addition to Mordan the room contained Bainbridge Martha, his chief of technical staff, and Longcourt Phyllis. His surprise at her presence was reinforced by annoyance at seeing she was armed.

"Good evening, Felix," Mordan answered mildly. "Why should it be protected?"

"Good grief! Aren't you going to resist attack?"

"But," Mordan pointed out, "there is no reason

to expect attack. This is not a strategic point. No doubt they plan to take the Clinic over later but the fighting will be elsewhere."

"That's what you think. I know better."

"Yes?"

"I was assigned to come here to kill you. A section follows me to seize the Clinic."

Mordan made no comment. He sat still, face impassive. Hamilton started to speak; Mordan checked him with a raised hand and said, "There are only three other men in the building. None of them are gunmen. How much time have we?"

"Ten minutes—or less."

"I'll inform the central peace station. They may be able to divert a few reserve monitors. Martha, send the staff home." He turned to the telephone.

The lighting flickered sharply, was replaced at once by a lesser illumination. The emergency lighting had cut in. No one needed to be told that Power Central was out. Mordan continued to try the phone—it was dead.

"The building cannot be held by two guns," he observed, as if thinking aloud. "Nor is it necessary. But there is just one point necessary to protect—the plasm bank. Our friends are not completely stupid. But it is still bad strategy. They forget that a trapped animal will gnaw off a leg. Come, Felix. We must attempt it."

The significance of the attack on the Clinic raced through Hamilton's mind. The plasm bank. The one here in the Capital's clinic was repository of the plasm of genius for the past two centuries.

If the rebels captured it, even if they did not win, they would have a unique and irreplaceable hostage. At the worst they could exchange it for their lives.

"What do you mean, 'two guns'?" demanded Longcourt Phyllis. "What about this?" She slapped her belt.

"I daren't risk you." Mordan answered. "You know why."

Their eyes locked for a moment. She answered with two words. "Fleming Marjorie."

"Hmm . . . I see your point. Very well."

"What is she doing here, anyhow?" demanded Hamilton. "And who is Fleming Marjorie?"

"She came here to talk with me—about you. Fleming Marjorie is another fifth cousin of yours. Quite a good chart. Come!" He started away briskly.

Hamilton hurried after him, thinking furiously. The significance of Mordan's last remarks broke on him with a slightly delayed action. When he understood he was considerably annoyed, but there was no time to talk about it. He avoided looking at Phyllis.

Bainbridge Martha joined them as they were leaving the room. "One of the girls is passing the word," she informed Mordan.

"Good," he answered without pausing.

The plasm bank stood by itself in the middle of a large room, a room three stories high and broad in proportion. The bank itself was arranged in library-like tiers. A platform divided it halfway up, from which technicians could reach the cells in the upper level.

Mordan went directly to the flight of stairs in the center of the mass and climbed to the platform. "Phyllis and I will cover the two front doors," he directed. "Felix, you will cover the rear door."

"What about me?" asked his chief of staff.

"You, Martha? You're not a gunman."

"There's another gun," she declared pointing at Hamilton's belt. Hamilton glanced down, puzzled. She was right. He had stuffed the gun he had taken from Monroe-Alpha under his belt. He handed it to her.

"Do you know how to use it?" asked Mordan.

"It will burn where I point it, won't it?"

"Yes."

"That's all I want to know."

"Very well. Phyllis, you and Martha cover the back door. Felix and I will take a front door apiece."

The balcony platform was surrounded by a railing waist high and not quite one solid piece, for it was pierced here and there with small openings—part of an ornamental design. The plan was quite simple—crouch behind the railing, spy out the doors through the openings and use them as loopholes through which to fire.

They waited.

Hamilton got out a cigaret, stuck it in his mouth and inhaled it into burning, without taking his eyes off the left-hand door. He offered the case to Mordan, who pushed it away.

"Claude, there's one thing I can't figure out . . ."

"So?"

"Why in the world didn't the government bust this up before it had gone so far? I gather that I wasn't the only stoolie in the set-up. Why didn't you smear it?"

"I am not the government," Mordan answered carefully, "nor am I on the Board of Policy. I might venture an opinion."

"Let's have it."

"The only certain way to get all of the conspirators was to wait until they showed themselves. Nor will it be necessary to try them—an unsatisfactory process at best. This way they will be exterminated to the last man."

Hamilton thought about it. "It does not seem to me that the policy makers are justified in risking the whole state by delaying."

"Policy makers take a long view of things. Biologically it is better to make sure that the purge is clean. But the issue was never in doubt, Felix."

"How can you be sure? We're in a sweet spot now, as a result of waiting."

"You and I are in jeopardy, to be sure. But the society will live. It may take a little time for the monitors to recruit enough militia to subdue them in any key points they may have seized, but the outcome is certain."

"Damnation," complained Hamilton. "It shouldn't be necessary to wait to stir up volunteers among the citizens. The police force should be large enough."

"No," said Mordan. "No, I don't think so. The police of a state should never be stronger or better armed than the citizenry. An armed citizenry, willing to fight, is the foundation of civil freedom. That's a personal evaluation, of course."

"But suppose they don't? Suppose these rats win? It's the Policy Board's fault."

Mordan shrugged. "If the rebellion is successful, notwithstanding an armed citizenry, then it has justified itself—biologically. By the way, be a little slow in shooting, if the first man comes through your door."

"Why?"

"Your weapon is noisy. If he is alone, we'll gain a short delay."

They waited. Hamilton was beginning to think that his time-piece had stopped, until he realized that his first cigaret was still burning. He glanced quickly back to his door, and said, "Psst!" to Mordan, and shifted his watching to the other door.

The man entered cautiously, weapon high. Mordan led him with his gunsight until he was well inside and had stepped out of direct line of sight of the door. Then he let him have it, neatly, in the head. Felix glanced at him, and noticed that it was a man he had had a drink with earlier in the evening.

The next two came in a pair. Mordan motioned for him not to shoot. He was not able to wait so long this time; they saw the body as soon as they were in the doorway. Hamilton noted with admiration that he was unable to tell which one had been shot first. They seemed to drop simultaneously.

"You need not honor my fire the next time," Mordan remarked. "The element of surprise will be lacking." Over his shoulder he called, "First blood, ladies. Anything doing there?"

"Not yet."

"Here they come!" Ba-bang! Bang! Hamilton had fired three times, winged three men. One of them stirred, attempted to raise himself and return the fire. He let him have one more bullet, which quieted him. "Thank you," said Mordan.

"For what?"

"That was my file secretary. But I would rather have killed him myself."

Hamilton cocked an eyebrow at him. "I think you once told me that a public official should try to keep his personal feeling out of his work?"

"That's true . . . but there is no rule saying I can't enjoy my work. I wish he had come in my door. I liked him."

Hamilton noted that Mordan had accounted for four more, silently, while Hamilton was so noisily stopping the rush at his own door. That made five at his door, one in between, and four at Mordan's. "If they keep this up, they'll have a barricade of living flesh," he commented.

"Formerly living," Mordan corrected. "Haven't you been at that same loophole a bit too long?"

"I stand corrected on both counts." He shifted

to another spot, then called back, "How is it coming, girls?"

"Martha got one," Phyllis sang out.

"Good for her! What's the matter with you?"

"I'm doing all right."

"Fine. Burn 'em so they don't wiggle."

"They don't," she stated briefly.

There were no more rushes. A portion of a head would peek out cautiously, its owner would blast once quickly without proper aim, the man would duck back. They returned the fire, but with little expectation of hitting anything. The targets never appeared twice in the same spot, and for split seconds only. They crept back and forth along the balcony, trying to enfilade the rooms beyond, but their antagonists had become cagy.

"Claude . . . I just thought of something funny."

"So?"

"Suppose I get killed in this. You get your own way in our argument, don't you?"

"Yes. What's the joke?"

"But if I get knocked over, you'll probably be dead too. You told me my deposit was listed only in your mind. You win and you lose."

"Not exactly. I said it was not on file. But it's identified in my will—my professional executor will carry out the plan."

"Oh, ho. So I'm a papa anyhow." He fired once at a shape that suddenly appeared in his door. There was a yelp of anguish, and the shape drew back. "Lousy," he deplored. "I must be losing my eyesight." He banked a slug off the floor in front of his door, letting it thereby ricochet loosely in the room beyond. He did the same through Mordan's door. "That's to teach 'em to keep their heads down. Look, Claude—if you had your choice, which would you prefer: for both of us to be knocked over and thereby insure your own way about my hypothetical offspring, or for both of us to get through it and be back where we started?"

Mordan considered the question. "I think I would rather try to argue around to my viewpoint. I'm afraid there isn't much of the martyr spirit in me."

"That's what I thought."

Somewhat later Mordan said, "Felix, I think they have taken to drawing our fire. I don't think that was a face I shot at last time."

"I believe you're right. I couldn't have missed a couple of times lately."

"How many shots have you left?"

Hamilton did not need to count; he knew—and it had been worrying him. He had had four clips when he left for the Hall of the Wolf—three in his belt, one in his gun, twenty-eight shots in all. The last clip was in his gun; he had fired two shots from it. He held up one hand, fingers spread. "How about you?"

"About the same. I *could* use half charge for this sparring." He thought a moment. "Cover both doors." He crawled rapidly away through the stacks to where the two women kept guard on the rear door.

Martha heard him and turned. "Look at this,

chief," she insisted, holding out her left hand. He looked—the first two joints of the forefinger were burned away and the tip of the thumb—cleanly cauterized. "Isn't that a mess?" she complained. "I'll never be able to operate again. No manipulation."

"Your assistants can operate. It's your brain that counts."

"A lot you know about it. They're clumsy—every blessed one of them. It's a miracle they can dress themselves."

"I'm sorry. How many charges have you left?"

The picture was no better here. Phyllis's lady's weapon had been only a twenty-gun to start with. Both Mordan's and Monroe-Alpha's were fifty-guns, but the gun expropriated from Monroe-Alpha had started the evening even more depleted than Mordan's. Phyllis had withdrawn Martha from anything more than stand-by when she had been wounded, planning to use the gun herself when her own was exhausted.

Mordan cautioned them to be still more economical with their shooting and returned to his post. "Anything happened?" he asked.

"No. What's the situation?"

Mordan told him.

Hamilton whistled tunelessly, his eye on his target. "Claude?"

"Yes, Felix."

"Do you think we are going to get out of this?"

"No, Felix."

"Hmmm . . . Well, it's been a nice party." A

little later he added, "Damn it—I don't want to die. Not just yet . . . Claude, I've thought of another joke."

"Let's have it."

"What's the one thing that could give life point to it—*real* point?"

"That," Mordan pointed out, "is the question I've been trying to answer for you all along."

"No, no. The question itself."

"You state it," Mordan parried cautiously.

"I will. The one thing that could give us some real basis for our living is to know *for sure* whether or not anything happens after we die. When we die, do we die all over—or don't we?"

"Hmm . . . granting your point, what's the joke?"

"The joke is on me. Or rather on my kid. In a few minutes I'll probably know the answer. But *he* won't. He's sitting back there right now—in a way—sleeping in one of those freezers. And there is no way on earth for me to let him know the answer. *But he's the one that will need to know.* Isn't that funny?"

"Hmm . . . If that's your idea of a joke, Felix, I suggest that you stick to parlor tricks."

Hamilton shrugged jauntily. "I'm considered quite a wit in some circles," he bragged. "Sometimes I wow myself."

"Here they come!" It was an organized rush this time, spreading fanwise from both doors. They were both very busy for perhaps two seconds, then it was over. "Any get through?"

"Two, I think," Mordan answered. "You cover the stairs. I'll stay here." It was not personal caution, but tactics. Mordan's eye and hand were fast, but Hamilton was the younger, abler man.

He watched the stairs on his belly, most of his body shielded by the stacks. He was lucky on the first shot—his man stuck his head up facing the other way. Hamilton sent him down with a hole in the back of his skull and his forehead blown away. He then shifted quickly to the far side of the stair well. But his gun was empty.

The second man came up fast. Hamilton slugged him with the empty weapon and grappled, trying to get inside his range. The man almost fought free, dragging them both part way into the staircase, but Hamilton jerked back on his head, hard. There was a crunch of bone; he went limp.

Hamilton reported back to Mordan.

"Good. Where's your gun?" Hamilton shrugged and spread his palms. "There ought to be two at the foot of the stairs," he suggested.

"You wouldn't last long enough to stoop over for them. You stay up here. Go back and get Martha's."

"Yes, sir."

He crawled back, explained what he wanted, and told Martha to hide in the stacks. She protested. "Chief's orders," he lied. Then to Phyllis, "How are you doing, kid?"

"All right."

"Keep your chin up and your head down." He glanced at the meters on both guns. They had the same charge. He holstered Monroe-Alpha's gun, shot a quick look at the door Phyllis was covering, then grabbed her chin, turned her face around, and kissed her quickly.

"That's for keeps," he said, and turned away at once.

Mordan reported no activity. "But there will be," he added. "We don't dare waste shots on casual targets and they will soon realize it."

It seemed an interminable wait. They grimly forbore accepting the targets they were offered. "I think," said Mordan at last, "that we had better expend one charge on the next thing that appears. It might cause a worthwhile delay."

"You don't have any silly notion that we are going to get out of this *now*, do you? I've begun to suspect that the monitors don't even know this point was attacked."

"You may be right. But we'll keep on."

"Oh, of course."

They had a target soon—plain enough to be sure that it was a man, and not a decoy. Mordan stung him. He fell in sight, but shots were scarce—he was allowed to crawl painfully back.

Hamilton looked up for a moment. "See here, Claude—it *would* be worthwhile, you know—to know what happens after the lights go out. Why hadn't anyone tackled it seriously?"

"Religions do. Philosophies do."

"That isn't what I mean. It ought to be tackled the same as any other—" He stopped. "Do you smell anything?"

Mordan sniffed. "I'm not sure. What does it smell like?"

"Sweetish. It—" He felt suddenly dizzy, a strange sensation for him. He saw two of Mordan. "Gas. They've got us. So long, pal." He tried to crawl to the passageway down which Phyllis was on duty, but he achieved only a couple of clumsy, crawling steps, fell on his face, and lay still.

CHAPTER TEN

"—the only game in town"

It was pleasant to be dead. Pleasant and peaceful, not monotonous. But a little bit lonely. He missed those others—serene Mordan, the dauntless gallantry of Phyllis, Cliff and his frozen face. And there was that funny little man, pathetic little man who ran the *Milky Way Bar*—what had he named him? He could see his face, but what had he named him? Herbie, Herbert, something like that—names didn't taste the same when words were gone. Why had he named him Herbert?

Never mind. The next time he would not choose to be a mathematician. Dull, tasteless stuff, mathematics—quite likely to give the game away before it was played out. No fun in the game if you knew the outcome. He had designed a game like that once, and called it *Futility*—no matter how you played, you had to win. No, that wasn't himself, that was a player called Hamilton. Himself wasn't Hamilton—not this game. He was a geneticist—that was a good one!—a game within a game. Change the rules as you go along. Move the players around. Play tricks on yourself.

"Don't you peek and close your eyes, And I'll give you something to make a s'prise!"

That was the essence of the game—surprise. You locked up your memory, and promised not to look, then played through the part you had picked with just the rules assigned to that player. Sometimes the surprises were pretty ghastly, though— he didn't like having his fingers burned off.

No! He hadn't played that position at all. That piece was an automatic, some of the pieces had to be. Himself had burned off that piece's fingers, though it seemed real at the time.

It was always like this on first waking up. It was always a little hard to remember which position Himself had played, forgetting that he had played all of the parts. Well, that was the game; it was the only game in town, and there was nothing else to do. Could he help it if the game was crooked? Even if he had made it up and played all the parts. But he would think up another game the next time. Next time . . .

His eyes didn't work right. They were open but he couldn't see anything. A hell of a way to run things—some mistake.

"Hey! What's going on here?"

It was his own voice. He sat up, the cloth fell from his eyes. Everything was too bright; his eyes smarted.

"What's the trouble, Felix?" He turned in the direction of the voice and strove to focus his aching eyes. It was Mordan, lying a few feet away from him. There was something he wanted to ask Mordan, but it escaped him.

"Oh. Claude. I don't feel right. How long have we been dead?"

"We aren't dead. You're just a bit sick. You'll get over it."

"Sick? Is that what it is?"

"Yes. I was sick once, about thirty years ago. It was much like this."

"Oh—" There was still something he wanted to ask Mordan, but he couldn't for the life of him recall what it was. It was important, too, and Claude would know. Claude knew everything—he made the rules.

That was silly. Still, Claude would know.

"Do you want to know what happened?" Mordan asked.

Maybe that was it. "They gassed us, didn't they? I don't remember anything after that." That wasn't quite right—there was something else. He couldn't recall.

"We were gassed, but it was done by our own monitors. Through the conditioning system. We were lucky. No one knew we were under siege inside, but they could not be sure that all of the staff were out of the building—else they would have used a lethal gas."

His head was clearing now. He remembered the fight in detail. "So? How many were left? How many did we fail to get?"

"I don't know exactly, and it's probably too late to find out. They are probably all dead."

"Dead? Why? They didn't burn them after they were down, did they?"

"No . . . But this gas we took is lethal without an immediate antidote—and I'm afraid that the therapists were a little bit over-worked. Our own people came first."

Hamilton grinned. "You old hypocrite. *Say! How about Phyllis?*"

"She's all right, and so is Martha. I ascertained that when I woke up. By the way, do you know that you snore?"

"Do I really?"

"Outrageously. I listened to your music for more than an hour. You must have had a heavier dose of gas than I had. Perhaps you struggled."

"Maybe. I wouldn't know. Say, where are we?" He swung his legs out of bed, and attempted to stand. It was a foolish attempt; he just missed falling on his face.

"Lie down," ordered Mordan. "You won't be fit for several hours yet."

"I guess you're right," Hamilton admitted, sinking back on the cushion. "Say, that's a funny feeling. I thought I was going to fly."

"We're next door to the Carstairs Infirmary, in a temporary annex," Mordan continued. "Naturally, things are a bit crowded today."

"Is the party all over? Did we win?"

"Of course we won. I told you the issue was never in doubt."

"I know, but I've never understood your confidence."

Mordan considered how to reply to this. "Perhaps," he said, "it would be simplest to state that they never did have what it takes. The leaders were, in most cases, genetically poor types, with conceit far exceeding their abilities. I doubt if any one of them had sufficient imagination to conceive logically the complexities of running a society, even the cut-to-measure society they dreamed of."

"They talked as if they did."

Mordan nodded. "No doubt. It's a common failing, and it's been with the race as long as it has had social organization. A little businessman thinks his tiny business is as complex and difficult as the whole government. By inversion, he conceives himself as competent to plan the government as the chief executive. Going further back in history, I've no doubt that many a peasant thought the job of the king was a simple one and that he could do it better if he only had a chance. What it boils down to is lack of imagination and overwhelming conceit."

"I would never have thought them lacking in imagination."

"There is a difference between constructive imagination and wild, uncontrolled daydreams. One is psychopathic—megalomania—unable to distinguish between fact and fancy. The other is hardheaded. In any case, the fact remains that they did not have a single competent scientist, nor a synthesist of any sort, in their whole organization. I venture to predict that, when we get

around to reviewing their records, we will find
that the rebels were almost all—all, perhaps—
men who had never been outstandingly successful
at anything. Their only prominence was among
themselves."

Hamilton thought this over to himself. He had
noticed something of the sort. They had seemed
like thwarted men. He had not recognized a face
among them as being anyone in particular outside
the Survivors Club. But inside the club they were
swollen with self-importance, planning this, de-
ciding that, talking about what they would do
when they "took over." Pipsqueaks, the lot of 'em.

But dangerous pipsqueaks, no matter what
Mordan said. You were just as dead, burned by a
childish man, as you would be if another killed
you.

"Felix, are you still awake?"

"Yes."

"Do you recall the conversations we were having during the fight?"

"Why, um—yes—yes, I think I do."

"You were about to say something when the gas
hit us." Hamilton was slow in replying. He recalled what had been on his mind but it was difficult to fit it into adequate words. "It's like this,
Claude. It seems to me that scientists tackle every
problem but the important ones. What a man
wants to know is 'Why?'—all that science tells him
is 'What.' "

" 'Why' isn't the business of science. Scientists
observe, describe, hypothecate, and predict.

'What' and 'How' are their whole field; 'Why' doesn't enter into it."

"Why shouldn't 'Why' enter into it? I don't want to know how far it is from here to the Sun; I want to know why the Sun is there—and why I am standing here looking at it. I ask what life is for, and they show me a way to make better bread."

"Food is important. Try going without it."

"Food isn't important after you've solved that problem."

"Were you ever hungry?"

"Once—when I was studying basic socio-economics. But it was just instructional. I never expect to be hungry again—and neither does anybody else. That's a solved problem and it answers nothing. I want to know What next? Where to? Why?"

"I had been thinking about these matters," Mordan said slowly, "while you were sleeping. The problems of philosophy seem to be unlimited, and it is not too healthy to dwell on unlimited questions. But last night you seemed to feel that the key problem, for you, was the old, old question as to whether a man was anything more than his hundred years here on earth? Do you still feel that way?"

"Yes . . . I think I do. If there was anything, anything more at all, after this crazy mix-up we call living, I could feel that there might be some point to the whole frantic business, even if I did not know and could not know the full answer while I was alive."

"And suppose there was not? Suppose that when a man's body disintegrates, he himself disappears absolutely. I'm bound to say I find it a probable hypothesis."

"Well— It wouldn't be cheerful knowledge, but it would be better than not knowing. You could plan your life rationally, at least. A man might even be able to get a certain amount of satisfaction in planning things better for the future, after he's gone. A vicarious pleasure in the anticipation."

"I assure you he can," Mordan stated, from his own inner knowledge. "But, I take it, either way, you would feel that the question you posed to me in our first interview was fairly answered."

"Mmm, yes."

"Whereupon you would be willing to co-operate in the genetics program planned for you?"

"Yes, *if.*"

"I don't propose to give you an answer here and now," Mordan answered equably. "Would you be willing to co-operate if you knew that a serious attempt was being made to answer your question?"

"Easy there! Wait a minute. You-win-and-I-lose. I ought to be entitled to look at the answer. Suppose you do assign someone to look into the matter and he comes back with a negative report—after I've fulfilled my part of the bargain?"

"It would be necessary for you to place credence in me. Such a research might not be completed in years, or in our lifetimes. But suppose I declare to you that such a research were to be attempted, seriously, hard headedly, all out, and no trouble spared, would you then consent to co-operate?"

Hamilton covered his face with his hands. There were myriad factors revolving in his brain—some of which he was not fully aware of, none of which he wished to talk about. "If you did—*if* you did—I think perhaps—"

"Here, here," a voice boomed in the room. "What's going on in here? Mustn't excite yourselves yet."

"Hello, Joseph," Mordan greeted the newcomer.

"Morning, Claude. Feel better?"

"Much."

"You still need sleep. Put yourself to sleep."

"Very well." Mordan closed his eyes.

The man called Joseph stepped up to Felix, felt his wrist, peeled back his eyelid, and examined the eye. "You'll do."

"I want to get up."

"Not yet. I want you to sleep for a few hours first. Look at me. You feel sleepy. You—"

Felix tore his gaze away from the man's eyes, and said, "Claude!"

"He's asleep. You can't possibly wake him."

"Oh. See here, you're a therapist, aren't you?"

"Certainly."

"Is there anything that can be done to cure snoring?"

The man chuckled. "All I can suggest is that you sleep through it. Which is what I want you to do now. You are sleepy. You are falling asleep. Sleep . . ."

When they let him go he tried to look up Phyllis. It was difficult to find her, to begin with, since the meager hospital accommodations of the city were overcrowded and she had been ministered to, as he had been, in temporary quarters. When he did find her, they wouldn't let him in—she was sleeping, they said. Nor were they inclined to give him any information as to her condition; he could show no claim on such knowledge and it was clearly in the private sphere.

He made such a nuisance of himself that he was finally told that she was entirely well, save for a slight indisposition pursuant to gas poisoning. He had to be contented with that.

He might have gotten himself into serious trouble had he been dealing with a man, but his argument was with a grimly inflexible matron, who was about twice as tough as he was.

He had the faculty of dismissing from mind that which could not be helped. Phyllis was not on his mind once he had turned away. He started for his apartment automatically, then recalled, for the first time in a good many hours, Monroe-Alpha.

The fool, the silly fool! He wondered what had happened to him. He was reluctant to inquire since to do so might give away his connection with the conspiracy. It seemed likely that he had already found some means to do that himself.

It did not occur to him then, or at any other time, to "do the honorable thing" by reporting

Monroe-Alpha. His morals were strictly pragmatic, and conformed to accepted code as closely as they did only through a shrewd and imaginative self-interest.

He called Monroe-Alpha's office—no, he was not there. He called his apartment. No answer. Temporarily blocked, he decided to go to his friend's apartment on the assumption that he might show up there first.

He got no response at the door. He knew the combination but ordinarily would not think of using it. This seemed to him an extraordinary occasion.

Monroe-Alpha was sitting in his lounging room. He looked up when Hamilton entered, but did not rise and said nothing. Hamilton walked over and planted himself in front of him. "So you're back."

"Yes."

"How long have you been back?"

"I don't know. Hours."

"You have? I signalled your phone."

"Oh, was that you?"

"Certainly it was. Why didn't you answer?"

Monroe-Alpha said nothing, looked at him dully, and looked away. "Snap out of it, man," Hamilton snapped, by now exasperated. "Come to life. The putsch failed. You know that, don't you?"

"Yes." Then he added, "I'm ready."

"Ready for what?"

"You've come to arrest me, haven't you?"

"Me? Great Egg! I'm no monitor."

"It's all right. I don't mind."

"Look here, Cliff." Hamilton said seriously. "What's gotten into you? Are you still filled up with the guff McFee dished out? Are you determined to be a martyr? You've been a fool—there's no need to be a damned fool. I've reported that you were an agent of mine." (In this he anticipated a decision he had made at the moment; he would carry it out later—if necessary.) "You're all in the clear. Well, speak up. You didn't get in on the fighting, did you?"

"No."

"I didn't think you would, after the hypno pills I stuffed down you. One more and you would have listened to the birdies. What's the trouble, then? Are you still fanatical about this damned Survivors Club tommyrot?"

"No. That was a mistake. I was crazy."

"I'll say you were crazy! But see here—you don't rate it, but you're getting away with it, cold. You don't have to worry. Just slide back in where you were and no one's the wiser."

"It's no good, Felix. Nothing's any good. Thanks, just the same." He smiled briefly and wanly.

"Well, for the love o'—I've a good mind to paste you right in the puss, just to get a rise out of you." Monroe-Alpha did not answer. His face he had let sink down into his hands; he showed in no way that he had even heard. Hamilton shook his shoulder.

"What's the matter? Did something else happen? Something I don't know about."

"Yes." It was barely a whisper.

"Do you want to tell me about it?"

"It doesn't matter." But he did start to tell of it; once started he went on steadily, in a low voice and without raising his head. He seemed to be talking only to himself, as if he were repeating over something he wished to learn by heart.

Hamilton listened uneasily, wondering whether or not he should stop him. He had never heard a man bare his secret thoughts as Monroe-Alpha was doing. It seemed indecent.

But he went on and on, until the whole pitiful, silly picture was mercilessly sharp. "And so I came back here," he concluded. He said nothing further, nor did he look up.

Hamilton looked amazed. "Is that all?"

"Yes."

"You're sure you haven't left anything out?"

"No, of course not."

"Then what, in the Name of the Egg, are you doing here?"

"Nothing. There wasn't anyplace else to go."

"Cliff, you'll be the death of me, yet. Get going. Get started. Get up off that fat thing you're sitting on and get a move on."

"Huh? Where?"

"After her, you bubble-brained idiot! Go find her."

Monroe-Alpha shook his head wearily. "You must not have listened. I tell you I tried to burn her."

Hamilton took a deep breath, let it out, then

said, "Listen to me. I don't know much about women, and sometimes it seems like I didn't know anything about them. But I'm sure of this—she won't let a little thing like you taking a pot shot at her stand in the way if you ever had any chance with her at all. She'll forgive you."

"You don't really mean that, do you?" Monroe-Alpha's face was still tragic, but he clutched at the hope.

"Certainly I do. Women will forgive anything." With a flash of insight he added, "Otherwise the race would have died out long ago."

CHAPTER ELEVEN

"—then a man is something more than his genes!"

I cannot say," remarked the Honorable Member from Great Lakes Central, "that I place high evaluation on Brother Mordan's argument that this project be taken up to get young Hamilton's consent to propagate. It is true that I am not entirely familiar with the details of the genetic sequence involved—"

"You should be," Mordan cut in somewhat acidly, "I supplied full transcript two days ago."

"I beg your pardon, brother. In those forty-eight hours I have held hearings steadily. The Mississippi Valley matter, you know. It's rather urgent."

"I'm sorry," Mordan apologized. "It's easy for a layman to forget the demands on a Planner's time."

"Never mind. No need for finicky courtesy among ourselves. I scanned the brief and the first sixty pages while we were assembling; that, with such previous knowledge of the case as I had, gives me a rough idea of your problem. But tell me, am I correct in thinking that Hamilton holds nothing exclusively in his chart? You have alternative choices?"

"Yes."

"You expected to finish with his descendent generation—how many generations would be required, using alternative choices?"

"Three additional generations."

"That is what I thought, and that is my reason for disagreeing with your argument. The genetic purpose of the sequence is, I think, of greater importance to the race, but a delay of a hundred years, more or less, is not important—not sufficiently important to justify an undertaking as major as a full effort to investigate the question of survival after death."

"I take it," put in the Speaker of the Day, "that you wish to be recorded as opposing Brother Mordan's proposal?"

"No, Hubert, no. You anticipate me—incorrectly. I am supporting his proposition. Notwithstanding the fact that I consider his reasons, though good, to be insufficient, I evaluate the proposal as worthwhile in itself. I think we should support it fully."

The Member from the Antilles looked up from the book he was reading (*not* rudeness; everyone present knew that he had parallel mental processes and no one expected him to waste half the use of his time out of politeness) and said, "I think George should amplify his reason."

"I will. We policy men are like a pilot who is attempting to do a careful job of conning his ship without having any idea of his destination. Hamilton has put his finger on the weak point in our whole culture—he should be a planner himself. Every decision that we make, although it is based on data, is shaped by our personal philosophies. The data is examined in the light of these philosophies. How many of you have an opinion about survival-after-death? I ask for a show of hands. Come now, be honest with yourselves."

Somewhat hesitantly they put their hands up—men and women alike, every one of them. "Now," the Great Lakes member continued, "the hands of those who are sure that their opinions are correct."

All of the hands went down, save that of the Member from Patagonia. "Bravo!" Rembert of the Lakes called out. "I should have guessed that you would be sure."

She took the cigar out of her mouth, said rather sharply, "Any fool knows that one," and went back to her needlework. She was over a hundred years old, and the only control natural in the Board. Her district had confirmed her tenure regularly for more than fifty years. Her eyesight was thought to be failing, but she had all of her own yellow teeth. Her wrinkled, mahogany features showed more evidence of Indian blood than Caucasian. They all claimed to be a little afraid of her.

"Carvala," Rembert said to her, "perhaps you can cut the matter short by giving us the answer?"

"I can't *tell* you the answer—and you wouldn't believe me if I did." She was silent for a moment, then added, "Let the boy do as he pleases. He will anyway."

"Do you support or oppose Mordan's proposition?"

"Support. Not that you're likely to go at it right."

There was a short silence. Every member in the chamber was hastily trying to recall when, if ever, Carvala had been proven to be on the wrong side of a question—in the long run.

"It would seem obvious to me," Rembert continued, "that the only rational personal philosophy based on a conviction that we die *dead*, never to rise again, is a philosophy of complete hedonism. Such a hedonist might seek his pleasure in life in very subtle, indirect, and sublimated fashions; nevertheless pleasure must be his only rational purpose—no matter how lofty his conduct may appear to be. On the other hand, the possibility of *something* more to life than the short span we see opens up an unlimited possibility of evaluations other than hedonistic. It seems to me a fit subject to investigate."

"Granting your point," commented the woman representing the Northwest Union, "is it our business to do so? Our functions and our authority are limited; we are forbidden by constitution to meddle in spiritual matters. How about it, Johann?"

The member addressed was the only priest *persona* among them, he being the Most Reverend Mediator to some millions of his co-religionists south of the Rio Grande. His political prominence was the more exceptional in that the great majority of his constituents were not of his faith. "I do not see, Geraldine," he replied, "that the constitutional restriction applies. What Brother Mordan proposes is a coldly scientific investigation. Its consequences may have spiritual implications, if there are positive results, but an unbiased investigation is no violation of religious freedom."

"Johann is right," said Rembert. "There is no subject inappropriate for scientific research. Johann, we've let you fellows have a monopoly of such matters for too long. The most serious questions in the world have been left to faith or speculation. It is time for scientists to cope with them, or admit that science is no more than pebble counting."

"Go ahead. I shall be interested in seeing what you can make of them—in laboratories."

Hoskins Geraldine looked at him. "I wonder, Johann, what your attitude will be if this research should turn up facts which controvert some one of your articles of faith?"

"That," he answered imperturbably, "is a matter for me to settle with myself. It need not affect this board."

"I think," observed the Speaker for the Day, "that we might now seek a preliminary expression of opinion. Some support the proposal—are any opposed?" There was no response. "Are any undecided?" There was still no response, but one member stirred slightly. "You wished to speak, Richard?"

"Not yet. I support the proposal, but I will speak to it later."

"Very well. It appears to be unanimous . . . It is so ordered. I will co-opt an instigator later. Now, Richard?"

The member-at-large for transient citizens indicated that he was ready. "The research does not cover enough territory."

"Yes?"

"When proposed as a means of persuading Hamilton Felix to accede to the wishes of the State geneticists, it was sufficient. But we are now undertaking it for itself. Is that not true?"

The Speaker glanced around the room, picking up nods from all but ancient Carvala—she seemed uninterested in the whole matter. "Yes, that is true."

"Then we should undertake not just one of the problems of philosophy, but all of them. The same reasons apply."

"We are under no necessity of being consistent, you know."

"Yes, I know, am I not trammeled by the meshes of verbal logic. I am interested. I am stimulated by the vista. I want us to extend the research."

"Very well. I am interested, too. I think we might well spend the next several days discussing it. I will postpone co-opting the instigator until we determine just how far we will go."

Mordan had been intending to ask to be excused, his mission accomplished, but at this new twist, fire and earthquake, garnished with pretty girls, could not have tempted him to leave. As a citizen, he was entitled to listen if he chose; as a distinguished synthesist himself, no one would think of objecting to his physical presence in the circle of discussion.

The member for transients went on. "We should enumerate and investigate all of the problems of philosophy, especially the problems of metaphysics and epistemology."

"I had thought," the Speaker said mildly, "that epistemology had been pretty well settled."

"Certainly, certainly—in the limited sense of agreeing on the semantic nature of symbolic communication. Speech and other communication symbols necessarily refer back to agreed-upon, *pointed-to* referent physical facts, no matter how high the level of abstraction, for communication to take place. Beyond that we cannot communicate. That's why Brother Johann and I can't argue about religion. He carries his around inside of him and can't point to what he means—as I carry mine. We can't even be sure that we disagree. Our notions about religion may be identical, but we can't talk about it *meaningfully*—so we keep quiet."

Johann smiled with untroubled good nature, but said nothing. Carvala looked up from her fancywork and said sharply, "Is this a development center lecture?"

"Sorry, Carvala. We agree on the method of symbol communication—the symbol is *not* the referent, the map is *not* the territory, the speech-sound is *not* the physical process. We go further and admit that the symbol *never* abstracts all of the details of the process it refers to. And we concede that symbols can be used to manipulate symbols . . . dangerously but usefully. And we agree that symbols should be structurally as similar as possible to the referents for communication purposes. To that extent epistemology is settled; but the key problem of epistemology—*how* we know *what* we know and what that knowledge means, we have settled by agreeing to ignore—like Johann and myself in re theology."

"Do you seriously propose that we investigate it?"

"I do. It's a key problem in the general problem of the personality. There is a strong interconnection between it and the object of Mordan's proposal. Consider—if a man 'lives' after his body is dead or before that body was conceived, *then a man is something more than his genes and his subsequent environment*. The doctrine of no-personal-responsibility for personal acts has become popular through the contrary assumption. I won't go into the implications—they must be evident to all of you—in ethics, in politics, in every field. But note the parallel between map-territory and gene-chart-and-man. These basic problems are all interrelated and the solution to any of them might be the key to all the others."

"You did not mention the possibility of direct communication without symbols."

"I implied it. That is one of the things we agreed to forget when we accepted the semantic negative-statements as the final word on epistemology. But it ought to be looked into again. There is *something* to telepathy, even if we can't measure it and manipulate it. Any man who has ever been happily married knows that, even if he's afraid to talk about it. Infants and animals and primitives have *some* use of it. Maybe we've been too smart. But the question ought to be reopened."

"Speaking of philosophical questions in general," put in the member from New Bolivar, "we have already agreed to subsidize one. Doctor Thorgsen's project—the ballistic stellarium—eidouraniun, I should call it. The origin and destination of the universe is certainly a classic problem of metaphysics."

"You are right," said the Speaker. "If we follow Richard's proposal, Doctor Thorgsen's project should be included."

"I suggest we did not allot Doctor Thorgsen enough credit."

"The subsidy could be increased, but he has not spent much of it. He seems to have little talent for spending money."

"Perhaps he needs abler assistants. There is Hargrave Caleb, and, of course, Monroe-Alpha Clifford. Monroe-Alpha is wasted in the department of finance."

"Thorgsen knows Monroe-Alpha. Perhaps Monroe-Alpha doesn't want to work on it."

"Nonsense! Any man likes a job that stretches his muscles."

"Then perhaps Thorgsen hesitated to ask him to help. Thorgsen is an essentially modest man, as is Monroe-Alpha."

"That seems more likely."

"In any case," the Speaker finished, "such details are for the instigator to consider, not the whole board. Are you ready for opinion? The question is Brother Richard's proposal in the broadest sense—I suggest that we postpone elaboration of the details of projects and methods until tomorrow and other morrows. In the meantime—does any member oppose?"

There was no opposition; there was full consent.

"So be it," said the Speaker. He smiled. "It seems we are about to attempt to walk where Socrates stumbled."

"Crawl, not 'walk,'" Johann corrected. "We have limited ourselves to the experimental methods of science."

"True, true. Well, 'he who crawls cannot stumble.' Now to other matters—we still have a state to govern!"

CHAPTER TWELVE

"Whither thou goest—"

How would you like," Felix asked Phyllis, "to have a half interest in a gladiator?"

"What in the world are you talking about?"

"This undertaking of Smith Darlington's—feetball. We are going to incorporate each employee's contract and sell it. Our agent thinks it will be a good investment, and, truthfully, I think he's right."

"Feetball," repeated Phyllis meditatively. "You did say something about it, but I never understood it."

"It's a silly business, at best. Twenty-two men get out on a large open place and battle with their bare hands."

"Why?"

"The excuse is to move a little plastic spheroid from one end of the place to the other."

"What difference does it make which end it's on?"

"None, really—but it's as reasonable as any other game."

"I don't get it," Phyllis decided. "Why should anyone fight unless he wants to kill someone?"

"You have to see it to understand it. It's exciting. I even found myself shouting."

"You!"

"Uh huh. Me. Old calm-as-a-cat Felix. It's going to take hold, I tell you. It's going to be popular. We'll sell permissions to view it physically and then all sorts of lesser rights—direct pick-up, recording, and so forth. Smith has a lot of ideas about identifying various combinations with cities and organizations and attaching color symbols to them and songs and things. He's full of ideas— an amazing young man, for a barbarian."

"He must be."

"Better let me buy you a piece of it. It's a pure spec proposition and you can get in cheap—now. It'll make you rich."

"What use have I for any more money?"

"I don't know. You might spend it on me."

"That's pretty silly. You're bloated with credit now."

"Well, that brings me around to another subject. When we're married you can really put your mind on helping me spend it."

"Are you on that subject again?"

"Why not? Times have changed. There is no obstacle anymore. I've come around to Mordan's way of thinking."

"So Mordan told me."

"He did? Egg's Name—everything goes on behind my back! Never mind. When do we stat the contract?"

"What makes you think we are going to?"

"Huh? Wait a minute—I thought that all that stood between us was a difference of opinion about children?"

"You thought too much. What I said was that I would never marry a man who didn't want children."

"But I understood you to say—" He got up and moved nervously around the room. "Say, Phil—don't you *like* me?"

"You're nice enough—in your own horrid way."

"Then what's the trouble?"

She did not answer.

Presently he said, "I don't know whether it makes any difference since you feel that way about it, but I love you—you know that, don't you?"

"Come here." He came near to where she was sitting. She took him by the ears and pulled his head down.

"Filthy, you big dope—you should have said that ten minutes ago." She kissed him.

Sometime later she said dreamily, "Filthy—"

"Yes, darling?"

"After we have Theobald we'll have a little girl and then another little boy, and then maybe another little girl."

"Um—"

She sat up. "What's the matter? Aren't you pleased at the prospect?" She looked at him closely.

"Sure, sure."

"Then why are you looking so glum?"

"I was thinking about Cliff. The poor lunk."

"Hasn't he found any trace of her yet?"

"Nary a trace."

"Oh, dear!" She put her arms around him and held him.

No sign of her in the Giant Forest, though he had cut the air back to the place. No woman had registered there with the given name of Marion. No one could he find who could identify her by his description. No ship had checked in there registered to such a person. Nor did the owners of the ships that had been there know such a person—several of them knew Marions, but not *the* Marion—although three of them had responded to the description closely enough to send him charging across country, with wildly beating heart, on errands which cruelly disappointed him.

There remained Johnson-Smith Estaire, at whose town house he had first seen her. He had consulted her at once, after his initial failure to find Marion still at the Park. No, she didn't recall such a person. "After all, my dear Master Monroe-Alpha, the place was simply *mobbed*."

Did she keep a guest list? Yes, of course; what kind of a hostess did he think she was? Could he see it? She sent for her social secretary.

There was no Marion on the list.

He went back again. Could she have been mistaken? No, there was no mistake. But people sometimes brought others along to such a party as that—had he thought of that? In that case she would have no record of it. Did she recall any such? No, she couldn't—it was too much to ask. Would it be too much to ask to copy the guest list? Not at all—anything to oblige.

But first he must listen to her. "It's becoming simply *impossible* to get servants at any *reasonable* wage." Couldn't he do something about it. "*Dear* Master Monroe-Alpha." In what way? He was the man who handled the dividend, wasn't he? That was the trouble—with the dividend so high they simply would *not* enter service unless you simply *bribed* them, my dear.

He tried to explain to her that he had no control over the dividend, that he was simply the mathematical go-between for the facts of economics and the Board of Policy. He could see that she did not believe him.

He decided not to tell her, since he wanted a favor from her, that he himself would not choose to work as a personal servant for another unless driven to it by hunger. He tried to suggest that she make use of the excellent automaton furniture manufactured by her husband, supplemented by the help of the service companies. But she would have none of it. "So common, my dear. I tell you *nothing* replaces a well-trained servant. I should think people of that class would take *pride* in such a profession. I'm sure *I* would if I were called to such a station in life."

Impatiently, but with aching care, he plodded through the list. Some of the addresses were outside the Capital, some as far away as South America—Johnson-Smith Estaire was a fashionable hostess. Those he could not question himself, not fast enough to satisfy the lump of misery inside him. He must needs hire agents to track them down. He did so; it took all the credit he had—personal service comes high!—he borrowed against his salary to make up the deficit. Two of the guests had died in the meantime. He set more agents to work, investigating tactfully their backgrounds and acquaintances, trying, trying to locate a woman named Marion. He dare not even leave these two deceased to the last, for fear the trail might grow cold.

The others, those living in the Capital, he investigated himself. No, we took no one with us to that party—certainly no one named Marion. Estaire's party?—let me see, she gives so many. Oh, that one—no, I'm sorry. Now let me think—do you mean Selby Marion? No, Selby Marion is a little tiny woman with bright red hair. Sorry, my dear fellow—care for a drink. No? What's the hurry?

Yes, surely. My cousin, Faircoat Marion. There's a stereo of her over there, on the organ. Not the one you're looking for? Well, signal me and tell me how you made out. Always glad to do a favor for a friend of Estaire's. Fine woman, Estaire—always lots of fun at her place.

We *did* take someone to that party—who was it, dear? Oh, yes, Reynolds Hans. He had some strange girl with him. No, I can't remember her name—do you, dear?—Me, I just call them all

Lollipops, if they're under thirty. But here's Reynolds' address; you might ask him.

Master Reynolds did not consider it an intrusion, no. Yes, he recalled the occasion—jolly brawl. Yes, he had escorted his cousin from Sanfrisco. Why, yes, her name *was* Marion—Hartnett Marion. How had he known her name?

Say, that's interesting—done something like that himself once. Thought he'd lost track of the girl, only she turned up the following week at another party. Married, though, and in love with her husband—fortunately.

No, he didn't mean that Marion was married, but this other girl—kid named Francine. Did he have a picture of his cousin? Well, now, let me see, he didn't think so. Wait now, he might have a flat pic, taken when they were kids, in a scrapbook somewhere. Where would that be? He was going to clean out this flat some day and throw away a lot of this junk—never could find anything when he wanted it. Here it is—that's Marion, in the front row, second from the left. Was that the girl?

It was she! It was *she*!

How fast can a skyracer be pushed? How many corners can a man cut without being patrolled? Go . . . go . . . go!

He paused for a moment and tried to still his racing heart, before signalling at the door. The scanner investigated him and the door dilated.

He found her alone.

He stopped when he saw her, unable to move, unable to speak, face white.

"Come in," she said.

"You . . . you'll receive me?"

"Of course. I've been waiting."

He searched her eyes. They were warm and tender still, albeit troubled. "I don't understand. I tried to burn you."

"You didn't mean to. You didn't want to."

"I— But . . . Oh, Marion, Marion!" He stumbled forward toward her, and half fell. His head was in her lap. He shook with the racking sobs of one who has not learned how to cry.

She patted his shoulder. "My dear. My dear."

He looked up at last and found that her face was wet, even though he had heard no sound of tears. "I love you," he said. He said it tragically, as if it were an irreparable harm.

"I know. I love you."

Much later, she said to him, "Come with me."

He followed her on out into another room, where she busied herself at her wardrobe. "What are you doing?"

"I've a few things to take care of first."

"First?"

"This time I'm coming with you."

On the way back he used the phrase "after we're married."

"You intend to marry me?"

"Of course. If you'll have me!"

"You would marry a control natural?"

"Why not?" He met the issue bravely, even casually.

Why not? Well, Roman citizens, proud of their

patrician Latin blood, could have told him. The
white aristocracy of the Old South could have, in
their little day, explained to him in detail why not.
"Aryan" race-myth apologists could have defined
the reasons. Of course, in each case the persons
giving the reasons would have had a different
"race" in mind when explaining the obscene hor-
ror he contemplated committing, but their reasons
would have been the same. Even Johnson-Smith
Estaire could have explained to him "Why not"—
and she would most certainly cut him off her list
for stooping to such an alliance. After all, kings
and emperors have lost their thrones for lesser
miscegenations.

"That's all I wanted to know," she said. "Come
here, Clifford."

He came, a little mystified. She raised her left
arm; he read the little figures tattooed there. The
registration number was—no matter. But the clas-
sification letter was neither the "B" of a basic
type, such as he bore, nor the "C" of a control
natural. It was X—experimental.

She told him about it a little later. Her hyper-
dexter great-grandparents had both been control
naturals. "Of course it shows a little," she said. "I
do catch colds, if I don't take my pills. And sometimes I forget. I'm a sloppy person, Clifford."

A child of these two, her dexter grandfather,
had been identified, rather late in life, as a mutation, probably favorable—almost certainly favorable. His mutation was no gross matter, easily
recognized, but was subtle and subliminal. It had

to do with emotional stability. Perhaps it would be easiest to say that he was more civilized than any man can be expected to be. Naturally, an attempt was made to conserve the mutation. She was one of the conservators.

CHAPTER THIRTEEN

*"No more privacy than a guppy
in an aquarium"*

Phyllis squealed at him as he got home. "Felix!"

He chucked aside the file case he had been carrying and kissed her. "What's the trouble, Flutterbrain?"

"This. Look. Read it." "It" was a stat of a handwritten message. He read aloud: " 'Espartero Carvala presents her compliments to Madame Longcourt Phyllis and prays permission to call on the morrow at half after sixteen hundred.' Hummm . . . You're shooting high, darling."

"But whatever am I to *do*?"

"Do? Why, you put out your hand, say 'How do you fare?' and then serve her something—tea, I suppose, though they say she drinks like a fish."

"Filthy!"

"What's the matter?"

"Don't joke with me. What am I to *do*? I can't entertain her. She's a Policy Maker—I wouldn't know what to *say* to her."

"Suppose she is on the Policy Board. She's human, ain't she? Our home is all right, isn't it?

Go down and buy yourself a new gown—then you'll feel fit for anything."

Instead of brightening up, she began to cry. He took her in his arms, and said, "There, there! What's the trouble? Did I say something wrong?"

She stopped and dabbed at her eyes. "No. Just nerves, I guess. I'm all right."

"You startled me. You never did anything like that before."

"No. But I never had a baby before, either."

"Yeah, that's right. Well, cry, if it makes you feel better. But don't let this old fossil get under your skin, kid. You don't have to receive her, you know. I'll call her and tell her you can't."

She seemed quite recovered from her unease. "No, don't do that. I'd really like to see her. I'm curious and I'm flattered."

They had discussed with each other the question as to whether Madame Espartero Carvala had intended to call on both of them, or Phyllis only. Felix was reluctant to be present if his presence was not expected; he was equally reluctant to fail to show proper urbanity by not being present to receive a distinguished visitor. As he pointed out to Phyllis, it was his home as well as hers. He telephoned Mordan, since he knew that Mordan was much closer to such mighty and remote people than himself. Mordan gave him no help. "She's a rule unto herself, Felix. She's quite capable of breaking every custom of polite conduct, if she chooses."

"Any idea why she's coming?"

"Not the slightest. Sorry." Mordan himself wondered, but was honest enough to admit that his guesses were unsound—no data; he simply did not understand the old girl, and knew it.

Madame Espartero Carvala settled the matter herself. She came stumping in, supporting herself with a heavy cane. Clutched in her left hand was a lighted cigar. Hamilton approached her, bowed, "Madame—" he began.

She peered at him. "You're Hamilton Felix. Where's your wife?"

"If Madame will come with me." He attempted to offer her his arm for support.

"I can manage," she said rather ungraciously. Nevertheless she clamped the cigar in her teeth and took his arm. He was amazed to find how little she weighed, judging by the pressure on his arm—but the grip of her fingers was firm. Once in the lounging room, in the presence of Phyllis, she said, "Come here, child. Let me look at you."

Hamilton stood by foolishly, not knowing whether to seat himself or leave. The old lady turned, noticing that he was still there and said, "You were very gracious to escort me in to your wife. I thank you." The formal politeness of the words were oddly at variance with her first, brittle remarks, but they were not delivered in warm tones. Felix realized that he had been clearly and unmistakably dismissed. He got out.

He went to his retiring room, selected a scroll-script, fitted it into the reader, and prepared to kill time until Carvala should leave. But he found himself unable to fix his attention on the story he selected. He found that he had used the rewind button three times and still had no notion of how the story started.

Damn! He thought—I might as well have gone to the office.

For he had an office—now. The thought made him smile a little. He was the man who was never going to be tied down, who had split his profits with a man-of-affairs rather than be troubled with business worries. Yet here he was, married, an expectant father, actually living at the same address as his wife, and—possessing an office! True, the office had nothing to do with his business affairs.

He found himself actually engaged in the Great Research which Mordan had promised. Carruthers Alfred, former member of the Board of Policy until he had retired to pursue his studies, had been co-opted as instigator for the enlarged project. He in turn had co-opted Hamilton, who had protested, that he was no synthesist, nor scientist. Nevertheless Carruthers wanted him. "You have an erratic and unorthodox imagination," he had said. "This job calls for imagination, the more heterodox the better. You needn't do routine research, if you don't want to—plenty of patient technicians for that."

Felix suspected that Mordan had had something to do with his selection, but did not press him about it. Mordan, Hamilton knew, had an over-rated opinion of his ability. He esteemed himself as a second-rater, a competent and high-powered man, but a second-rater nonetheless. That chart that Mordan talked about—you could not compress a man into a diagram and hang him on a wall. He was not that chart. And didn't he know more about himself, from sitting on the inside, than any genetic technician could learn by peering down the double barrel of a 'scope?

But he had to admit he was glad that he had been invited into the project—it interested him. He had realized quite early that the enlarged project had not been taken up just to circumvent his balkiness—the transcript of authorization had shown him that. But he did not feel cheated— Mordan had delivered everything that he had promised, and Felix had become interested in the project for its own sake—both projects. Both the great public project of the Great Research and the private matter of himself, Phyllis, and their child to come.

He wondered what the little tyke would be like.

Mordan seemed confident that he knew. He had shown them the diploid chromosome chart resulting from their carefully chosen gametes, expounding on how the characteristics of the two parents would be combined in the child. Felix was not so sure; in spite of his own reasonably thorough knowledge of genetic theory and technique he was not convinced that all of a human being's multifold complexity could be wrapped up in a little blob of protoplasm smaller than a pin point.

It was not *reasonable*. There had to be more to a man than that.

Mordan had seemed to find it highly desirable that he and Phyllis possessed so many Mendelian characteristics in common. It not only, he pointed out, made the task of selection of gametes much simpler and shorter, but also insured reinforcement of those characteristics, genetically. Paired genes would be similar, instead of opposed.

On the other hand, Hamilton found that Mordon favored the alliance of Monroe-Alpha and Hartnett Marion, although they were as dissimilar as two persons could be. Hamilton pointed out the inconsistency in reasoning. Mordan had been unperturbed. "Each genetic case is a discrete individual. No rule in genetics is invariable. They complement each other."

It was certainly obvious that Marion had made Cliff happy, happier than Felix had ever seen him.

The big dope.

He had long been of the opinion that what Cliff needed was a keeper, to lead him around on a string, fetch him indoors when it rained, and tickle him when he pouted. (Not that the opinion subtracted from his very real devotion to his friend.)

Marion seemed to qualify on all counts. She hardly let him out of her sight. She worked with him, under the euphemistic title of "special secretary."

" 'Special secretary'?" Hamilton said, when

Monroe-Alpha told him about it. "What does she do? Is she a mathematician?"

"Not at all. She doesn't know a thing about mathematics—but she thinks I'm wonderful!" He grinned boyishly—Hamilton was startled to see how it changed his face. "Who am I to contradict her?"

"Cliff, if you keep that up, you'll have a sense of humor yet."

"*She* thinks I have one now."

"Perhaps you have. I knew a man who raised warthogs once. He said they made the flowers more beautiful."

"Why did he think that?" Monroe-Alpha was puzzled and interested.

"Never mind. Just what is it that Marion does?"

"Oh, a lot of little things. Keeps track of things I forget, brings me a cup of tea in the afternoon. Mostly she's just here when I want her. When a concept won't come straight and my head feels tired, I look up and there's Molly, just sitting there, looking at me. Maybe she's been reading, but when I look up I don't have to say anything— she's looking back at me. I tell you it helps, I never get tired anymore." He smiled again.

Hamilton realized with sudden insight that there never had been anything wrong with Monroe-Alpha except that the poor boob had never been happy. He had no defenses against the world—until now. Marion had enough for both of them.

He had wanted to ask Cliff what Hazel thought

of the new arrangements, but hesitated to do so, despite their close friendship. Monroe-Alpha brought it up himself. "You know, Felix, I was a little worried about Hazel."

"So?"

"Yes. I know she had said she wanted to enter a divorce, but I hadn't quite believed her."

"Why not?" Felix had inquired blandly.

Monroe-Alpha had colored. "Now, Felix, you're just trying to get me mixed up. Anyhow, she seemed positively relieved when I told her about Marion and me. She wants to take up dancing again."

Felix thought with regret that it was a mistake for a retired artist to attempt a comeback. But Cliff's next words made him realize he had been hasty. "It was Thorgsen's idea—"

"Thorgsen? Your boss?"

"Yes. He had been telling her about the outstations, particularly the ones on Pluto, of course, but he mentioned Mars and the rest, I suppose. They don't get much recreation, other than canned shows and reading." Hamilton knew what he meant, although he had never thought much about it. With the exception of the tourist cities on Luna there was nothing to attract human beings to the other planets, save for exploration and research. The devoted few who put up with the unearthly hardships necessarily lived a monklike existence. Luna was a special case, naturally; being practically in Earth's front yard and an easy jump, it was as popular for romantic holidays as Southpole had once been.

"She got the idea, or Thorgsen suggested it to her, of getting together a diversified travelling troupe to play a circuit of all the outposts."

"It doesn't sound commercial."

"It doesn't have to be. Thorgsen took the matter up for subsidy. He argued that, if research and exploration were necessary, then morale of the personnel involved was a government matter, in spite of the longstanding policy against government participation in the entertainment business, luxury business, or fine arts."

Hamilton whistled. "Nice going! Why, that principle was almost as rock solid as civil rights."

"Yes, but it was a matter of constitution. And the Planners are no fools. They don't necessarily follow precedent. Look at this job we're on."

"Yes, surely. Matter of fact, that was what I dropped in to see you about. I wanted to see how you were getting along." At the time of this conversation Hamilton was feeling his way into the whole picture of the Great Research. Carruthers had given him no fixed instructions, but she told him to spend a few weeks sizing up the problem.

The phase of the research occupying Monroe-Alpha's attention—Thorgsen's project, the Grand Eidouraniun—was much further advanced than any other aspect of the whole project, since it had been conceived originally as a separate matter before the Great Research, which included it, had been thought of. Monroe-Alpha had come into it rather late, but Hamilton had assumed that his friend would be the dominant figure in it. This, Monroe-Alpha maintained, was not true.

"Hargrave is much more fitted for this sort of work than I am. I take my directions from him—myself, and about sixty others."

"How come? I thought you were tops in the numbers racket."

"I have my specialty and Hargrave knows how to make the best use of it. You apparently have no idea of how diversified and specialized mathematics is, Felix. I remember a congress I attended last year—more than a thousand present, but there weren't more than a dozen men there I could really talk to, or understand."

"Hmmm . . . What does Thorgsen do?"

"Well, naturally, he isn't much use in *design*—he's an astrophysicist, or, more properly, a cosmic metrician. But he keeps in touch and his suggestions are always practical."

"I see. Well—got everything you want?"

"Yes," admitted Monroe-Alpha, "unless you should happen to have concealed, somewhere about your person, a hypersphere, a hypersurface, and some four-dimensional liquid, suitable for fine lubrication."

"Thanks. You can hand me back my leg now. I see I've been wrong again—you *are* acquiring a sense of humor."

"I am quite serious about it," Cliff answered without cracking a smile, "even though I haven't the slighest idea where I could find such nor how I could manipulate it if I did."

"For *why*? Give."

"I would like to set up a four-dimensional integrator to integrate from the solid surface of a four-dimensional cam. It would greatly shorten our work if we could do such a thing. The irony of it is that I can describe the thing I want to build, in mathematical symbology, quite nicely. It would do work, which we now have to do with ordinary ball-and-plane integrators and ordinary three-dimensional cams, in one operation whereas the system we use calls for an endless series of operations. It's a little maddening—the theory is so neat and the results are so unsatisfactory."

"I grieve for you," Hamilton had answered, "but you had better take it up with Hargrave."

He had left soon after that. It was evident that those human calculating machines needed nothing from him, and that they knew what they were doing. The project was important—damned important, he thought it was—to investigate what the Universe had been and what it would become. But it was certainly a long-distance matter and he himself would never live to see the end of it. Cliff had told him with a perfectly straight face that they hoped to check their preliminary calculations in a matter of three or three-and-a-half centuries. After that they could hope to build a really worthwhile machine which might tell them things they did not already know.

So he dismissed the matter. He admired the

sort of intellectual detachment which would permit men to work on such a scale, but it was not his horse.

The Great Research in its opening phases seemed to fall into half a dozen major projects, some of which interested him more than others because they gave some hope of producing results during his lifetime. Some, however, were almost as colossal as the building of the Grand Eidouraniun. The distribution of life through the physical universe, for example, and the possibility that other, nonhuman intelligences existed somewhere. If there were such, then it was possible, with an extremely high degree of mathematical probability, that some of them, at least, were more advanced than men. In which case they might give Man a "leg up" in his philosophical education. They might have discovered "Why" as well as "How."

It had been pointed out that it might be extremely dangerous, psychologically, for human beings to encounter such superior creatures. There had been the tragic case of the Australian Aborigines in not too remote historical times—demoralized and finally exterminated by their own sense of inferiority in the presence of the colonizing Anglish.

The investigators serenely accepted the danger; they were not so constituted as to be able to do otherwise.

Hamilton was not sure it *was* a danger. To some it might be, but he himself could not conceive of

a man such as Mordan, for example, losing his
morale under any circumstances. In any case it
was a long-distance project. First they must reach
the stars, which required inventing and building
a starship. That would take a bit of doing. The
great ships which plied the lonely reaches between the planets were simply not fast enough.
Some new drive must be found, if the trips were
not to take generations for each leg.

That they would find life elsewhere in the universe he was quite sure, although a millennia of
exploration might intervene. After all, he considered, the universe was roomy! It had taken Euro-
peans four centuries to spread throughout the two
continents of the "New World"—what about a
galaxy!

But Life they would find. It was not only an
inner conviction; it was just short of scientific
fact, for it was a tight inference of only one stage
from established fact. Arrhenius the Great had set
forth the brilliant speculation, sometime around
the beginning of the XXth century, that life-potent
spores might be carried from planet to planet,
from star to star, pushed along by light pressure.
The optimum size for motes to be carried along
by light pressure happens to be on the same order
as the sizes of bacilli. And bacilli spores are practically unkillable—heat, cold, radiation, time—they
sleep through it until lodged in a favorable environment. Arrhenius calculated that spores could
drift to Alpha Centauri in around nine thousand
years—a mere cosmic blink of the eye.

If Arrhenius were right, then the universe was populated, not just the earth. It mattered not whether life had originated first on earth, first elsewhere, or in many different neighborhoods, once started it had to spread. Millions of years before spaceships it had spread—if Arrhenius were right. For spores alone, lodging and multiplying, would infect an entire planet with whatever forms of life were suited to that planet. Protoplasm is protean; any simple protoplasm can become any complex form of life under mutation and selection.

Arrhenius had been spectacularly vindicated, in part, in the early days of interplanetary exploration. Life had been found on all the planets, save Mercury and Pluto; even on Pluto there were signs of feeble, primitive life in the past. Furthermore, protoplasm seemed to be much the same wherever found—incredibly varied but presumably related. It was disappointing not to have found recognizable intelligence in the solar system—it would have been nice to have had neighbors! (The poor degenerate starveling descendants of the once-mighty Builders of Mars can hardly be described as intelligent—except in charity. A half-witted dog could cheat them at cards.)

But the most startling and satisfying vindication of Arrhenius lay in the fact that *spores* had been trapped out in space itself, in the supposedly-sterile raw vacuum of space!

Hamilton admitted that he did not expect the search for other living intelligences to bear fruit

during his tenure on Terra, unless they got a
hump on themselves in dreaming up that starship
and then hit the jackpot on the first or second
try. And again it was not his forte—he might cook
up a few gadgets for them as auxiliary mechanicals in making the ship more livable, but for the
key problem, motive power, he was about twenty
years too late in specializing. No, keep in touch,
kibitz a little, and report to Carruthers—that was
all he could do.

But there were still several other research possibilities already underway, things that had to do
with human beings, with men, in their more eso-
teric and little-studied aspects. Things that nobody knew anything about anyhow and which he
could, therefore, tackle on an equal footing with
others, catch-as-catch-can, and no holds barred.
Where does a man go after he's dead? And, con-
versely, where does he come from? He made a
mental note of that latter—it suddenly occurred
to him that most of the attention had been given
to the first half of the paired question. What is
telepathy and how do you make it tick? How is it
that a man can live another life in his dreams?
There were dozens more, all questions science
had refused to tackle because they were too slip-
pery—had in fact walked away from like a dis-
gruntled cat. All of them related to some
troublesome characteristic of the human personality—whatever that was—and any of them might
lead to an answer as to *purpose—meaning.*

He felt toward these questions the free and easy

attitude of the man who was asked if he could pilot a rocket: "I don't know—I've never tried." Well, he would try. And he would help Carruthers see to it that many others tried, strongly, consistently, following out every approach that could be thought of, and keeping meticulous, full, scientific records. They would track down the Ego, trap it, and put a band on its leg.

What was an ego? He didn't know, but he knew he was one. By which he did not mean his body, nor, by damn, his genes. He could localize it—on the centerline, forward of his ears, back of his eyes, and about four centimeters down from the top of the skull—no, more like six. That was where he *himself* lived—when he was home—he would bet on it, to the nearest centimetre. He *knew* closer than that, but he couldn't get in and measure it. Of course, he wasn't home all the time.

Hamilton could not figure out just why Carruthers wanted him, but then, he had not been present at an exchange between Mordan and Carruthers. "How is my Problem Child getting along?" Mordan had inquired.

"Quite well, Claude. Quite well indeed."

"What are you using him for?"

"Well . . ." Carruthers pursed his lips. "I'm using him as a philosopher, only he does not know it."

Mordan chuckled. "Better not let him know. I think he might be offended to be called a philosopher."

"I shan't. Really, he's quite useful to me. You know how impossible most specialists are, and how pedantic most of our brother synthesists."

"Tut, tut. Such heresy."

"Isn't it, though? But Felix is useful to me. He has an active, uninhibited mind. His mind *prowls*."

"I told you he was a star line."

"Yes, you did. Every now and then you genetics laddies come out with the right answer."

"May your bed spring a leak," Mordan answered. "We can't always be wrong. The Great Egg must love human beings, he made a lot of them."

"Same argument applies to oysters, only more so."

"That's different," said Mordan. "*I'm* the one who loves oysters. Have you had dinner?"

Felix sat up with a start. The house phone at his elbow was chiming. He flipped the come-along tab and heard Phyllis's voice. "Felix, my dear, will you come in and say goodbye to Madame Espartero?"

"Coming, dear."

He returned to the lounge, feeling vaguely unsettled. He had forgotten the presence of the ancient Planner.

"Madame, will you graciously permit—"

"Come here, lad!" she said sharply. "I want to see you in the light." He came forward and stood before her, feeling somewhat as he always had as a child when the development center therapists checked over his growth and physical development. Damnation, he thought, she looks at me as if I were a horse and she a buyer.

She stood up suddenly and grasped her stick. "You'll do," she stated, as if the knowledge somehow annoyed her. She extracted a fresh cigar from somewhere about her person, turned to Phyllis, and said, "Goodbye, child. And thank you." Whereupon she started for the door.

Felix had to hurry to catch up with her and let her out.

Felix returned to Phyllis, and said savagely, "A man that'ud do that 'ud be challenged."

"Why, Felix!"

"I detest," he stated, "these damned emphatic old women. I have never seen why politeness should be the obligation of the young and rudeness the privilege of age."

"Why, Felix, she's not like that at all. I think she's a dear."

"She doesn't act like it."

"Oh, she doesn't mean anything by that. I think she's just always in a hurry."

"Why should she be?"

"Wouldn't you be—at her age?"

He hadn't thought of it from that point of view. "Maybe you're right. Sands of time, and so forth. What did the two of you talk about?"

"Oh—lots of things. When I expected the baby and what we were going to name him and what plans we had for him and things."

"I'll bet she did most of the talking."

"No, I did. Occasionally she put in a question."

"Do you know, Phyllis," he said soberly, "one of the things I like least about the whole business of you and me and *him* is the quivering interest that outsiders take in it. No more privacy than a guppy in an aquarium."

"I know what you mean, but I didn't feel that way with her. We talked women talk. It was nice."

"Hrummph!"

"Anyway, she didn't talk much about Theobald. I told her we intended to have a little sister for Theobald presently. She was very much interested. She wanted to know when, and what plans we had for *her*, and what we intended to name her. I hadn't thought about that. What do you think would be a nice name, Felix?"

"Egg knows—seems to me that's rushing matters a little. I hope you told her that it would be a long, long time."

"I did, but she seemed a little disappointed. But I want to be *myself* for a while, after Theobald comes. How do you like the name 'Justina'?"

"Seems all right," he answered. "What about it?"

"She suggested it."

"She did? Whose baby does she think it's going to be?"

CHAPTER FOURTEEN

"—and beat him when he sneezes"

Now, Felix, don't get yourself excited."

"But dammit, Claude, she's been in there a long time!"

"Not very long. First babies are often a little slow arriving."

"But—Claude, you biologist johnnies should have worked out something better than this. Women shouldn't have to go through with this."

"Such as?"

"How should I know? Ectogenesis, maybe."

"We could practice ectogenesis," Mordan answered imperturbably, "if we wished. It has been done. But it would be a mistake."

"Egg's sake—why?"

"Contra-survival in nature. The race would be dependent on complex mechanical assistance to reproduce. The time might come when it wasn't available. Survivor types are types that survive in difficult times as well as easy times. An ectogenetic race couldn't cope with really hard, primitive conditions. But ectogenesis isn't new—it's been in use for millions of years."

"No, I suppose it—Huh? How long did you say?"

"Millions of years. What is egg-laying but ectogenesis? It's not efficient; it risks the infant zygotes too hazardously. The great auk and the dodo might still be alive today, if they had not been ectogenetic. No, Felix, we mammals have a better method."

"That's all right for you to say," Felix replied glumly. "It's not your wife that's concerned."

Mordan forebore to answer this. He went on, making conversation. "The same applies to any technique which makes life easier at the expense of hardiness. Ever hear of a bottle-baby, Felix? No, you would not have—it's an obsolete term. But it has to do with why the barbarians nearly died out after the Second Genetic War. They weren't all killed, you know—there are always survivors, no matter how fierce the war. But they were mostly bottle-babies, and the infant-generation thinned out to almost nothing. Not enough bottles and not enough cows. Their mothers could not feed them."

Hamilton raised a hand irritably. Mordan's serene detachment—for such he assumed it to be—from the events at hand annoyed him.

"The deuce with that stuff. Got another cigaret?"

"You have one in your hand," Mordan pointed out.

"Eh? So I have!" Quite unconsciously he snuffed

it out, and took another one from his own pouch. Mordan smiled and said nothing.

"What time is it?"

"Fifteen-forty."

"Is that all? It must be later."

"Wouldn't you be less jumpy if you were inside?"

"Phyllis won't let me. You know how she is, Claude—a whim of steel." He smiled, but there was no gayety in it.

"You are both rather dynamic and positive."

"Oh, we get along. She lets me have my own way, and later I found out I've done just what she wanted me to do."

Mordan had no difficulty in repressing his smile. He was beginning to wonder at the delay himself. He told himself that his interest was detached, impersonal, scientific. But he had to go on telling himself.

The door dilated; an attendant showed herself. "You may come in now," she announced with brisk cheeriness.

Mordan was closer to the door; he started to go in first. Hamilton made a long arm, grabbed him by the shoulder. "Hey! What goes on here? Who's the father in this deal, anyhow?" He pushed himself into the lead. "You wait your turn."

She looked a little pale. "Hello, Felix."

"Hello, Phil." He bent over her. "You all right?"

"Of course I'm all right—this what I'm for." She looked at him. "And get that silly smirk off your face. After all, you didn't *invent* fatherhood."

"You're sure you're all right?"

"I'm fine. But I must look a fright."

"You look beautiful."

A voice at his ear said, "Don't you want to see your son?"

"Eh? Oh—sure!" He turned and looked. Mordan straightened up and stood out of the way. The attendant held the baby up, half inviting him to hold it, but he kept his arms down and looked it over gingerly. It seemed to have the usual number of arms and legs, he thought, but that bright orange color—well, he didn't know. Maybe it was normal.

"Don't you approve of him?" Phyllis asked sharply.

"Huh? Sure, sure. It's a beautiful baby. He looks like you."

"Babies," said Phyllis, "don't look like anyone, except other babies."

"Why, Master Hamilton," put in the attendant, "how you are sweating! Don't you feel well?" Transferring the baby with casual efficiency to her left arm, she picked up a pad and wiped his forehead. "Take it easy. Seventy years in this one location and we've never lost a father."

Hamilton started to tell her that the gag was ancient when the establishment was new, but he restrained himself. He felt a little inhibited, a rare thing for him. "We'll take the child out for a while," the attendant went on. "Don't stay too long."

Mordan excused himself cheerily and left.

"Felix," she said thoughtfully, "I've been thinking about something."

"So?"

"We've got to move."

"Why? I thought you liked our place."

"I do. but I want a place in the country."

He looked suddenly apprehensive. "Now, darling, you know I'm not the bucolic type."

"You don't have to move if you don't want to. But Theobald and I are going to. I want him to be able to get himself dirty and have a dog and things like that."

"But why be so drastic? All development centers run to the air, sunshine, and the good earth motif."

"I don't want him spending all his time in development centers. They're necessary, but they're no substitute for family life."

"*I* was raised in development centers."

"Take a look at yourself in the mirror."

The child grew in no particularly spectacular fashion. He crawled at a reasonable age, tried to stand, burned his fingers a few times, tried to swallow the usual quota of unswallowable objects.

Mordan seemed satisfied. So did Phyllis. Felix had no criteria.

At nine months Theobald attempted a few words, then shut up for a long time. At fourteen months he began speaking in sentences, short and of his own structure, but sentences. The subjects of his conversation, or, rather, his statements, were consistently egocentric. Normal again—no one expects an infant to write essays on the beauties of altruism.

"That," remarked Hamilton to Mordan one day, hooking a thumb toward where Theobald sat naked in the grass, trying to remove the ears from an unco-operative and slightly indignant puppy, "is your superchild, is he not?"

"Mm, yes."

"When does he start doing his miracles?"

"He won't do miracles. He is not unique in any one respect; he is simply the best we can conceive in every respect. He is uniformly *normal*, in the best sense of the word—optimum, rather."

"Hmm. Well, I'm glad he doesn't have tentacles growing out of his ears, or a bulging forehead, or something like that. Come here, son."

Theobald ignored him. He could be deaf when he chose; he seemed to find it particularly difficult to hear the word "No." Hamilton got up, went over and picked him up. He had no useful purpose in mine; he just wanted to cuddle the child for a while for his own amusement. Theobald resisted being separated from the pup for a moment, then accepted the change. He could soak up a great deal of petting—when it suited him. If it really did not suit him he could be extremely unco-operative.

Even to the extent of biting. He and his father had put in a difficult and instructive half hour in his fifteenth month settling the matter. Beyond cautioning Felix to be careful not to damage the brat Phyllis had let them have it out. Theobald did not bite anymore, but Felix had a permanent, small, ragged scar on his left thumb.

Hamilton was almost inordinately fond of the child, although he was belligerently off-hand in his manner. It hurt him that the child did not really seem to care anything about him and would as readily accept petting and endearments from "Uncle Claude"—or a total stranger—if he happened to be in the mood to accept anything of the sort.

On Mordan's advice and by Phyllis's decision (Felix was not offered a vote in the matter—she was quite capable of reminding him that *she*, and not he, was a psycho-pediatrician) Theobald was not taught to read any earlier than the usual age of thirty months, although experimental testing showed that he could comprehend the basic idea of abstracted symbols a little earlier than that. She used the standard extensionalized technique of getting a child to comprehend symbolic grouping-by-abstracted-characteristics while emphasizing individual differences. Theobald was rather bored with the matter and appeared to make no progress at all for the first three weeks. Then he seemed suddenly to get the idea that there might be something in it for him—apparently by recognizing his own name on a stat which Felix had transmitted from his office, for shortly thereafter he took the lead in his own instruction and displayed the concentrated interest he was capable of.

Nine weeks after the instruction began it was

finished. Reading was an acquired art; further instruction would merely have gotten in his way. Phyllis let him be and restricted her efforts in the matter of seeing to it that only such reading matter was left in his reach as she wished him to attempt. Otherwise he would have read anything he could lay hands on; as it was she had to steal scrolls from him when she wanted him to exercise or eat.

Felix worried around the child's obsession with printed matter. Phyllis told him not to. "It will wear off. We've suddenly extended his psycho field; he's got to explore it for a while."

"It didn't with me. I still read when I should be doing something else. It's a vice."

He read stumblingly and with much subvocalization and was, of course, forced to call for help frequently when he ran on to symbols new to him and not sufficiently defined by context. A home is not as well equipped for extensional instruction as a development center. In a center no words appear in a primer which are not respresented by examples which can be pointed to, or, if the words are action symbols, the actions are such that they can be performed there and then.

But Theobald was through with primers before he should have been and their home, although comfortably large, would have needed to be of museum size to accommodate samples in groups of every referent he inquired about. Phyllis's resourcefulness and histrionic ability were stretched to the limit, but she stuck to the cardinal principle of semantic pedagogy: never define a new symbol in terms of symbols already known if it is possible to point to a referent instead.

The child's eidetic memory first became evident in connection with reading. He read rapidly if badly and remembered what he read. Not for him was the childish custom of cherishing and rereading favorite books. A once-read scroll was to him an empty sack; he wanted another.

"What does 'infatuated' mean, Mama?" He made this inquiry in the presence of his father and Mordan.

"Hmmm," she began guardedly, "tell me what words you found it sitting with."

" 'It is not that I am merely infatuated with you, as that old goat Mordan seems to think—' I don't understand that either. Is Uncle Claude a goat? He doesn't look like one."

"What," said Felix, "has that child been reading now?" Mordan said nothing, but he cocked a brow at Felix.

"I think I recognize it," Phyllis said in an aside to Felix. Then, turning back to the child, she added, "Where did you find it? Tell Phyllis."

No answer.

"Was it in Phyllis's desk?" She knew that it had been; there was secreted in there a bundle of stats, mementos of the days before she and Felix had worked out their differences. She had the habit of rereading them privately and secretly. "Tell Phyllis."

"Yes."

"That's out of bounds, you know."

"You didn't see me," he stated triumphantly.

"No, that is true." She thought rapidly. She wished to encourage his truthfulness, but to place a deterrant on disobedience. To be sure, disobedience was more often a virtue than a sin, but— Oh, well! She tabled the matter.

Felix muttered, "That child seems to have no moral sense whatsoever."

"Have you?" she asked him, and turned back to Theobald.

"There was lots more, Mama. Want to hear it?"

"Not just now. Let's answer your two questions first."

"But Phyllis," Felix interrupted.

"Wait, Felix. I've got to answer his questions."

"Suppose you and I step out into the garden for a smoke," Mordan suggested. "Phyllis is going to be fairly busy for a while."

Quite busy. "Infatuated" was, in itself, quite a hurdle, but how to explain to a child in his forty-second month the allegorical use of symbols? She was not entirely successful; Theobald referred to Mordan indiscriminately thereafter as "Uncle Claude" or "Old Goat."

Eidetic memory is a Mendelian recessive. Both Phyllis and Felix had the gene group for it from one ancestor; Theobold had it from both his parents, by selection. The potentiality, masked as recessive in each of his parents, was therefore effective in him. Both "recessive" and "dominant" are relative terms; dominants do not cancel recessives like symbols in an equation. Both Phyllis and Felix had excellent, unusual memories. Theobald's memory was well-nigh perfect.

Recessive Mendelian characteristics are usually undesirable ones. The reason is simple—dominant characteristics get picked over by natural selection every generation. Natural selection—the dying out of the poorly equipped—goes on day in and day out, inexorable and automatic. It is as tireless, as inescapable, as entropy. A really bad dominant will weed itself out of the race in a few generations. The worst dominants appear only as original mutations, since they either kill their bearers, or preclude reproduction. Embryo cancer is such a one—complete sterility is another. But a recessive may be passed on from generation to generation, masked and not subjected to natural selection. In time a generation may arrive in which a child receives the recessive from both parents—up it pops, strong as ever. That is why the earlier geneticists found it so hard to eliminate such recessives as hemophilia and deaf-mutism; it was impossible, until the genes in question were charted by extremely difficult indirect and inferential means, to tell whether or not an adult, himself in perfect health, was actually "clean." He might pass on something grisly to his children. Nobody knew.

Felix demanded of Mordan why, in view of the bad reputation of recessives, eidetic memory should happen to be recessive rather than dominant.

"I'll answer that twice," said Mordon. "In the

first place the specialists are still arguing as to why some things are recessives, and others dominants. In the second place, why call eidetic memory a desirable trait?"

"But—for Egg's sake! You *selected* for it for Baldy!"

"To be sure we did—for Theobald. 'Desirable' is a relative term. Desirable for *whom*? Complete memory is an asset only if you have the mind to handle it; otherwise it's a curse. One used to find such cases occasionally, before your time and mine—poor simple souls who were bogged down in the complexities of their own experience; they knew every tree but could not find the forest. Besides that, forgetting is an anodyne and a blessing to most people. They don't need to remember much and they don't. It's different with Theobald."

They had been talking in Mordan's office. He took from his desk a file of memoranda, arranged systematically on perhaps a thousand small punched cards. "See this? I haven't looked it over yet—it's data the technicians supply me with. Its arrangement is quite as significant as its content—more so, perhaps." He took the file and dumped the cards out onto the floor. "The data are still all there, but what use is it now?" He pressed a stud on his desk; his new file secretary entered. "Albert, will you please have these fed into the sorter again? I'm afraid I've randomed them."

Albert looked surprised, but said, "Sure, chief," and took the pied cards away.

"Theobald has the brain power, to speak loosely, to arrange his data, to be able to find it when he wants it, and to use it. He will be able to see how what he knows is related to its various parts, and to abstract from the mass significantly related details. Eidetic memory is a desirable trait *in him*."

No doubt—but sometimes it did not seem so to Hamilton. As the child grew older he developed an annoying habit of correcting his elders about minutiæ, in which he was always maddeningly accurate. "No, Mother, it was not last Wednesday; it was last Thursday. I remember because that was the day that Daddy took me walking up past the reservoir and we saw a pretty lady dressed in a green jumpsuit and Daddy smiled at her and she stopped and asked me what my name was and I told her my name was Theobald and that Daddy's name was Felix and that I was four years and one month old. And Daddy laughed and she laughed and then Daddy said—"

"That will do," said Felix. "You've made your point. It was Thursday. But it is not necessary to correct people on little things like that."

"But when they're wrong I have to tell them!"

Felix let it ride, but he reflected that Theobald might need to be inordinately fast with a gun when he was older.

Felix had developed a fondness for country life, little as he had wanted to undertake it. Had it not been for his continuous work on the Great Research he might have taken up horticulture seriously. There was something deeply satisfying, he found, in making a garden do what he wanted it to do.

He would have spent all his holidays fussing with his plants, if Phyllis had concurred. But her holidays were less frequent than his, since she had resumed putting in one shift a day at the nearest primary development center as soon as Theobald was old enough to need the knocking around he would get from other children. When she did have a holiday she liked to go somewhere—a flying picnic, usually.

They had to live near the Capital, because of Felix's work, but the Pacific was only a little over five hundred kilometres west of them. It was convenient to pack a lunch, get to the beach in time for a swim and a nice, long, lazy bake, then eat.

Felix wanted to see the boy's reaction the first time he saw the ocean. "Well, son, this is it. What do you think of it?"

Theobald scowled out at the breakers. "It's all right," he grudged.

"What's the matter?"

"The water looks sick. And the sun ought to be off *that* way, not there. And where's the big trees?"

"What big trees?"

"The high slim ones, with big bushes at the top."

"Hmmm . . . what's wrong with the water?"

"It ain't *blue*."

Hamilton walked back to where Phyllis lay on

the sand. "Can you tell me," he said slowly, "whether or not Baldy has ever seen stereos of royal palms—on a beach, a tropical beach?"

"Not that I know of. Why?"

"Think back. Did you use such a picture to extensionalize for him?"

"No, I'm sure of that."

"You know what he's read—has he seen any flat-picture like that."

She checked back through her excellent and well-arranged memory. "No, I would have remembered it. I would never have put such a picture in his way without explaining it to him."

The incident occurred before Theobald had been entered at the development center; what he had seen, he had seen at home. Of course it was possible that he had seen it in a news or story cast in the receiver at home, but he could not start the machine himself and neither of them recalled such a scene. Nevertheless, it was damned funny.

"What did you start to say, dear?"

Hamilton gave a slight start. "Nothing, nothing at all."

"What kind of 'nothing'?"

He shook his head. "Too fantastic. My mind was wandering."

He went back to the boy and attempted to pump him for details in an effort to ferret out the mystery. But Theobald was not talking. In fact, he was not even listening. He said so.

On a similar occasion but much later an event

occurred which was quite as disturbing, but a little more productive. Felix and the boy had been splashing in the surf, until they were quite tired. At least Felix was, which made a majority with only one dissent. They lay down on the sand and let the sun dry them. Presently the salt drying on the skin made them itch, as it has a habit of doing.

Felix scratched Theobald between the shoulder blades—that awkward spot—and reflected to himself how catlike the child was in many ways, even to the sybaritic way in which he accepted this small sensuous pleasure. Just now it suited him to be petted; a moment later he might be as haughty and distant as a Persian tom. Or he might decide to cuddle.

Then Felix lay on his stomach, Theobald straddled his back and returned the favor. Felix was beginning to feel rather catlike himself—it felt so good! when he began to be aware of a curious and almost inexplicable phenomenon.

When one human monkey does another the great service of scratching him, delightful as it is, it never *quite* hits the spot. With infuriating obtuseness, despite the most careful coaching, the scratcher will scratch just above, just below, all around the right spot, but never, never, never quite on it, until, in sheer frustration, the scratchee will nearly dislocate his shoulder going after it for himself.

Felix was giving Theobald no instructions; in fact, he was nearly falling asleep under the warm relaxing ecstasy of his son's ministrations, when he suddenly snapped to attention.

Theobald was scratching where Felix itched.

The exact spot. An area of sensation had only to show up for him to pounce on it and scratch it out of existence.

This was another matter that had to be taken up with Phyllis. He got up and explained to her what had happened, attempting the meanwhile to keep it from the child's attention by suggesting that he go for a run down the beach—"But don't go in more than ankle deep."

"Just try him," he added, when he had told her of it. "He can do it. He really can."

"I'd like to," she said. "But I can't. I'm sorry to say that I am still fresh and clean and free from vulgar distresses."

"Phyllis—"

"Yes, Felix?"

"What kind of a person can scratch where another person itches?"

"An angel."

"No, seriously."

"You tell me."

"You know as well as I do. That kid's a telepath!"

They both looked down the beach at a small, skinny, busy silhouette. "I know how the hen felt that hatched the ducks," said Phyllis softly. She got quickly to her feet. "I'm going in and get some salt on me, and let it dry. I've got to find out about this."

CHAPTER FIFTEEN

"Probably a blind alley—"

Hamilton Felix took his son into the city the next day. There were men attached to the Great Research who knew much more about such things than either he or Phyllis; he wished them to examine the boy. He took Theobald to his office, supplied him with a scroll and a reader, a dodge that would tie him to one spot almost as effectively as if he were chained down, and called Jacobstein Ray by telephone. Jacobstein was in charge of a team investigating telepathy and related phenomena.

He explained to Jake that he was unable to leave his own office at the moment. Could Jake drop over, or was he tied up? Jake could and would; he arrived a few minutes later. The two men stepped into an adjoining room, out of earshot of the child. Felix explained what had taken place on the beach and suggested that Jake look into it.

Jake was willing and interested. "But don't expect too much from it," he cautioned. "We've demonstrated telepathy in young children time and again, under circumstances which made it a statistical certainty that they were receiving information by no known physical means. But there was never any control in the business, the child was never able to explain what was going on, and the ability faded away to nothing as the child grew up and became more coherent. It seems to shrivel away just like the thymus gland."

Hamilton looked alert. "Thymus gland? Any correlation?"

"Why, no. I just used that as a figure of speech."

"Mightn't there be?"

"It seems most unlikely."

"Everything about this business seems most unlikely. How about putting a crew on it? A good biostatician and one of your operators?"

"I will if you wish."

"Good. I'll stat an open voucher to your office. It's probably a blind alley, but you never know!"

Let us add that it *was* a blind alley. Nothing ever came of it, but a slight addition to the enormous mass of negative information constituting the main body of scientific knowledge.

Felix and Jake went back into the room where Theobald sat reading. They seated themselves first, in order to be on the same level as the child, and Felix performed the introduction with proper attention to the enormous and vulnerable dignity of a child. He then said:

"Look, sport, Dad wants you to go with Jake

and help him with some things for an hour or so. How about it?"

"Why?"

That was a tough one. With less-than-adult minds it had been found to be optimum procedure to keep them from knowing the purpose of the experimentation. "Jake wants to find out some things about the way your mind works. He'll talk with you about it. Well . . . will you help him?"

Theobald thought about it.

"It will be a favor to Dad." Phyllis could have warned him against that approach. Theobald had been rather slow in reaching the degree of social integration necessary to appreciate the cool pleasure of conferring benefits on others.

"Will *you* do me a favor?" he countered.

"What do you want?"

"A flop-eared buck." The boy had been raising rabbits, with some adult assistance; but his grandiose plans, if unchecked, would have resulted in their entire home being given over to fat, furry rodents. Nevertheless, Hamilton was somewhat relieved to find the favor desired was no larger.

"Sure thing, sport. You could have had one anyhow."

Theobald made no answer, but stood up, signifying his willingness to get on with it.

After they had gone Hamilton considered the matter for a moment. A new buck rabbit was all right; he did not mind that as much as he would have minded a new doe. But something had to be done fairly soon, or else his garden would have to be abandoned.

Theobald seemed to be working out, with the busy and wholehearted collaboration of his rabbits, an interesting but entirely erroneous neo-Mendelian concept of inherited characteristics. Why, he wanted to know, did white bunnies sometimes have brown babies? Felix pointed out that a brown buck had figured in the matter, but soon bogged down, and turned the matter over to Mordan—accepting as inevitable the loss of face involved. Theobald, he knew, was quite capable now of being interested in the get of a flop-eared buck.

The boy had formulated an interesting, but decidedly specialized, arithmetic to keep his records of rabbits, based on the proposition that one plus one equals at least five. Hamilton had discovered it by finding symbols in the boy's rabbit note book with which he was unfamiliar. Theobald boredly interpreted them for him.

Hamilton showed the records to Monroe-Alpha the next time Monroe-Alpha and Marion showed up at his home. He had regarded it as an amusing and insignificant joke, but Clifford took it with his usual dead seriousness. "Isn't it about time you started him on arithmetic?"

"Why, I don't think so. He is a little young for it—he's hardly well into mathematical analysis." Theobald had been led into mathematical symbology by the conventional route of generalized geometry, analysis, and the calculi. Naturally, he had not been confronted with the tedious, inane, and specialized mnemonics of practical arithmetic—he was hardly more than a baby.

"I don't think he is too young for it. I had devised a substitute for positional notation when I was about his age. I imagine he can take it, if you don't ask him to memorize operation tables." Monroe-Alpha was unaware that the child had an eidetic memory and Hamilton passed the matter by. He had no intention of telling Monroe-Alpha anything about Theobald's genetic background. While custom did not actually forbid such discussion, good taste, he felt, did. Let the boy alone, let him keep his private life private. He and Phyllis knew, the geneticists involved had to know, the Planners had had to know since this was a star line. Even that he regretted, for it had brought such intrusions as the visit of that old hag Carvala.

Theobald himself would know nothing, or very little, of his ancestral background until he was a grown man. He might not inquire into it, or have it brought to his attention, until he reached something around the age Felix had been when Mordan called Felix's attention to his own racial significance.

It was better so. The pattern of a man's inherited characteristics was racially important and inescapable anyhow, but too much knowledge of it, too much thinking about it, could be suffocating to the individual. Look at Cliff—damned near went off the beam entirely just from thinking about his great-grandparents. Well, Marion had fixed *that*.

No, it was not good to talk too much about such things. He himself had talked too much a short time before, and had been sorry ever since. He had been telling Mordan his own point of view about Phyllis having any more children—after the baby girl to come, of course. Phyllis and he had not yet come to agreement about it; Mordan had backed up Phyllis. "I would like for you two to have at least four children, preferably six. More would be better but we probably would not have time enough to select properly for that many."

Hamilton almost exploded. "It seems to me that you make plans awfully easy—for other people. I haven't noticed you doing *your* bit. You are pretty much of a star line yourself—how come? Is this a one-way proposition?"

Mordan had kept his serenity. "I have not refrained. My plasm is on deposit, and available if wanted. Every moderator in the country saw my chart, in the usual course of routine."

"The fact remains that you haven't done much personally about children."

"No. No, that is true. Martha and I have so many, many children in our district, and so many yet to come, that we hardly have time to concentrate on one."

From the peculiar phraseology Hamilton gained a sudden bit of insight. "Say, you and Martha are married—*aren't you?*"

"Yes. For twenty-three years."

"Well, then . . . but, why—"

"We *can't*," Mordan said flatly, with just a shade less than his usual calm. "She's a mutation . . . sterile."

Hamilton's ears still burned to think that his big mouth had maneuvered his friend into making such a naked disclosure. He had never guessed the relationship; Martha *never* called Claude anything but "chief"; they used no words of endearment, nor let it creep otherwise into their manner. Still, it explained a lot of things—the rapport-like co-operative between the technician and the synthesist, the fact that Mordan had shifted to genetics after starting a brilliant career in social administration, his intense and fatherly interest in his charges.

He realized with a slight shock that Claude and Martha were as much parents of Theobald as were Phyllis and himself—foster parents, godparents. Mediator parents might be the right term. They were mediator parents to hundreds or thousands, he didn't know how many.

But this wasn't getting his work done—and he would have to go home early today, because of Theobald. He turned to his desk. A memorandum caught his eye—from himself to himself. Hmmm . . . he would have to get after that. Better talk to Carruthers. He swung around toward the phone.

"Chief?"

"Yes, Felix."

"I was talking with Doctor Thorgsen the other day, and I got an idea—may not be much in it."

"Give." Way out on far Pluto, the weather is cold. The temperature rarely rises above eighteen degrees centigrade *absolute* even on the side toward the sun. And that refers to high noon in the open sunlight. Much of the machinery of the observatories is exposed to this intense cold. Machinery that will work on Terra will not work on Pluto, and vice versa. The laws of physics seem to be invariable but the characteristics of materials change with changes in temperature—consider ice and water, a mild example.

Lubricating oil is a dry powder at such temperatures. Steel isn't steel. The exploring scientists had to devise new technologies before Pluto could be conquered.

Not only for mobiles but for stabiles as well— such as electrical equipment. Electrical equipment depends on, among other factors, the resistance characteristics of conductors; extreme cold greatly lowers the electrical resistance of metals. At thirteen degrees centigrade absolute lead becomes a super-conductor with no resistance whatsoever. An electric current induced in such lead seems to go on forever, without damping.

There are many other such peculiarities. Hamilton did not go into them—it was a sure thing that a brilliant synthesist such as his chief had all the gross facts about such matters. The main fact was this: Pluto was a natural laboratory for low temperature research, not only for the benefit of the observatories but for every other purpose.

One of the classic difficulties of science has to

do with the fact that a research man can always think of things he wants to measure before instruments for the purpose have been devised. Genetics remained practically at a standstill for a century before ultramicroscopy reached the point where genes could really be seen. But the peculiar qualities of superconductors and near superconductors gave physicists an opportunity, using such chilled metals in new instruments, to build gadgets which would detect phenomena more subtle than ever before detected.

Thorgsen and his colleagues had stellar bolometers so accurate and so sensitive as to make the readings of earlier instruments look like a casual horseback guess. He claimed to be able to measure the heat from a flushed cheek at ten parsecs. The colony on Pluto even had an electro-magnetic radiation receiver which would—sometimes—enable them to receive messages from Terra, if the Great Egg smiled and everyone kept their fingers crossed.

But telepathy, if it was anything physical at all—whatever "physical" may mean!—should be detectable by some sort of a gadget. That the gadget would need to be extremely sensitive seemed a foregone conclusion; therefore, Pluto seemed a likely place to develop one.

There was even some hope to go on. An instrument—Hamilton did not remember what it had been—had been perfected there, had worked satisfactorily, and then had performed very erratically indeed—when the two who had perfected it attempted to demonstrate it in the presence of a crowd of colleagues. It seemed sensitive to living people.

To *living* people. Equivalent masses, of blood temperature and similar radiating surfaces, did not upset it. But it grew querulous in the presence of human beings. It was dubbed a "Life Detector"; the director of the colony saw possibilities in it and instigated further research.

Hamilton's point to Carruthers was this: might not the so-called life detector be something that was sensitive to whatever it was they called telepathy? Carruthers thought it possible. Would it not then be advisable to instigate research along that line on Terra? Decidedly. Or would it be better to send a team out to Pluto, where low temperature research was so much more handy? Go ahead on both lines, of course.

Hamilton pointed out that it would be a year and a half until the next regular ship to Pluto. "Never mind that," Carruthers said. "Plan to send a special. The Board will stand for it."

Hamilton cleared the phone, turned it to recording, and spoke for several minutes, giving instructions to two of his bright young assistants. He referred to his next point of agenda.

In digging back into the literature of the race it had been noted that the borderline subjects of the human spirit with which he was now dealing had once occupied much more of the attention of the race than now was the case. Spiritism, apparitions, reports of the dead appearing in dreams with messages which checked out, "Ghosties, and Ghoulies, and things that go Flop in the Dark" had once obsessed the attention of many. Much of the mass of pseudo-data seemed to be psychopathic. But not all of it. This chap Flammarion, for example, a professional astronomer (or was he an astrologer?—there used to be such, he knew, before space flight was developed)—anyhow, a man with his head screwed on tight, a man with a basic appreciation for the scientific method even in those dark ages. Flammarion had collected an enormous amount of data, which, if even one per cent of it was true, proved survival of the ego after the physical death beyond any reasonable doubt.

It gave him a lift just to read about it.

Hamilton knew that the loose stories of bygone days did not constitute evidence of the first order, but some of it, after examination by psychiatric semanticians, could be used as evidence of the second order. In any case, the experience of the past might give many a valuable clue for further research. The hardest part of this aspect of the Great Research was to know where to start looking.

There were a couple of old books, for example, by a man named Doon, or Dunn, or something of the sort—the changes in speech symbols made the name uncertain—who had tediously collected records of forerunner dreams for more than a quarter of a century. But he had died, no one had followed up his work, and it had been forgotten. Never mind—Dunn's patience would be vindicated; over ten thousand careful men, in addition to their other activities, made a practice of recording their dreams immediately on wakening, before speaking to anyone or even getting out of bed. If dreams ever opened a window to the future, the matter would be settled, conclusively.

Hamilton himself tried to keep such records. Unfortunately, he rarely dreamed. No matter— others did, and he was in touch with them.

The old books Hamilton wished to have perused were mostly obscure and few translations had ever been made; idiom presented a hazard. There were scholars of comparative lingo, of course, but even for them the job was difficult. Fortunately, there was immediately at hand a man who could read Anglish of the year 1926 and for at least the century preceding that date—a particularly rich century for such research, as the scientific method was beginning to be appreciated by some but the interest in such matters was still high—Smith John Darlington—or J. Darlington Smith, as he preferred to be called. Hamilton had co-opted him. Smith did not want to do it. He was very busy with his feetball industry—he had three associations of ten battle groups each, and a fourth forming. His business was booming; he was in a fair way to becoming as rich as he wanted to be, and he disliked to spare the time.

But he would do it—if the man who gave him his start in business insisted. Felix insisted.

Felix telephoned him next. "Hello, Jack."

"Howdy, Felix."

"Do you have any more for me?"

"I've a stock of spools shoulder high."

"Good. Tube them over, will you?"

"Sure. Say, Felix, this stuff is awful, most of it."

"I don't doubt it. But think how much ore must be refined to produce a gram of native radium. Well, I'll clear now."

"Wait a minute, Felix. I got into a jam last night. I wonder if you could give me some advice."

"Certainly. Give." It appeared that Smith, who, in spite of his financial success, was a brassarded man and technically a control natural, had inadvertently given offense to an armed citizen by refusing to give way automatically in a public place. The citizen had lectured Smith on etiquette. Smith had never fully adjusted himself to the customs of a different culture; he had done a most urbane thing—he had struck the citizen with his closed fist, knocking him down and bloodying his nose. Naturally, there was the deuce to pay, and all big bills.

The citizen's next friend had called the following morning and presented Smith with a formal challenge. Smith must either accept and shoot it out, apologize acceptably, or be evicted from the city bodily by the citizen and his friends, with monitors looking on to see that the customs were maintained.

"What ought I to do?"

"I would advise you to apologize." Hamilton saw no way out of it; to advise him to fight was to suggest suicide. Hamilton had no scruples about suicide, but he judged correctly that Smith preferred to live.

"But I can't do that—what do you think I am, a nigger?"

"I don't understand what you mean. What has your color to do with it?"

"Oh, never mind. But I can't apologize, Felix. I was ahead of him in line. Honest I was."

"But you were brassarded."

"But . . . Look, Felix, I want to shoot it out with him. Will you act for me?"

"I will if you request it. He'll kill you, you know."

"Maybe not. I might happen to beat him to the draw."

"Not in a set duel you won't. The guns are cross-connected. Your gun won't burn until the referee flashes the signal."

"I'm fairly fast."

"You're outclassed. You don't play feetball yourself you know. And you know why."

Smith knew. He had planned to play, as well as manage and coach, when the enterprise was started. A few encounters with the men he had hired soon convinced him that an athlete of his own period was below average in this present period. In particular his reflexes were late. He bit his lip and said nothing.

"You sit tight," said Felix, "and don't go out of your apartment. I'll do a little calling and see what can be worked out."

The next friend was polite but regretful. Awfully

sorry not to oblige Master Hamilton but he was
acting under instructions. Could Master Hamilton
speak with his principal? Now, really, that was
hardly procedure. But he admitted that the circumstances were unusual—give him a few minutes, then he would phone back.

Hamilton received permission to speak to the
principal; called him. No, the challenge could not
be lifted—and the conversation was strictly under
the rose. Procedure, you know. He was willing to
accept a formal apology; he did not really wish to
kill the man.

Hamilton explained that Smith would not accept the humiliation—could not, because of his
psychological background. He was a barbarian
and simply could not see things from a gentleman's point of view. Hamilton identified Smith as
the Man from the Past.

The principal nodded. "I know that now. Had
I known that before, I would have ignored his
rudeness—treated him as a child. But I didn't
know. And now, in view of what he did—well, my
dear sir, I can hardly ignore it, can I?"

Hamilton conceded that he was entitled to satisfaction, but suggested it would make him pub-
licly unpopular to kill Smith. "He is rather a
public darling, you know. I am inclined to think
that many will regard it as murder to force him
to fight."

The citizen had thought of that. Rather a di-
lemma, wasn't it?

"How would you like to combat him physically—punish him the way he damaged you, only more so?"

"Really, my dear sir!"

"Just an idea," said Hamilton. "You might think about it. May we have three days grace?"

"More, if you like. I told you I was not anxious to push it to a duel. I simply want to curb his manners. One might run into him anywhere."

Hamilton let it go, and called Mordan, a common thing when he was puzzled. "What do you think I ought to do, Claude?"

"Well, there is no real reason why you should not let him go ahead and get himself killed. Individually, it's his life; socially, he's no loss."

"You forget that I am using him as a translator. Besides, I rather like him. He is pathetically gallant in the face of a world he does not understand."

"Mmm . . . well, in that case, we'll try to find a solution."

"Do you know, Claude," Felix said seriously, "I am beginning to have my doubts about this whole custom. Maybe I'm getting old, but, while it's lots of fun for a bachelor to go swaggering around town, it looks a little different to me now. I've even thought of assuming the brassard."

"Oh, no, Felix, you mustn't do that!"

"Why not? A lot of people do."

"It's not for you. The brassard is an admission of defeat, an acknowledgement of inferiority."

"What of it? I'd still be myself. I don't care what people think."

"You're mistaken, son. To believe that you can

live free of your cultural matrix is one of the easiest fallacies and has some of the worst consequences. You are part of your group whether you like it or not, and you are bound by its customs."

"But they're only customs!"

"Don't belittle customs. It is easier to change Mendelian characteristics than it is to change customs. If you try to ignore them, they bind you when you least expect it."

"But dammit! How can there be any progress if we don't break customs?"

"Don't break them—avoid them. Take them into your considerations, examine how they work, and make them serve you. You don't need to disarm yourself to stay out of fights. If you did you would get into fights—I know you!—the way Smith did. An armed man need not fight. I haven't drawn my gun for more years than I can remember."

"Come to think about it, I haven't pulled mine in four years or more."

"That's the idea. But don't assume that the custom of going armed is useless. Customs always have a reason behind them, sometimes good, sometimes bad. This is a good one."

"Why do you say that? I used to think so, but I have my doubts now."

"Well, in the first place an armed society is a polite society. Manners are good when one may have to back up his acts with his life. For me, politeness is a *sine qua non* of civilization. That's a personal evaluation only. But gunfighting has a strong biological use. We do not have enough things to kill off the weak and the stupid these days. But to stay alive as an armed citizen a man has to be either quick with his wits or with his hands, preferably both. It's a good thing.

"Of course," he continued, "our combativeness has to do with our ancestry and our history." Hamilton nodded; he knew that Mordan referred to the Second Genetic War. "But we have preserved that inheritance intentionally. The Planners would not stop the wearing of arms if they could."

"Maybe so," Felix answered slowly, "but it does seem like there ought to be a better way to do it. This way is pretty sloppy. Sometimes the bystanders get burned."

"The alert ones don't," Mordan pointed out. "But don't expect human institutions to be efficient. They never have been; it is a mistake to think that they can be made so—in this millennium or the next."

"Why not?"

"Because we *are* sloppy, individually—and therefore collectively. Look at a cageful of monkeys, at your next opportunity. Watch how they do things and listen to them chatter. You'll find it instructive. You'll understand humans better."

Felix grinned. "I think I see what you mean. But what am I to do about Smith?"

"If he gets out of this, I think he had better wear a gun after this. Perhaps you can impress on him then that his life will depend on the softness of his words. But for the present—I know this chap he challenged. Suppose you suggest me as referee."

"Are you going to let them *fight*?"

"In my own way. I think I can arrange for them to fight barehanded." Mordan had delved back into his encyclopedic memory and had come out with a fact that Hamilton would not fully appreciate. Smith had come from a decadent period in which handfighting had become stylized as fist fighting. No doubt he was adept in it. It was necessary for one not to use the gun with which he was adept; it was equitable that the other not use fists, were he adept in their use. So Mordan wished to referee that he might define the rules.

It is not necessary to give overmuch attention to that rather unimportant and uncolorful little man, J. Darlington Smith. Hamilton was forced to withdraw as next friend, since Carruthers needed him at the time, and did not therefore see the encounter. He learned of it first by discovering that Smith was immobilized in an infirmary, suffering from some rather unusual wounds. But he did not quite lose the sight of his left eye and his other damages were mostly gone in a couple of weeks.

All of which happened some days later than the conversation with Mordan.

Hamilton turned back to his work. There were various little matters to attend to. One team of researchers in particular belonged to him alone. He had noticed when he was a boy that a physical object, especially a metallic one, brought near to his forehead above the bridge of the nose seemed to produce some sort of a response inside the head, not connected, apparently, with the physiological senses. He had not thought of it for many years, until the Great Research had caused him to think of such things. Was it real, or was it imagination? It was a mere tightening of the nerves, an uneasy feeling, but distinct and different from any other sensation. Did other people have it? What caused it? Did it mean anything?

He mentioned it to Carruthers who had said, "Well, don't stand there speculating about it. Put a crew to work on it."

He had. They had already discovered that the feeling was not uncommon but rarely talked about. It was such a little thing and hard to define. Subjects had been found who had it in a more marked degree than most—Hamilton ceased being a subject for experimentation himself.

He called the crew leader. "Anything new, George?"

"Yes and no. We have found a chap who can distinguish between different metals nearly eighty per cent of the time, and between wood and metal every time. But we are still no nearer finding out what makes it tick."

"Need anything?"

"No."

"Call me if you need me. Helpful Felix the Cheerful Cherub."

"Okay."

It must not be supposed that Hamilton Felix

was very important to the Great Research. He was not the only idea man that Carruthers had, not by several offices. It is probable that the Great Research would have gone on in much the same fashion, even during his lifetime, even if he had not been co-opted. But it would not have gone in quite the same way.

But it is hard to evaluate the relative importance of individuals. Who was the more important?—the First Tyrant of Madagascar, or the nameless peasant who assassinated him? Felix's work had *some* effect. So did that of each of the eight-thousand-odd other individuals who took part at one time or another in the Great Research.

Jacobstein Ray called back before he could turn his mind to other matters. "Felix? You can come over and take your young hopeful away, if you will."

"Fine. What sort of results?"

"Maddening. He started out with seven correct answers in a row, then he blew up completely. Results no better than random—until he stopped answering at all."

"Oh, he did, did he?" remarked Hamilton, thinking of a certain flop-eared buck.

"Yes indeed. Went limp on us. I'd as leave try to stuff a snake down a hole."

"Well, we'll try another day. Meanwhile I'll attend to *him*."

"I'd enjoy helping you," Jake said wistfully.

Theobald was just sitting, doing less than nothing, when Felix came in. "Hello, sport. Ready to go home?"

"Yes."

Felix waited until they were in the family car and the pilot set on home before bracing him. "Ray tells me you didn't help him very well."

Theobald twisted a string around his finger. He concentrated on it.

"Well, how about it? Did you, or didn't you?"

"He wanted me to play some stupid games," the child stated. "No sense to them."

"So you quit?"

"Yeah."

"I thought you told me you would help?"

"I didn't *say* I would."

Felix thought back. The child was probably right—he could not remember. But he had had a feeling of contract, the "meeting of minds."

"Seems to me there was mention of a flop-eared rabbit."

"But," Theobald pointed out, "you said I could have it anyhow. You told me so!"

The rest of the trip home was mostly silence.

CHAPTER SIXTEEN

The Quick and the Dead

Madame Espartero Carvala called again, unexpectedly and with no ceremony. She simply called by telephone and announced that she was coming to see them. She had informed Phyllis on the previous occasion that she expected to come back and see the baby. But more than four years had passed with no word from her; Phyllis had given up expecting her. After all, one does not thrust oneself on a member of the cosmically remote Board of Policy!

They had seen references to her in the news: Madame Espartero re-confirmed without opposition. Madame Espartero offers her resignation. The Grand Old Lady of the Board in failing health. Madame Espartero's alternate selected by special election. Carvala rallies in her fight for life. Planners honor sixtieth year of service of the Oldest Member. Stereo-stories and news bits—she had become an institution.

Felix had thought when he saw her last that she looked older than any human being could. He realized when he saw her this time that he had been mistaken. She was still more incredibly frail and shrunken and she seemed to move with great effort. She compressed her lips tightly with each movement.

But her eye was still bright, her voice was still firm. She dominated her surroundings.

Phyllis came forward. "We are delighted. I never expected to see you again."

"I told you I was coming back to see the boy."

"Yes, I remember, but it has been a long time and you did not come."

"No sense in looking a child over until he has shaped up and can speak for himself! Where is he? Fetch him in."

"Felix, will you find him?"

"Certainly, my dear." Felix departed, wondering how it was that he, a grown man and in full possession of his powers, could permit a little old woman, ripe for cremation, to get him so on edge. It was childish of him!

Theobald did not want to leave his rabbits. "I'm busy."

Felix considered the plan of returning to the lounge and announcing that Theobald would receive Madame Espartero, if at all, at the rabbit run. But he decided that he could not do such a thing to Phyllis. "Look, son, there is a lady in there who wants to see you."

No answer.

"Make up your mind," Felix announced cheerfully. "Will you walk or do you prefer to be dragged? It makes no difference to me."

Theobald looked slowly up his father's sheer two meters and, without further comment, started for the house.

"Madame Espartero, this is Theobald."

"So I see. Come to me, Theobald." Theobald stood fast.

"Go to her, Theobald." Phyllis spoke briskly; the boy complied at once. Felix wondered why it was that the child obeyed his mother so much more readily than his father. Damn it, he was good to the child and just with him. There must have been a thousand times when he had refrained from losing his temper with him.

Madame Carvala spoke to him in a low voice, too low for either Felix or Phyllis to catch. He glowered and tried to look away, but she insisted, caught his eye, and held it. She spoke again, and he answered, in the same low tones. They talked together for some minutes, quite earnestly. Finally she straightened up in her chair and said in a louder tone, "Thank you, Theobald. You may go now."

He fled out of the house. Felix looked longingly after him, but decided he had to stay. He selected a chair as far across the room as manners permitted, and waited.

Carvala selected another cigar, puffed until she was the center of a cloud of blue smoke, and turned her attention exclusively to Phyllis. "He's a sound child," she announced. "Sound. He'll do well."

"I'm happy that you think so."

"I don't *think* so, I *know* so." They talked for a while longer about the boy, small talk. Felix had a feeling that the old woman was improvising until she was ready with whatever was on her mind.

"When do you expect to have his sister?"

"I am ready any time," replied Phyllis. "I have been for months. They are selecting for her now."

"What are they selecting for? Anything different from the boy?"

"Not in any major respect—except one. Of course there will be plenty of variation from what Theobald is, because in so many, many of the alternatives no attempt will be made to make a choice."

"What is the one major respect you spoke of?"

Phyllis told her of it. Since the coming child was to be a girl, its chromosome pattern would contain *two* X-chromosomes, one from each of its parents. Now philoprogenitiveness is, of course, a sex-linked characteristic. Hamilton, be it remembered, lacked it to a moderate degree. Theobald derived his one X-chromosome from his mother; Mordan confidently expected that he would be normal in his desire to have children of his own when he became old enough for such things to matter to him.

But his projected little sister would inherit from both her parents in this respect. She might be rather cool to the matter of having children. However, if she did have, then *her* offspring need not be handicapped by any lack in this highly desirable survival trait; since she would pass on to her heirs but one of her two X-chromosomes, by selection, she could transmit only that of her mother. Hamilton's undesirable trait would be eliminated forever.

Carvala listened carefully to this explanation— or rather to that small portion of it Phyllis had found it necessary to relate—and nodded cheerfully. "Put your mind at rest, child. It won't matter a bit." She offered no elaboration of her words.

She talked of other matters for a while, then said suddenly, "Any time now, I take it?"

"Yes," Phyllis agreed.

Carvala stood up and took her departure as suddenly as she came. "I hope we will have the honor of your presence again, Madame," Felix said carefully.

She stopped, turned, and looked at him. She took her cigar from her mouth and grinned. "Oh, I'll be back! You can count on that."

Felix stood scowling at the door through which she had left. Phyllis sighed happily. "She makes me *feel good*, Felix."

"She doesn't me. She looks like a corpse."

"Now, Filthy!"

Felix went outside and looked up his son. "Hi, sport."

"H'lo."

"What did she have to say to you?"

Theobald muttered something in which Felix caught only the term "cuss boss!"

"Take it easy, son. What did she want?"

"She wanted me to promise her something."

"And did you?"

"No."

"What was it?"

But Theobald wasn't listening again.

After a late and pleasant supper in the cool of the garden Felix turned on the news, rather idly. He listened lackadaisically for a while, then suddenly called out, "Phyllis!"

"What is it?"

"Come here! Right away!"

She ran in; he indicated the spieling, flickering box:

"—dame Espartero Carvala. She appears to have died instantly. It is assumed that she stumbled near the top of the escalator, for she seemed to have fallen, or rolled, the entire flight. She will long be remembered, not only for her lengthy tenure on the Board, but for her pioneer work in—" Phyllis had switched it off. Felix saw that she had tears in her eyes, and refrained from the remark he had intended to make about her cockiness in saying that she would be sure to be back.

Hamilton did not think it advisable to take Theobald back to Jacobstein Ray again; he felt that an antipathy had already grown up. But there were others engaged in telepathy research; he selected a crew and introduced Theobald to them. But he had formed a theory about the former failure; the methods used then had been the simple methods considered appropriate for young children. This time they told Theobald what they were attempting to do and started him out with tests intended for adults.

He could do it. It was as simple as that. There had been other cases equally clear cut, and the research leader cautioned Felix not to expect too much, as telepathically sensitive children tended to fade out in the talent—which Felix knew. But he could do it. Theobald, at least within the limits of the conditions, could read minds.

So Felix called Mordan again, told him again of what was on his mind. Did Mordan think that Theobald was a mutation?

"Mutation? No, I have no data to go on."

"Why not?"

" 'Mutation' is a technical term. It refers only to a *new* characteristic which can be inherited by Mendelian rules. I don't know what this is. Suppose you find out for me first what telepathy *is*—then I'll tell you whether or not Theobald can pass it on—say, about thirty years from now!"

Well, that could wait. It sufficed that Theobald was telepathic—at least for the present. The projected telepath gadget, which had derived from the Plutonian "Life Detector," was beginning to show promise. It had been duplicated in the auxiliary cold laboratory beneath the outskirts of Buenos Aires and had performed in the same fashion as on Pluto. It had been greatly refined, once the researchers knew the direction in which they were driving, but it had presented grave difficulties.

One of the difficulties had been straightened out in a somewhat odd fashion. The machine, while responsive to sentient beings (it would not respond to plants, nor to animal life of low form), did little else—it was not a true telepath. There was a cat, of doubtful origin, which had made itself the lab mascot—moved in and taken possession. While the gadget was sensitized the operator had stepped back without looking and stepped on pussy's tail. Pussy did not like it and said so.

But the technician acting as receiver had liked it even less; he had snatched off the headset, yelping. It had screamed at him, he alleged.

Further experimentation made it evident that the machine was especially sensitive to the thalamic storm aroused by any sudden violent emotion. Mere cool celebration had much less effect on it. However, banging a man on the thumb did not count. The man expected it, and delayed his reaction, routing it through the "cooler" of the forebrain. The emotion had to be strong and authentic.

Many tails were stepped on thereafter; many cats sacrificed their temporary peace of mind to the cause of science.

Theobald developed a strange antipathy for his mother's company during the period when she was expecting the arrival of his sister. It upset Phyllis; Felix tried to reason him out of it. "See here, sport," he said, "hasn't mama been good to you?"

"Yeah. Sure."

"Then what's the trouble? Why don't you like her?"

"I like her all right . . . but I don't like *her*." He

pointed and his meaning was unmistakable. Felix held a hurried whispered consultation with his wife. "How about it, Phil? I thought we hadn't let him in on the news yet?"

"I haven't."

"I didn't—that's sure. Do you suppose Claude—no, Claude wouldn't spill it. Hmmm . . . well, there's only one other way he could have found out . . . he found out for himself." He looked at his son with a deeply wrinkled brow; it might not be too convenient, he was thinking, to have a telepathic member of the household. Well, it might wear off—it frequently did.

"We'll have to play it as it lies. Theobald."

"Wha'cha want?"

"Is it your little sister whom you don't like?"

The boy scowled and indicated assent.

("It's probably nothing but natural jealousy. After all, he's been the big show around here all his life.") He turned again to his son. "Look here, sport—you don't think that little sister will make any difference in how mama and daddy feel about *you*, do you?"

"No. I guess not."

"A little sister will be a lot of fun for you. You'll be bigger than she will be, and you'll know a lot more, and you'll be able to show her things. You'll be the important one."

No answer.

"Don't you *want* a baby sister?"

"Not *that* one."

"Why not?"

He turned completely away. They heard him mutter, "Old cuss boss!" Then he added distinctly, "and her cigars *stink*."

The threesome was adjourned. Phyllis and Felix waited until the boy was asleep, and, presumably, with his telepathic ability out of gear. "It seems pretty evident," he told her, "that he has identified Carvala in his mind with Justina."

She agreed. "At least I'm relieved to know that it isn't *me* he has a down on. Just the same, it's serious. I think we had better call in a psychiatrist."

Felix agreed. "But I'm going to talk to Claude about it, too."

Claude refused to be upset by it. "After all," he said, "it's perfectly natural that blood relatives should dislike each other. That's a prime datum of psychology. If you can't condition him to put up with her, then you'll have to rear them apart. A nuisance, but that's all."

"But how about this fixation of his?"

"I'm not a psychiatrist. I wouldn't worry too much about it. Children frequently get some funny notions. If you ignore them, they generally get over them."

So the psychiatrist thought, too. But he was totally unable to shake Theobald's conviction in the matter. He had made his point, he stuck to it, and he refused to argue.

It was a matter of prime significance, aside from Theobald's fantastic delusion, that a telepathic person had been able to locate a person whom he had never seen and whose existence he had no reason to suspect. It was a fair-sized brick in the Great Research. Dutifully, Hamilton reported the affair to Carruthers.

Carruthers was intensely interested. He asked questions about it, took the matter home with him, and nursed it. The next day he called Felix to explain a plan he had conceived. "Mind you," he said, "I'm not urging you to do this. I'm not even asking you. It's your wife, and your baby, and your boy. But I think it's a unique opportunity to advance the Research."

Felix thought about it. "I'll let you know tomorrow."

"How would you like," he said to Phyllis, when they were alone that night, "to go to Buenos Aires to have Justina?"

"Buenos Aires? Why there?"

"Because there is the only telepath machine on Earth. And it can't be moved out of the cold laboratory."

CHAPTER SEVENTEEN

Da Capo

I've got it again." The receiver for the telepath made the announcement grimly. The gadget was still cantankerous; during the past few days it had worked beautifully part of the time—about twenty minutes in all!—and had refused to come to life the rest of the time. It seemed to have soaked up some of the contrariness of the subtle life-force it tapped.

"What are you getting?"

"Feels like a dream. Water, long stretches of water. Shore line in the back with mountain peaks." A recorder at his elbow took down everything he said, with the exact times.

"Are you *sure* it's the baby?"

"Sure as I was yesterday. Everybody is different over it. They *taste* different. I don't know how else to express it. Hold on! Something else . . . a city, a damn big city, bigger than Buenos Aires."

"Theobald," said Mordan Claude gently, "can you still hear her?" Mordan had been brought because Felix conceded that Claude had a handier way with the child than Felix. The child could not hear the telepath receiver where they had spotted him, although Claude could cut in through an earphone. Phyllis, of course, was in another room, busy with her fundamental affairs . . . it made no difference to the gadget, nor to Theobald. Felix had a roving assignment, privileged to make a nervous nuisance out of himself to anyone.

The boy leaned back against Mordan's thigh. "She's not over the ocean any more," he said. "She's gone to Capital City."

"Are you sure it's Capital City?"

"Sure." His voice was scornful. "I've been there, ain't I? And there's the tower."

Beyond the partition someone was asking, "A modern city?"

"Yes. Might be the Capital. It's got a pylon like it."

"Any other details?"

"Don't ask me so many questions—it breaks into the revery . . . she's moving again. We're in a room . . . lot of people, all adults. They're talking."

"What now, son?" Claude was saying.

"Aw, she's gone to that party again."

Two observers, standing clear of the activity were whispering. "I don't like it," the short one said. "It's ghastly."

"But it's happening."

"But don't you realize what this means, Malcolm? Where can an unborn child get such concepts?"

"Telepathically from its mother, perhaps. The brother is certainly a telepath."

"No, no, no! Not unless all our ideas of cerebration are mistaken. Conceptions are limited to experiences, or things similar to experiences. An unborn child has experienced nothing but warmth and darkness. It *couldn't* have such conceptions."

"Ummm."

"Well—answer me!"

"You've got me—I can't."

Someone was saying to the receiver, "Can you make out any of the people present?"

He raised his headset. "Quit bothering me! You drive it out with my own thoughts when you do that. No, I can't. It's like dream images . . . I think it is a dream. I can't feel anything unless she thinks about it."

A little later. "Something's happening . . . the dream's gone. Uneasy . . . it's very unpleasant . . . she's resisting it . . . it's . . . it's . . . Oh, Great—it's awful . . . it hurts! *I can't stand it!*" He tore off his headset, and stood up, white and shaking. At the same instant Theobald screamed.

It was a matter of minutes only when a woman came out the door of Phyllis' room and motioned to Hamilton.

"You can come in now," she said cheerfully.

Felix got up from where he was kneeling with Theobald. "Stay with Uncle Claude, Sport," he said, and went in to his wife.

CHAPTER EIGHTEEN

"Beyond This Horizon—"

It was nice to be able to come to the beach again. It was swell that Phyllis felt up to such little expeditions. It was pleasant to lie in the sun with his family and soak up comfort.

Things had not turned out the way he had planned, but things rarely did. Certainly he would never have believed all this a few years back ... Phyllis and Baldy, and now Justina. Once he had asked Claude to tell him the meaning of life—now he did not care. Life was good, whatever it was. And the prime question had been answered for him. Let the psychologicians argue it all they pleased—there was some kind of life after this one—where a man might find out the full answer.

For the main question: *"Do we get another chance?"* had been answered—by the back door. There was something more to the ego of a new-born child than its gene pattern. Justina had answered that, whether she knew it or not. She had brought memory patterns with her; she had lived before. He was convinced of that. Therefore, it was a dead-sure cinch that the ego went somewhere after the body disintegrated. Where, he would worry about when the time came.

It did seem extremely likely that Justina did not know what she had proved (and of course there was no way of asking her). Her telepathic patterns after she was born were meaningless, confused, as one would expect of a baby. Shock amnesia the psychologicians had decided to call it. Being born must be something like being awakened out of a sound sleep by a dash of cold water in the face. That would shock anybody.

He had not made up his mind yet whether he wanted to continue active in the Great Research, or not. He might just be lazy and raise dahlia bulbs and kids. He didn't know. Most of it was pretty long-distance stuff, and he personally was satisfied. Take that work Cliff was on—centuries and then some. Cliff had compared the job with that of trying to figure out the entire plot of a long stereostory from just one flash frame.

But they would finish it—some day. Theobald wouldn't see it, but he would see more of it than Felix, and his *son* would see still more. His sons would roam the stars—no limit.

It was nice that Theobald seemed to have gotten over that ridiculous fixation identifying Justina with Old Carvala. True, he did not seem actually fond of the baby, but that was expecting a lot. He seemed more puzzled by her, and interested. There he was, leaning over the baby's basket. He really did seem—

"Theobald!"

The boy stood up straight quickly.

"What were you doing?"

"Nothing." Maybe—but it *looked* as if he had pinched her.

"Well, I think you had better find another place to do it. The baby needs to sleep now."

The boy shot a quick glance at the infant and turned away. He walked slowly down toward the water.

Felix settled back, after glancing at Phyllis. Yes, she was still asleep. It was a good world, he assured himself again, filled with interesting things. Of which the most interesting were children. He glanced at Theobald. The boy was a lot of fun now, and would be more interesting as he grew up—if he could refrain from wringing his cussed little neck in the meantime!

OUTSTANDING SCIENCE FICTION FROM

☐ **THE BEST OF TREK #17 edited by Walter Irwin and G. B. Love.** From the first five-year mission to the far distant future, fascinating new explorations of the Star Trek universe. From Trek® magazine. (454383—$4.99)

☐ **THE BEST OF TREK #18 edited by Walter Irwin and G. B. Love.** This book more than lives up to its fine tradition and offers brand new articles on everything from a one-on-one interview with Robin Curtis about her role as Saavik, a show-by-show rating of *The Next Generation*, and a resolution to the long-standing debate about whether Data is merely a Spock clone. No matter what your favorite topics, characters, or episodes, you'll find something new about them here. (454634—$4.99)

☐ **RED DWARF: *Infinity Welcomes Careful Drivers* by Grant Naylor.** An international best-seller! Not since *Hitchhiker's Guide to the Galaxy* has there been such a delightful excursion into the wackiest regions of the unknown universe! (452011—$4.99)

☐ **RED DWARF: BETTER THAN LIFE by Grant Naylor.** Trapped aboard the starship Red Dwarf, David Lister must get back to reality and escape from the game. "Better Than Life", where his own mind creates the world in which he lives. But can he do it without the help of the computer Holly before he dies or the Red Dwarf is destroyed? (452313—$4.99)

☐ **DR. DIMENSION by John DeChancie and David Bischoff.** Dr. D. and four of his colleagues are lost in spacetime and caught in the middle of a war between two super-races of aliens. Will they get home—that is if one still exists? (452526—$4.99)

☐ **DR. DIMENSION: MASTERS OF SPACETIME by John DeChancie and David Bischoff.** Can a questionable robot actually help Dr. Dimension and his sidekick, Troy, escape the trash planet? (453549—$4.99)

Prices slightly higher in Canada.

Buy them at your local bookstore or use this convenient coupon for ordering.

PENGUIN USA
P.O. Box 999 — Dept. #17109
Bergenfield, New Jersey 07621

Please send me the books I have checked above.
I am enclosing $_____ (please add $2.00 to cover postage and handling). Send check or money order (no cash or C.O.D.'s) or charge by Mastercard or VISA (with a $15.00 minimum). Prices and numbers are subject to change without notice.

Card #_____ Exp. Date _____
Signature_____
Name_____
Address_____
City _____ State _____ Zip Code _____

For faster service when ordering by credit card call **1-800-253-6476**

Allow a minimum of 4-6 weeks for delivery. This offer is subject to change without notice.

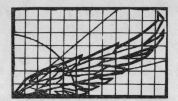

IF YOU LIKE VIRTUAL WORLD...
YOU'LL *LOVE* THE REAL THING!

BATTLETECH®

In the year 3058, mankind fights its interstellar battles from the cockpits of huge, humanoid war machines called BattleMechs. Far superior to any conventional force, these fearsome 'Mechs effortlessly crush everything in their paths. Five star-spanning nations spent generations in these 'Mechs fighting for dominance over human-occupied space, but when an unfamiliar foe crushed the best the Inner Sphere had to offer using more advanced BattleMech technology, the squabbling Houses banded together to defeat the invaders. Now the Successor Lords race against time and each other to achieve technological superiority and once again rule the battlefield.

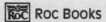